PALM BEACH BONES

A CHARLIE CRAWFORD MYSTERY (BOOK 4)

TOM TURNER

TRIBECA PRESS

Published by Tribeca Press.

www.tomturnerbooks.com

Palm Beach Bones/Tom Turner – 1st ed.

Print ISBN: 978-1-546-74311-8

JOIN TOM'S AUTHOR NEWSLETTER

Get the latest news on Tom's upcoming novels when you sign up for his free author newsletter at **tomturnerbooks.com/news**.

ONE

CRAWFORD AND OTT WERE EYEBALLING THE BODY THAT LAY ON the beach behind The Breakers. Ott was down in a crouch; Crawford was snapping photos on his iPhone. Even for veteran detectives from the mean streets of New York and Cleveland, it was not a pretty sight. The dead man appeared to be in his sixties, wearing khaki pants and a blue shirt. It was apparent that creatures of the sea had had their way with him. A bullet hole in the middle of his chest indicated that someone of the human species had as well. The victim's skin was slug white and wrinkled and he had a bulky Breitling watch that was still ticking even though his heart no longer was.

It was 6:30 a.m. An early morning beach stroller had called Palm Beach PD an hour ago with shock and horror in her voice. Crawford had been at the station at the time of the call, while Ott had come to the scene directly from his house.

"Shot him somewhere on the beach then dragged him into the water," Ott weighed in, glancing up at Crawford. "Or maybe dumped him from a boat."

Crawford nodded as he took another photo with his iPhone.

"Hawes on his way?" Ott asked.

Bob Hawes had been the medical examiner for Palm Beach County for twenty-five years. Way longer than he should have been, as far as Crawford was concerned.

"Yeah, should be any minute," said Crawford.

Crawford looked up and saw a kid and a dog walking toward them. He held up his hand and walked in their direction. "Sorry son, but you can't come any closer."

The boy's eyes were big. "Is that man okay?"

"You're going to have to turn around and go back," Crawford said, pointing over the boy's shoulder.

"Okay," said the boy reluctantly, still eyeing the body. Then he turned, gave a tug on the dog's leash, and started walking away.

Three uniforms came down to the beach, having parked in one of The Breakers' parking lots. Crawford put a hand up to his mouth and shouted to them. "You guys got any tape?"

One of them, Stan Gilhuley, held up a roll of yellow crime-scene tape.

"Good. I need you over there, Stan." He pointed to where the boy had just come from. "And Jon, over there," he pointed to the other side of the beach. "Don't let anyone get anywhere close."

He looked up at The Breakers and saw a cluster of people looking down at them. One had a pair of binoculars and two others had cameras. He saw a cameraman from WPEC news, the CBS affiliate.

"Tape off the path, Hal," Crawford told the third cop, "between those two trees." He pointed to two Chinese podocarpus. "Make sure those people stay up there," Crawford said. "Even the press."

"Especially the press," Ott mumbled.

Then Crawford saw the figure of Bob Hawes part the crowd, no doubt telling the public to make way so he could get to the crime scene before the clueless cops messed it up. Hawes wore gray flannel pants and a shirt that looked more like a pajama top, totally inappropriate for a June day that was already north of eighty degrees.

Ott hadn't noticed the ME yet; he was busy taking notes in his vintage leather-bound notebook that he'd had since way back when.

"Hawes is about to make his entrance," Crawford said under his breath.

Ott groaned as he stood up straight and pocketed the notebook.

A few moments later, Hawes walked up to them, his black Corfam high-gloss tie shoes having taken on a few spoonfuls of sand.

"Boys," Hawes said with a nod to Crawford and Ott before he looked down at the body. "Ho-lee shit." His eyes were as big as the gut hanging over his white plastic belt.

"What?" Crawford asked.

"That's Clyde Loadholt."

"Who's Clyde Loadholt?"

"He was chief of police here fifteen years ago," Hawes said, bending down for a closer look. "That watch...he got that when he retired. Clyde was a damn fine chief. Everyone loved the guy."

Crawford didn't point out the obvious: everyone except at least one.

TWO

THE THWACK-THWACK-THWACKING OF A HELICOPTER'S BLADE broke the silence of the group huddled around the corpse on the beach.

Crawford looked up as it got closer.

"Jesus," Ott said. "What the hell—"

He shook his head as Crawford walked toward the helicopter, waving his hands. But it just kept coming, lower by the second. It got to right above where the body was, only about twenty-five feet above them, its rotors kicking up a sandstorm.

A pretty woman, her hair flying in all directions, was leaning out the passenger side, snapping pictures.

Crawford yelled through the cloud of sand, "Get out of here, you're wrecking our scene!"

The woman looked down at him, smiled, waved, and just kept snapping.

Ott, a mile-wide frown on his face, pulled out his Glock and pointed it. "Outta here! *Right now!*"

The woman's smile disappeared but she snapped off a few last shots. Then she lowered her camera, reached into her pocket, pulled something out, and tossed it from the helicopter. It fluttered down toward the beach.

The helicopter started to rise, then headed inland.

Ott shook his head, brushing sand out of his thinning hair as he watched the helicopter disappear. "You believe that shit?"

"Guess you made the six o'clock news, waving your piece," Crawford said.

"Which means I'll be hearing from Rutledge," Ott said referring to Norm Rutledge, the current chief of police.

Crawford nodded. "You can count on it."

A uniform brought something over to Crawford and handed it to him. "This is what she tossed," he said.

It was a business card. It read: Alexa Dillon, *Palm Beach Morning News*.

Ott read it over Crawford's shoulder. "Gotta hand it to her. She got the money shot for tomorrow's edition."

CRAWFORD HAD BEEN OUT OF TOWN FOR THE PAST WEEK. He had been up in Connecticut and had just flown down from JFK airport the night before. *Family emergency* was how he had explained it to Norm Rutledge and when Rutledge pressed him for details he just repeated it.

Palm Beach had been homicide-free for the last five months, so his timing had been good.

Cam, Crawford's twenty-nine year old brother, was the family emergency. Cam had checked himself into Clairmount, located in the pastoral hills of New Canaan, Connecticut. Clairmount, as the website said, specialized in 'the treatment of psychiatric and addictive disorders,' and was a, 'unique and extraordinary place that helps people find the path back to mental health and wellness.'

It was clear Cam hadn't yet found the path.

Along with their older brother, Evan, Cam had followed their father's footsteps and had gone into the investment-banking business. Both Cam and Evan had become phenomenally successful and were now principals in the same New York hedge fund.

Because of the ten-year age difference, Crawford and Cam had never been too close. But they still got on the phone every month or so and talked football or what different family members were up to.

Cam was smart, funny, handsome, and *very* rich, but he'd also landed the Crawford family's depression gene. It didn't help that he had a marriage that was shaky at best because of a wife who obeyed her marriage vows only about six days out of seven.

Cam told Charlie that on the night before he was scheduled to check into Clairmount he had gone to a bar in the meatpacking district of Manhattan and parked himself on a barstool until the place closed down. Then—seven drinks later—he had gotten into his car and, with the companionship of a fifth of Johnny Walker Blue, had GPS'd his way up to New Canaan. He got there around 6:00 a.m., so he'd had some time to kill before Clairmount opened at nine. He then proceeded to pull out a small, dark bottle of white powder and powered through it for the next hour.

Needless to say, Cam hadn't made the best first impression with the staff when he'd staggered into reception that morning.

A week later, Crawford had walked into his brother's residence, a large Tudor home called Brook House—one of many on the Clairmount campus—and found Cam in the middle of a heated Monopoly game with five women. The brothers shared a long hug and Cam clapped Charlie on the back so hard it was like he was trying to dislodge a chicken bone from his throat.

"Your brother cheats," one of the Monopoly players announced to Crawford right off the bat.

"I could have told you that," Crawford said, as Cam introduced him to the women at the table. It was an odd mix from age twenty to around sixty.

"He always ends up on Chance," one named Emily said.

"And *never* goes to jail," said another named Cynthia.

"Speaking of jail," Cam announced. "My brother here's a cop—well, actually a detective—so you better be nice to him. Did you ever hear about that case where a guy called the Taxidermist killed all those people in Manhattan?"

Two of the women nodded.

"Well, Charlie here solved it," Cam said, beaming with pride.

"Wait, didn't you date that actress, Gwendolyn Hyde?" A younger woman asked.

Crawford's face reddened.

"He doesn't like to talk about that," Cam said in a conspiratorial whisper to his new friends.

After Cam had cheated his way to victory, he and Crawford went out on the porch of the house, which had an idyllic view of a swift-moving brook. A family of ducks waddled into their periphery a few minutes later.

"So how's it going here, Cam?" Crawford asked. "Something tells me it's not all fun and games."

"It's all right." Cam had never been a complainer. "We go to classes, they're teaching us this thing called DBT, which stands for... shit, I forget. It's all about trying to get our heads straight. Then we've got AA and Al-Anon every night. Hey, if you gotta be at a place like this, I guess this is as good as any."

"Doing you any good, you think?"

"Yeah, maybe. They're also doing ECT on me. Know what that is?"

Crawford shook his head.

"Electroconvulsive therapy. First, they put you out, then zap you with electric shocks."

Crawford felt an unexpected protective impulse. "Christ, you don't mean like in *One Flew over the Cuckoo's Nest?*"

Cam laughed and held up a hand. "No, no, it's come a long way from that. Got a pretty good track record fighting depression. Oh, now I remember: DBT stands for Dialectical Behavior Therapy."

Crawford shrugged. "Whatever the hells that means."

"I know, right?" Cam said.

"So when do you get out?" Crawford asked.

"I'm not sure yet, but they tell me most people are here for a month or so."

"And that's okay with Grey?" Grey Macleod owned Trajectory Partners, Cam's hedge fund employer.

"Yeah, he's okay with it," Cam said.

Fact was, he had to be, since Cam was the star at Trajectory Partners. Crawford had read articles about his brother in the *Wall Street Journal* and the *Financial Times* and Cam had even been featured on Jim Cramer's TV show *Mad Money*.

"So Evan's pinch-hitting?" Crawford asked.

Evan, as far as the three brothers went, was the odd man out. Charlie and Cam had been athletes, Evan was on the debate team. Charlie and Cam had been kids who liked to have a good time, Evan was the serious one. Charlie and Cam got by with Cs, Evan straight As. Charlie and Cam were popular with girls, Evan was popular with librarians.

"Yeah, he'll be all right," Cam said.

"Doesn't make you a little nervous?"

Cam laughed. "Nah, he won't lose us any clients."

"I hope this isn't a sore subject, but what about Charlotte?" Crawford asked of Cam's wife.

"Ah, it's a little sore," Cam said. "She's seeing some guy on the side. I'm not supposed to know about it, of course. She went out to the Canyon Ranch for her annual tune-up. And whaddaya know, the guy was out there too."

"Sorry, man," Crawford said. He had always had his doubts about Charlotte, particularly when she flirted with him a couple of times.

"Yeah, well, this time it's definitely over." Cam shook his head. "Hey, not like I was husband of the year. Can we talk about you now?"

"Same old, same old," Crawford said. "Arrest guys, put 'em in jail."

"Somehow I think there's a little bit more to it than that," Cam said. "How're you liking Palm Beach?"

"I mostly like it," Crawford said.

"I've got a couple clients who have houses down there," Cam said. "What about Mort, how's that gnarly, old bastard doing?"

"Still fat and cranky," Crawford said, then he turned serious. "You think you're gonna be okay?"

"Yeah, yeah, I'll be fine," he said. "But quitting the booze might be a challenge."

"Well, I got a hotel room nearby for the next couple days. Maybe I can get into your Monopoly game."

Cam shook his head. "Naw, you don't need to stick around. I'll be okay."

"I know," Crawford said. "But the murder business is a little slow at the moment."

Until Clyde Loadholt's body drifted up behind The Breakers like a beached whale.

THREE

Susie Loadholt, the sixty-four-year-old widow of Clyde Loadholt, dabbed at her eyes. She had a pink Kleenex box in her lap at her two-story colonial in West Palm Beach. Her sister was sitting next to her, an arm around her shoulder, kissing her consolingly every thirty seconds or so.

Crawford—six three, one eighty, who everyone said looked like that polo player in the Ralph Lauren ads except with dirty blond hair —sat across from her. Ott—five seven, two thirty, sometimes mistaken for Palm Beach PD's janitor— had a chair next to Crawford's.

"All I can tell you was he said he was going to see someone on a boat somewhere," Susie said sniffling.

"Clyde wasn't the most communicative man in the world," the sister offered.

Crawford nodded. "But he didn't tell you who the person was or the location of the boat?"

Susie Loadholt shook her head. "No, that was all he said."

"And, Mrs. Loadholt, what did you think when Clyde didn't come home last night?" Ott asked.

Susie pulled another tissue out of the box. "I thought it was very strange. I called him on his cell a bunch of times starting at around eleven. Never slept a wink. Then this morning, I got the call from Norm."

Norm Rutledge, Crawford and Ott's boss. He'd been chief of police in Palm Beach ever since Clyde Loadholt retired.

"So Clyde never said anything else about who he was going to see last night?" Ott asked.

"She already told you," the sister said with an irritated look.

Susie Loadholt held up her hand. "I can handle this, Mavis," she said. "He did say one thing. He was going to repair an old wound. That was it."

Or maybe open up a new one, Crawford thought. "And you didn't happen to ask him what he meant by that?"

"No," Susie said.

"Mrs. Loadholt," Ott waded in again, "did Clyde say anything recently about someone he might have had trouble with, a disagreement with, or mention anyone who might have threatened him?"

Susie shook her head and sniffled again as her sister planted yet another kiss on her rouged cheek.

"How about back when he was police chief?" Crawford asked. "I know that was quite a while ago, but was there ever anyone he told you about, someone who, as my partner asked, might have threatened him or posed a danger to him?"

"Oh my God, that was ten years ago," the sister said. "How could she possibly remember?"

"Enough, Mavis," said Susie, turning to Crawford. "No, I don't remember anything at all like that. Clyde didn't exactly go around arresting hard-core criminals. It was Palm Beach, after all. He was—well, you know, the chief. Spent most of his time supervising his men. Probably the same as Norm Rutledge."

Crawford nodded. "Mrs. Loadholt, please understand, we have to ask you a few tough questions."

"I'm a big girl, Detective."

"Did Clyde, as far as you know, owe anyone money?"

Mavis burst out laughing.

"What's so damn funny?" Susie Loadholt turned to her sister.

"You know perfectly well," Mavis said. "Clyde never spent a dime. So how could he ever owe anyone money?"

Susie squinted her eyes and balled up her fists. "Why don't you just say he was cheap, Mavis," Susie said. "Did it occur to you that the poor man just died. I mean, for God's—"

"You're right," Mavis patted her sister's arm. "I'm sorry. I'll be quiet."

Crawford glanced over at Ott who was scratching away at his notebook and trying to hide a smirk.

"Mrs. Loadholt," Crawford began again, "by any chance, did Clyde gamble at all?"

Susie drew her head back. "If you want to call a friendly poker game where you'd win or lose fifty dollars, then, yes, he gambled."

"But not any trips to Las Vegas or betting with bookies, anything like that?"

Mavis looked like she wanted to jump in but was biting her tongue.

"Mostly he just liked to do his Sudoku and watch baseball on TV," Susie said.

Mavis couldn't hold back. "Football too," she added.

Susie turned on her. "Jesus, Mavis, who was married to him? You or me?"

"Just sayin' he was a big Dolphins fan."

Susie shook her head, threw up her hands, and gave Crawford a tired look. "Maybe you should be interviewing her."

FOUR

CRAWFORD AND OTT WERE IN ONE OF THEIR LEAST FAVORITES places in the world: Norm Rutledge's office. Rutledge had pictures of his family on all four walls—the ultimate loving husband and dad. But, on the sly, as just about everyone but his wife knew, he had something going with one of the women uniforms. Before that it had been a new female employee down at CSEU, the department's Crime Scene Evidence Unit.

"He was a good man," Rutledge said. "Ran a tight ship. Palm Beach couldn't have had a better guy at the helm."

The clichés always rolled off Rutledge's tongue. Nautical and otherwise.

"Do you remember him butting heads with anyone?" Ott asked, taking a swig from a water bottle.

"Everybody in this job butts heads with someone from time to time," Rutledge said.

"But not usually to the point where it gets 'em killed," Crawford said, looking up at a picture of Rutledge, his wife, and two sons dressed in chocolate brown sweaters and cracking smiles like they'd just heard a real knee-slapper.

"I don't really know," Rutledge said with a shrug. "Kinda lost touch with the man. We used to have lunch every once in a while after he retired. He had this poker game with a bunch of guys."

"Who was in the game?" Ott asked.

Rutledge leaned back in his faux-leather chair, looked out his window, and scratched his head. "Nobody you'd know. Mostly a buncha retired guys. A lawyer named Chuck Mitchell, I think he still practices. A guy who ran the dog track in West Palm. Another guy who—" Crawford watched as Rutledge suddenly bolted upright in his chair, his eyes enormous. "*Ho-ly Christ!* Judge Meyer! Yeah, Rich Meyer was in the game."

Crawford leaned forward. "Who is he?"

"Rich Meyer was a judge who got killed about three years back. Up in Jupiter," Rutledge said. "Official verdict was that it was a home invasion. But I wasn't sold on that."

"Why?"

"Cause whoever did it didn't take a thing."

Crawford glanced over at Ott, who was writing furiously now. It had taken place before he and Ott had come down to Palm Beach. Probably right around the time when Ott was swearing off shoveling snow in Cleveland and Crawford was going through a painful divorce in New York City.

"You thinking there might be a connection, Norm?" Crawford asked.

"I sure as hell think you guys oughta look into it."

Crawford nodded. "We're on it."

Ott nodded. "Okay, I need you to give me a list of everyone in that poker game, including phone numbers and addresses if you have them."

Rutledge nodded, his eyes as bright as Crawford had seen them in a long time. "Sure, no problem."

"So," said Crawford, "we got a police chief and we got a judge. Both played in the same poker game and both got shot and killed. Seems like a connection, not a coincidence, right?" Crawford had the jazzed-up feeling he got when he had something by the tail, even if it was a slippery tail. "So I'll do a quick hypothetical: two guys in the law enforcement business, one of whom, a police chief, arrests a guy for something, then another guy, a judge, throws the book at him and sends the guy away for a long time..."

"So the guy, who's in jail," Ott picked up on the thread, "hires someone on the outside to pop the judge and the police chief?"

A frown drifted across Crawford's face. "Only problem with that is the timing. Ten years after Loadholt retired is a pretty long time for the guy to wait to finally get revenge. And why three years between Meyer and Loadholt?"

Ott nodded. "So maybe the guy got someone to take out Meyer while he was inside, then recently got out and did Loadholt himself?"

Crawford nodded. "Maybe," he said. "There're a lot of possible scenarios. Especially if a guy was doing a long bit and thinking twenty-four/seven about the guys who put him in. But I still got a problem—if it's the same guy—with him waiting three years to do Loadholt."

"When did Meyer retire?" Ott asked Rutledge.

"I don't know exactly. Right around the same time as Loadholt, I think."

"You remember any big cases," Crawford started, "where maybe a guy on trial got up after the judge sentenced him and said he was gonna get him?"

"Seen too many movies, Crawford," said Rutledge.

"Hey, I got news for you," Ott told Rutledge. "Shit like that happens in real life. Trust me, I've seen it."

Crawford glanced at Ott. "Bet the boys up in Jupiter looked into that possibility back when Meyer was killed."

"I would think so," Ott said with a shrug.

Crawford turned to Rutledge. "Anyone else in the house when Meyer got killed? A wife, a girlfriend?"

"Yeah, as I remember it, his wife was there. Shirley, I think her name was."

Crawford got up from his chair. "Let's go, Mort," he said. "We've got some digging to do."

Ott followed Crawford out the door. "I know what that means," he said in the hallway. "*I've* got some digging to do."

Crawford laughed. "Hey, just so happens you're a hell of a lot better at it than me."

Ott shook his head. "Translation: I don't really wanna do that shit," he said. "Butter me up like I'm some kind of Einstein of research."

"Well, you are."

"Come on, Charlie, don't go blowin' smoke."

On the way back to their offices Crawford said how that was the first time in his two and a half years on the job in Palm Beach that he could ever remember Rutledge actually being helpful on a case. Ott said that wasn't true, he was helpful on the last one. Crawford racked his brain to remember Rutledge's contribution. Finally he asked Ott what he had done on the last one.

"Stayed the fuck out of the way," Ott replied.

FIVE

CRAWFORD WAS ALREADY FIFTEEN MINUTES LATE FOR HIS dinner with Rose Clarke at Malachi's in Citiplace. He had been on the phone with Judge Meyer's widow setting up a meeting for the following morning. He was going to drive up to her house in Jupiter and meet at nine before her morning bridge game.

He had just gotten another call from a woman who identified herself as Alexa Dillon. The name didn't register at first. Then he remembered: the card fluttering down to the sand a few feet from Clyde Loadholt's corpse.

"Oh, yeah, you're the one who messed up my crime scene," he said. "I've run across aggressive reporters before—"

"Freedom of the press, Charlie," the woman interrupted. "I don't remember Palm Beach Police Department owning the air space above a public beach."

He already didn't like her. And wasn't thrilled about her calling him Charlie.

"So you went to journalism *and* law school?"

"Just a girl trying to get a story," she said. "Not mess up your crime scene."

"Too late," Crawford said. "That's what a helicopter blowing sand does."

"I'm sorry," she said, like she actually meant it. "How 'bout I buy you a drink to make up for it?"

Yup, aggressive was the word.

"Thanks for the offer," he said. "But I'm pretty busy."

"Come on. I don't bite."

"Thanks," he said. "But I gotta go."

He clicked off.

ROSE WAS A GOOD FRIEND, NOT TO MENTION OCCASIONAL LOVER of Crawford's. It was almost like sex with no strings, or in the parlance of the day, they were *friends with benefits*. Rose was also the most successful real-estate broker in not just Palm Beach but in the whole Sunshine State as well. They were just occasional lovers because they both knew that Crawford's true love was Dominica McCarthy, a stunning crime-scene tech at Palm Beach PD. Only problem was, Dominica and Crawford were on hiatus at the moment.

Long story.

Rose was five ten and blond. She had a daily training session with a Romanian trainer who had made her into a shapely, gym-trim hardbody with absolutely no droops or jiggling body parts. Besides selling homes and exercising, another thing Rose liked to do was talk about people—just this side of gossip. Trouble was, she knew she had to hold her tongue around most people. But with Crawford, due to the nature of his job and his natural discreet manner, she knew she could blab away to her heart's content and be sure he'd never repeat a word.

That suited Crawford, who liked to listen way more than talk. But mainly, it was the fact that Rose was an incredible asset to him. She knew everyone, particularly the Palm Beach elite, and nothing happened without her knowing about it. Rose was quite happy to share what she knew with Crawford—for a price. Sometimes a lunch, sometimes a dinner, and sometimes, well, a sexual favor wouldn't be an inaccurate description.

"So the group started last month when five of us got together at Marla Fluor's house—"

"Who's she again?" Crawford asked, having heard that name before, but not remembering from where.

"She was like the first woman partner at Goldman Sachs," Rose said. "Something like that. Country girl from South Carolina originally, endowed a law school up in Columbia, I think it was."

Crawford nodded and took a pull on his Bud.

"The idea being women mentoring other women," she patted Crawford's hand. "'Cause as much as we love you, you guys still don't give us a fair shake. Still have that glass ceiling we have to crash through and don't pay us as much as you pay yourselves."

Crawford put up his hands in protest. "Whoa. Whoa. What is this 'you' stuff? I don't have anything to do with it, and just so you know, I think what you're doing is great."

Rose high-fived him. "Why aren't all men as smart as you, Charlie?"

Crawford shrugged. "So keep going. How's it work?"

"Well, like I said, we basically mentor women. You know, invest in their businesses. Use our contacts to help 'em get to the next level."

Crawford nodded. "Who else is in the group?"

"Well, except for me, just about everyone's from the Forbes 400," Rose said. "I mentioned Marla Fluor. Then there's Elle T. Graham, she started that Silicon Valley company Groupthink, and Diana Quarle—"

"The designer, right?" Crawford said. "Has that big house on Everglades Island."

"Yup. And Beth Jastrow, owns two Las Vegas casinos," Rose said.

"Wait a minute, a woman owns Vegas casinos?"

Rose nodded, a little scorn showing. "You're getting dangerously close to sounding sexist, Charlie."

"I'm sorry, I just don't think of a woman—" he cut himself off, not wanting to get any further into the dog house. "Know what it kinda sounds like to me?"

"What?"

"That TV show, *Shark Tank*, where people come on and pitch their products, companies and stuff."

"Yeah, I've seen it," Rose said. "All of 'em on it are pretty pleased with themselves. Think they're the smartest people on the planet. The difference is we're all on the same team and don't bid against each other or take a piece of their businesses. Sometimes we front capital, but with no interest. And if the business goes under, well, then that's our tough luck. But that's not gonna happen, not the way we screen 'em."

"Sounds like a helluva good thing," Crawford said.

"Oh and I forgot something."

"What's that?"

"We don't have anybody like that bald, obnoxious guy, Mr. Wonderful," Rose said, shaking her head. "What about you, Charlie? What's new in the murder game?"

"Funny you should ask," Crawford said. "After almost six months of it being quiet, we had a murder this morning. Guy who used to be police chief, matter-of-fact."

"Really?" Rose said, cocking her head. "What's his name?"

"Clyde Loadholt. Retired about ten years ago."

Rose shook her head. "I vaguely remember the name. How'd it happen?"

Crawford explained how Loadholt had washed up on the beach behind The Breakers with a single bullet in the chest. Then he mentioned the connection to Judge Meyer. Rose had heard of Meyer, said he'd been known as a pretty tough judge. The waiter came and refilled Rose's glass of rosé and got Crawford another Bud.

"So are we gonna sleep together tonight, Charlie?" Rose asked casually after a sip.

Crawford smiled at her. "Jesus, Rose, direct much?" he said. "You know, that expression has always amused me. I mean, it sounds like we go get into our pajamas, climb into bed, you get your pillow, I get mine, then we just quietly nod off."

Rose laughed. "Jesus, Charlie, it's called a euphemism. So that would be a *no*...?"

Crawford put his hands up. "Hang on," he said, then like he was pondering. "So after careful consideration, Rose..." dramatic pause, "you talked me into it."

Rose shook her head and laughed. "Real tough sell, aren't you, Charlie."

SIX

CRAWFORD ROLLED OUT OF ROSE CLARKE'S PLACE AT SIX THIRTY in the morning. As he drove out of her long driveway with the crunchy, white pebbles, he thought he might be able to get used to a place like 1241 South Ocean Boulevard. Twelve rooms, a pool, and—not that he had first-hand knowledge on the subject—one of the best ocean views around.

Only problem was, he wasn't in love with Rose.

As he pulled up to his one-bedroom West Palm Beach condo with a view of the vast Publix parking lot, the reality of his own humble existence kicked him in the teeth.

He showered in his tight shower that never had enough water pressure, toweled off in his pocket-sized bathroom, got dressed, and walked the ninety-odd steps to Dunkin' Donuts. Janelle, with the big smile and gold tooth, greeted him with his go-to: a regular extra dark and two blueberry donuts. He deluded himself into thinking the fruit-themed donuts were somehow good for him, even though they had glazed sugar coating them like salt spray on a life preserver and weighed in at 263 calories each.

A HALF HOUR LATER HE WAS AT SHIRLEY MEYER'S HOUSE IN Jupiter. It was a far cry from Rose's place, but was a neat, brick ranch on a cul-de-sac in a nice, middle-class neighborhood. A few late-model Detroit cars were parked on the street and bougainvillea grew up the sides of several neighboring houses.

Crawford parked, got out, walked up the path to number 23 Bellemead Court, and hit the doorbell. A woman in a pantsuit and short gray hair opened the door and welcomed Crawford in.

A few minutes later, he was sitting in a club chair in Mrs. Meyer's chintz-dominated living room with a cup of coffee and a saucer in his lap.

"First, Mrs. Meyer, let me just say, I really appreciate you taking the time to meet me and let me ask you some questions about your husband's death."

Shirley Meyer smiled and nodded. "You're very welcome, Detective. It was a terrible time back then, as I'm sure you can imagine."

Crawford nodded. "I certainly can," he said. "If you wouldn't mind, can you tell me exactly how it happened?"

She sighed then nodded back at him. "Sure. Richard and I were coming home from dinner at a restaurant with friends and he unlocked the front door, and as we walked in, I saw this person standing to the left of the foyer with a gun."

"Can you describe that person? Age? How he was dressed? Short? Tall? Average? As many details as possible would be helpful."

Shirley Meyer took a sip of her coffee. "As I told the detectives at the time, I was surprised by how short he was."

"So what would you say...five six or so?"

"If that, maybe more like five four," she said. "I couldn't tell how old he was because he had this nylon stocking over his face. But if I had to guess, I'd say twenties or thirties. He was wearing this bulky jacket and black running shoes."

Crawford nodded as he wrote in his notebook.

"So the man said, very calmly, 'I want all your jewelry.' He said it in this voice that seemed like he was trying to disguise his real voice. It was high and almost squeaky, more like a teenage boy's voice."

"What did you do?"

"Well, Richard said, 'I've got a thousand dollars in cash and I'll write you a check,' because we both—me in particular—had some expensive jewelry in our walk-in."

"And what did he say?"

"He actually laughed and said, 'So I cash your check and they just give me the money. Nobody arrests me?' He was being sarcastic."

Crawford smiled. "I got that."

"Then Richard started to say something," she put her hands over her eyes, "and the man shot him. Just like that. Then he ran out the door and didn't take anything with him."

Shirley Meyer sagged in her seat and began sobbing. Crawford put the coffee cup and saucer down and reached across and patted her on the arm. "I'm sorry, Mrs. Meyer, for making you go through it again. Me and my partner are going to re-open the case, maybe we'll have better luck this time around."

Shirley Meyer looked up at him, as tears ran down her cheeks. "I hope you do. It was so cold-blooded and, and...so unnecessary."

"I know what you mean," Crawford said.

She smiled, dabbing at her eyes with a handkerchief. "I'm okay now," she said. "I just had to get it out of my system."

Crawford didn't want to press it too hard. "Would it be all right if I asked you just one or two more questions?"

"Of course. I don't have to leave for my bridge game for forty-five minutes."

"Thanks," Crawford said, leaning back in his chair. "Could I ask you about the poker game your husband played in at Clyde Loadholt's house?"

She put her hand up to her mouth. "Oh, God, poor Clyde, I saw what happened on the news last night—" then it hit her. "Are you thinking maybe it was the same person?"

Crawford exhaled. "We really have no idea. It's possible. But you know how it is. We have to pursue everything."

She nodded.

"So tell me about the poker game, if you would. They played every week, correct?"

She nodded, frowned, and then lowered her voice. "I didn't approve of it."

"What do you mean?"

"Well, back about twenty years ago, I heard from one of the other wives that their games got pretty rowdy. Lots of drinking and carrying on."

"What do you mean, 'carrying on'?"

She shook her head slowly then sighed deeply. "I heard they once had a female stripper there."

Crawford sat back in his chair. "You mean a stripper came to Clyde Loadholt's house?"

She let out a long, slow sigh. "Yes, according to Joanna Mitchell. She's the wife of Chuck Mitchell, who was one of the regulars."

"How did she find out?"

"Chuck came home drunk, smelling of cheap perfume. She got it out of him. After that I told Richard I didn't want him to go anymore."

"What did he say?"

"He denied everything," she said. "Told me that was crazy, there were no strippers. It was just a regular old poker game."

Crawford stroked his chin, looked out the window then turned back to her. "Did you believe him?"

She thought for a second. "Let's just say, I half did."

"What do you mean by that exactly?"

"That maybe they had a stripper one time, maybe more," she said, "but Richard didn't touch her. That's what I hoped, anyway."

Crawford nodded, thinking there probably wasn't any more he could get out of Shirley Meyer. But what she had told him was very useful. He asked her next for a list of the men who played in the game. He and Ott had gotten one from Susie Loadholt, but he figured she might have forgotten someone.

He thanked her and stood up to go as she wrote out the list.

As she walked him to the door, he thanked her and said, 'have a nice card game,' knowing it was going to be a whole lot tamer than the one her husband used to play in.

SEVEN

Using the pseudonym Libbie, she had hitchhiked up to Florida State Prison in Starke, Florida, fifteen years ago. She had twenty-six dollars and some change in the back pocket of her blue jeans and a backpack that contained the rest of her worldly goods. She had made up a pretty convincing story about how she was Aileen Wuornos's step-sister, and Aileen either went along with it because she was desperate for a visitor or had no clue whether she had a step-sister or not.

Nobody at Starke called her Aileen. She was, and had been from the first day she arrived shackled in chains, the Crazy Bitch. And, the fact was, she liked the nickname. Because if there was one thing Aileen Wuornos was, it was perverse.

Through a two-inch, clear, plexiglass window at the prison, under the close scrutiny of a grim-faced, linebacker of a guard, the two talked through microphones. They had a long conversation and if the bitch wasn't crazy she was at least disjointed and rambled all over the place in her endless monologues. At first she seemed to be saying that she was a victim, that she had been raped by all of the men she killed;

then she said how she hated "human life" and if she ever got out of jail she'd do it all over again.

Well, of course, there was no way in hell she was ever getting out of jail except in a body bag.

Then the Crazy Bitch launched into her childhood and it was even worse than Libbie suspected. Her father and mother were truly a pair of five-star losers. Her mother was fourteen when she married her father, and two years later her mother filed for divorce. Shortly after that her father was sent to jail for, among other things, molesting a child, and ended up hanging himself there. Then the Crazy Bitch's mother abandoned her and her brother, so they were dumped on their grandparents. Turned out, the grandparents were just as bad as the parents. Maybe worse.

At the mention of her grandparents, Libbie was one hundred percent tuned in. Not only had the Crazy Bitch's grandfather sexually assaulted her, according to her anyway, but so had her brother and a friend of her grandfather by whom she became pregnant at the age of fifteen. That was also the same year she got thrown out of the house by her grandparents and ended up camping out in the woods behind her house, turning tricks with neighborhood kids, supporting herself as a teenage hooker.

Libbie couldn't believe what she was hearing. Her childhood had been pretty mild by comparison, even though there were more than a few parallels.

The Crazy Bitch had stopped at one point and asked, "Why are you so interested in my pathetic, fucked-up life anyway?"

Libbie mumbled an answer but the Crazy Bitch didn't seem to be listening. Instead she just changed a few words and repeated the same question. "Why the hell do you care about me? Why are you here? Do you want to play me in another fuckin' movie or something? Or write another book about me? I'm so sick of all that shit."

Libbie just laughed it off and explained that she was neither an actress nor a writer, just someone who was concerned and could relate to her life. Even though the Crazy Bitch's life made hers look like the proverbial day at the beach.

Then Aileen went into detail about the murders—all six of them. "Woulda been seven," she said, laughing in her off-kilter way, "but they couldn't find the bastard's body."

"But I heard your lawyers were going to appeal," Libbie said. "Try to get a new trial."

The Crazy Bitch shook her head so hard that tiny unidentifiable objects fell out of her hair. "Good fuckin' luck." Then she paused and spoke softly, "I'm not sure I want to live any longer in this fucked up world anyway. I been on death row for ten goddamn years now. Let's get this shit over with, for chrissake."

She then swerved off on another tangent, which quickly turned into a rant. "Matron bitches here piss in my food, spit in it, throw dirt in it, trying to push me over the brink so I'll wind up committing suicide before the execution. Put me through these nasty strip-searches, make my handcuffs so tight they cut off the circulation in my hands. No water pressure so I'm taking showers using the sink in my fuckin' cell. Nobody treats a dog like that." Then she detoured off onto what could best be described as the twilight zone, describing how her mind "was being tampered with and tortured at BCI and how her head was being crushed with sonic pressure."

Libbie listened patiently, but really wanted to go back to her tortured family life. The thing she could relate to the most.

But when she asked her again about it and the Crazy Bitch didn't want to talk about it anymore. She just dismissed it by saying, "Let me ask you this: how many teenage girls do you know who got raped by both her brother and grandfather and had their grandfather's asshole buddy's kid. All that while turning tricks in the woods behind the house they just got kicked out of?"

Libbie thought about it for a second, but didn't answer. She did know someone who half those things had happened to.

Herself.

EIGHT

CRAWFORD HAD JUST GOTTEN OFF THE PHONE WITH HIS brother, Cam. Cam was telling him how the craving for alcohol had subsided and how he really believed what he was learning at Clairmount was working. He added that he was going to the gym every day and was the reigning king on the tennis court.

When Crawford had been up there the week before, he and Cam had had a rousing mixed doubles match with two of Cam's friends from the Monopoly game. Clairmount had once been the forty-acre home of a New York industrialist and had an old clay tennis court, which had seen better days. But, despite a weed or two growing out of the clay, it was playable. Crawford's partner had been a sixty-year-old woman who said she played a lot as a kid but didn't remember how to keep score anymore. Cam's partner was a young hard body who showed up in a crop top and gym shorts and insisted on shouting orders at him on every point.

But Cam didn't seem to mind that, or the fact that she played three-quarters of the court. A few patients, looking for a yuk or having nothing better to do, showed up to watch. Final score: Cam and his partner won in a tie-breaker, though Crawford's partner accused Cam of calling a lot of shots out that were clearly in.

Crawford left the next day after he and Cam had a long walk around the Clairmount grounds. Crawford was pretty convinced that Cam was going to make it. He had seemingly embraced everything he was learning at Clairmount and their success rate, Crawford had heard, was impressive.

On the plane ride back to West Palm Beach, Crawford had thought about Cam the whole way. How was it possible, he wondered, that a guy as smart, successful, kind, humorous, and generous as his brother, had fallen to such depths? It wasn't as though he had had a lousy childhood or any handicap to overcome. Cam basically, to use the cliché of the day, had been born on second base and had all the tools to get to home plate in a slow walk. But then Crawford remembered, that wasn't exactly true, because even as a kid Cam was periodically stricken with crippling waves of depression. Where getting out of bed was a major effort, and lying awake in bed was a dark place to churn and spin things into a terrible thick stew of sadness, ennui, and anxiety. But anyone looking at Cam would think, *Man, talk about a guy who's got it made.*

The morning's call from Cam confirmed the hope he'd felt on the plane ride home: Cam, he felt certain, would get out of Clairmount with the monkey off his back. Or at the very least, the monkey was going to weigh a hell of a lot less.

The Loadholt case, however, was not going to solve itself. Crawford met Ott in his office at 10:00 a.m. to catch each other up on what they had learned the day before.

First, Ott told him about having spoken to the lead Jupiter detective on Judge Meyer's murder. They had spoken for about twenty minutes, but it could have been accomplished in ten seconds. Long story short, the Jupiter cops came up blank, not even one clue. It had been sitting in the cold case file for a long time now.

Then Crawford told Ott about his conversation with Shirley Meyer.

"Strippers, huh?" said Ott. "Closest my game comes to that is when Martha Boland passes a bowl of pretzels in a tank top. Ain't pretty, let me tell ya."

Crawford laughed and leaned back in his chair. "Sounds like these guys hit the booze pretty hard," Crawford said. "Hopefully we can see all the players today. I've got the dog-track guy at one. Other two haven't called back yet."

The three regulars in Clyde Loadholt's poker game were Chuck Mitchell, the lawyer, Rob Jaworski, who used to manage the dog track in West Palm, and Lem Richey, who owned a few local Jiffy Lubes.

Crawford's phone rang. He punched the green button. "Crawford."

"Hello, Detective, this is Chuck Mitchell, you called me?"

"Yes, thanks for getting back to me, Mr. Mitchell. I'm one of the detectives on the murder of Clyde Loadholt. Me and my partner would like to meet with you, ask you some questions. Later this morning okay?"

"Ah, sure," said Mitchell. "Say eleven o'clock?"

Crawford glanced over at Ott. "Eleven good?"

Ott nodded.

"We can come to you, if you give me your address," Crawford said.

"Sure," Mitchell said and gave him the address of his office in West Palm Beach.

———

CRAWFORD AND OTT WERE IN A WHITE CAPRICE. OTT WAS AT the wheel going over the bridge to Chuck Mitchell's office.

"So I was listening to Steely Dan on the way in, that one called *The Definitive Collection*." Ott said.

Crawford nodded. "Yeah, great album, bullshit title, though."

Ott looked offended. "Whaddaya mean?"

"I mean, 'definitive collection'?" Crawford said. "Hey, it's only rock n' roll."

Ott smiled. *"But I like it...*as Mick would say."

"Yeah, but *Definitive Collection* oughta be for a wall full of Picasso's or something."

Ott shook his head and shot Crawford a skeptical glance. "I think you're overthinking it, Charlie."

"Maybe, but we *are* talking about Steely Dan here. Don't get me wrong, good, but the Stones...now that's a band with a definitive collection."

"Can't argue there."

"Know what I'd put at the top of the list?"

"Of what?"

"Stones' songs," Crawford said. "'Shattered,' 'Emotional Rescue,' 'Dead Flowers' and, of course, 'Paint it Black.'"

Ott stopped at a light and looked over. "Okay, all good, but what about 'Street Fightin' Man,' 'Play with Fire,' and 'Monkey Man'?"

"'Monkey Man'? You kiddin'? Not even top twenty," Crawford said as his cell phone rang.

He clicked it. "Hello."

"Hi, this is Lem Richey for Detective Crawford."

"Thanks for getting back to me, Mr. Richey," Crawford said. "I'm one of the detectives on the Clyde Loadholt murder. My partner and I would like to sit down with you. You got time this afternoon?"

"Sure. Whenever you say," Richey said.

"How about two?" Crawford said. "Know where the station house is on South County?"

"Course I do," Richey said. "Hey, I was a buddy of Clyde Loadholt, don't forget."

"Of course," Crawford said. "See you then."

"Jiffy Lube guy," he told his partner.

Ott drove them into an underground garage. "You s'pose these boys are gonna cop to the stripper visit?"

Crawford chuckled. "I wouldn't count on it."

Ott pulled into a spot on the second level of the underground garage. "I just don't get how you'd be able to concentrate on cards if you got a stripper flashin' her ta-ta's in your face."

Crawford smiled and shook his head. "But you might be willing to give it a try, right?"

NINE

CHUCK MITCHELL'S LAW OFFICE HAD A SECOND-RATE
reception area and was in a second-rate office building. Worst of all
was the magazine selection: *Readers Digest, Motor Trend, Bon
Appetit*, and the one Ott had just picked up.

"Never even heard of this." He held up a copy of *Sport's Illus-
trated Kids*. "What's it give you, junior high school soccer scores?"

"Got me," Crawford shrugged as a bald man in his sixties walked
in from the back.

"Detective Crawford?" the man said.

Crawford stood up and shook his hand. "And my partner, Detective Ott."

Then Ott shook Mitchell's hand.

"Come on back," Mitchell said turning.

The three went back and sat down in Mitchell's office.

"Sorry about what happened to your friend," Crawford said.

"Yeah, poor bastard," said Mitchell. "What a way to go."

Crawford and Ott nodded.

"We understand your poker game was still going strong, and
Clyde was still in it," Crawford said.

"Yeah, he wouldn't have missed it. He stayed sharp in retirement. Guy won way more than he lost."

Ott put his notebook down on the back of Mitchell's desk. "Mr. Mitchell, in all the conversations you fellas had over the years, did Clyde ever talk about anyone he was afraid might be out to get him? Someone who threatened him? Anything at all like that?"

Mitchell leaned back in his chair and cupped his chin. "Not really. Palm Beach is hardly a place with a lot of murderers and bad guys running around. Or guys making threats. Know what I mean?"

Crawford nodded. "He said something to his wife about meeting with someone to 'repair an old wound,'" Crawford said. "So we're thinking it might go way back. How long were you in the poker game?"

"From the beginning," Mitchell said. "The whole thing was actually my idea. Started out Rich Meyer, Clyde, Will Barnes and me. Then Will Barnes moved down to Lauderdale. So we got Lem Richey and Rob Jaworski in. Thing's been going for over twenty-five years."

"Every week, right?"

"Yeah, well, pretty much," said Mitchell. "We had a few canceled. But it was almost as regular as going to church."

If church was a place with strippers and lots of booze.

"Do you remember any conversations between Clyde and Rich Meyer about someone Clyde may have arrested and where Meyer was the judge?" Crawford asked.

"I see where you're going," Mitchell said. "A connection between Clyde and Rich's murder. Never thought about that before. Sorry, I can't remember anything at all like that. And that's something I'd probably remember."

"Nothing at all?"

"No, sorry," Mitchell said, shaking his head.

Crawford glanced over at Ott and thought he recognized Ott going into his wind-up, about to throw his high, hard curveball. His eyes got all squinty and he started breathing a beat faster.

"Mr. Mitchell," Ott started. "I went back a little ways. Before you opened your practice as a defense attorney, you worked as a prosecutor, correct?"

"Correct. Fourteen years."

"So what occurred to me is that maybe there was a case or two where Clyde Loadholt was the arresting officer, you were the prosecutor, and Rich Meyer was the judge." Ott said. "Then I took it a little further and wondered, could there be someone out to get all three of you?"

Mitchell looked chilled by the idea. "Talk about something I'd remember. It's a good theory, but it never happened. I was in quite a few trials where Rich presided, but I never prosecuted any case where Clyde was the arresting officer or involved in any way. I know that for a fact."

Ott shrugged and smiled. "Hey, you know how it is, half of what we do is theorize."

"And ninety percent of the time it doesn't pan out," Crawford said. "So not once were the three of you tied up in the same case?"

Mitchell shook his head. "Not once. Hey, I'd love to help you catch the guy but that never happened. If it had, I guess I'd be afraid I was next in line."

"Just throwing stuff at the wall," said Crawford. "Seeing if anything sticks."

Crawford looked over at Ott. Seemed like he was out of questions and theories. "You have anything else, Mort?"

Ott shook his head.

"Oh, yeah," Crawford said, like it was an afterthought, "one last thing. I heard something about...strippers at the poker games?"

Mitchell flushed crimson red. "Just once. It was a night I didn't play. I...I...I,..." He seemed to run out of gas.

"So you don't—"

"I don't want to talk about it," Mitchell said, his eyes circling the ceiling. "'Cause I wasn't there."

"But what—"

"End of story," Mitchell said. This time he stared Crawford straight in the eyes.

"Okay, Mr. Mitchell," Crawford said, pulling a card out of his wallet and handing it to Mitchell. "Thanks for your time. You think of anything else, anything at all, give me a call, please."

All three stood up. Crawford shook hands with Mitchell then Ott did. "I definitely will," said Mitchell. "Good luck catching the guy. I'll sleep a lot better once you've got him."

Crawford and Ott walked out of his office and to an elevator.

"That stripper thing," Ott said, pressing the elevator button. "Ol' Chuck didn't seem real comfortable on that subject."

"Yeah, like he had a spotless attendance record at the game, except that one time," Crawford said.

"I'm thinking there might be something to the stripper," Ott said as they walked out of the elevator.

Crawford turned to Ott in the lobby of the building. "So you thinkin' she goes and kills the judge, then three years later lures Loadholt out on a boat and kills him?"

"Hey, coulda happened," Ott said with a shrug. "I see 'skeptical Charlie' plastered all over your face. Hey, man, I'm just a guy lookin' for a link."

"I know. So am I," Crawford sighed, walking toward the Caprice. "Like you said to Mitchell, half of what we do is theorize."

"Yeah," Ott said. "And, like you said, ninety percent of the time it doesn't pan out."

"Yeah," said Crawford. "But probably more like ninety-nine percent."

TEN

The Mentors, as the five women called themselves, referred to it as the power booth. Off to the left and in the rear of Madeline's, a restaurant across from the Palm Beach Publix. There were three on one side and two on the other. The three on the one side—according to Forbes—represented a net worth of more than six billion dollars. They were, in no particular order, Marla Fluor, Elle T. Graham, and Diana Quarle. On the other side were Rose Clarke and Beth Jastrow, rich but nowhere near as rich as the other three.

Marla Fluor was, in fact, the first woman partner at Goldman Sachs. She had gone on to start her own investment fund, which had beaten the Dow in nineteen out of the past twenty years. Elle T. Graham was a woman from a little town in New Hampshire who had ended up in Silicon Valley at the age of twenty-two after graduating from Harvard. She had been a big player in a company called Wesabe, which went on to be one of the biggest crash-and-burns in Silicon Valley history. But she landed on her feet and launched Grouptank, which had been, and still was, a major homerun. Diana Quarle was right up there with Tory Burch in designing trendy women's clothes and shoes, all of which sported the distinctive Q. She now had more than nine hundred shops in high-end locations.

Beth Jastrow was a classic rags-to-riches story. With no college degree, she had started out as an eighteen-year-old cocktail waitress on a riverboat casino on the Mississippi. Then she moved up to black-jack dealer, after which she became the manager of a drop team that collected and transported the casino's daily revenues, and by age twenty-eight was the vice president of casino operations. Now, at age thirty-seven, thanks to a Chinese backer, she had a silent majority interest in two Las Vegas casinos.

Then there was Rose Clarke. Poorer by a few hundred million, Rose could hold her own in business and just about any other arena.

They were discussing a woman that their group was taking under their wing to try to help bring to a higher level of business success.

"I've never seen hustlers like the Vietnamese," Marla Fluor was saying. "I mean that in a very positive way. So the backstory on Sandy is she now has three shops and wants to go wide and franchise the whole operation."

She was talking about a thirty-year-old woman named Sandy Lu, who had two nail-and-spa salons in West Palm and one in Lake Worth.

"Think she's a little premature?" asked Beth, "West Palm, Lake Worth...the world?"

"Yeah, I do," Marla said. "But I like her spirit, and her ambition. Plus she's got a really great concept. She packs more into a thousand-square-foot space than I've ever seen before. Her gross is over three million for the one on Belvedere alone. And her gross per square foot is off-the-charts."

"Jesus," Rose said, after polishing off a bite of her Caesar-salad-hold-the-croutons-cause-it-might-be-fattening."That's incredible. Know what her net is?"

"Twenty-five percent," Marla said. "Five hundred K. Then close to four hundred between the other two."

"So what's she need us for?" Beth asked.

"Lots of things," Marla said. "She's plowed a lot of the money back into the spas and doesn't have a lot of capital on hand. And franchising is capital-intensive. But mainly she needs help with the big picture, not to mention our contacts."

"I'm in," Beth said.

"Me too," Diana said. "I can help her with my retail connections."

Behind their booth, the door opened and Crawford and Ott walked in.

"Jesus, who's that?" Diana asked as the men strolled to the counter.

Rose swung around. "Oh, that's two of Palm Beach's finest. Detective Charlie Crawford is the one I believe you're referring to. And his partner, Mort Ott."

"He's gorgeous," Diana said. She did not mean Ott.

"And single," Rose said, choosing not to mention her special relationship with him.

"Is he the guy who used to be up in New York?" Diana asked. "Had a thing with that actress for a while?"

Rose nodded. "Yeah, Gwendolyn Hyde."

"How do you know so much about him?" Marla asked.

Rose batted her eyelashes and looked down. "We're friends."

"What kind of friends?"

"All right, you two," Elle said. "You sound like a couple of cheerleaders getting all hot and bothered about the quarterback. Can we please get back to Sandy Lu?"

"Yeah, we're supposed to be captains of industry," Beth said. "Not a bunch of pom-pom girls."

"I SAW YOUR GIRLFRIEND WHEN WE CAME IN," OTT SAID, sitting down at the counter.

Crawford shook his head. "I don't have a girlfriend, my chubby little friend," Crawford said.

"Cut the shit, Charlie," Ott said. "That wasn't you coming out of a certain house on the ocean this morning when I was on my way in to the station?"

Crawford groaned and snuck a look up at Rose's table.

Diana, Marla and Rose were all giving him fluttery little hand waves.

ELEVEN

Rob Jaworski, the man who'd once managed the dog track in West Palm Beach, arrived at the station at exactly one. Crawford guessed he was in his early seventies. He was slightly stooped, had watery eyes, and walked very slowly.

But, boy, could he talk.

He spent the better part of forty-five minutes theorizing about the possible suspects in the death of his poker-playing friend, Clyde Loadholt. His first suspect was a man, Jaworski had no idea what his name was, who, many years ago, had cut off Loadholt in his car on Dixie Highway. The incident had quickly escalated and, long story short, the man had first thrown a full can of Coke at Loadholt's car, then pulled a gun out of his glove compartment and waved it threateningly at Loadholt as they both were doing fifty.

Loadholt had called for back up as he stayed behind the man at a safe distance.

After the man was pulled over and arrested, he clocked in at 0.126 on the drunkometer and, a month later, made the mistake of representing himself at his trial. He ended up spending a week in jail, lost his job because the story made the front page of the *Palm Beach*

Morning News, and eventually his wife left him. Then, one day, according to Jaworski, he called up Loadholt again and threatened to burn his house down. Loadholt arrested him again. And again, the man, who was drunk at the time he made the call, went back to jail, after once more trying to act as his own attorney.

"How long ago was this?" Crawford asked.

Jaworski thought for a second, doing the math. "Oh, maybe twenty-two, twenty-three years ago."

"You really think that twenty-two, twenty-three years later that man would decide to lure Clyde onto a boat and kill him?" Crawford asked.

Jaworski threw his hands up in the air. "I don't know," he said. "Maybe he got drunk again and figured Clyde was the reason his whole life was in the shitter. You never know, the man was a complete hothead."

Crawford glanced over at Ott, who was chewing the tip of his pen, apparently having decided he didn't need to take notes anymore.

"Got any more thoughts on the matter, Mr. Jaworski?" Ott looked like he wasn't sure he should ask.

"Well, matter-of-fact, I do," Jaworski said.

Ott didn't look surprised.

"There was this cop who, according to Clyde, was dirty," Jaworski said. "I can't remember exactly what he did, something to do with taking bribes from somebody."

Couldn't get much more general than that, thought Crawford, thrumming his fingers on his desk.

"Or, no, I remember what it was. Somehow Clyde found out about a contractor bribing someone on a government project. Yeah, yeah, that's what it was."

"So what happened?" Ott asked, restlessly.

"Clyde had him drummed out of the department," Jaworski snapped his fingers, "just like that. No pension. No nothing. Clyde didn't tolerate any of his guys not walking the straight and narrow, so everyone said."

Crawford looked at Ott, like...*had he missed something?* Ott looked baffled too.

"Wait, you said the guy was a contractor, not a cop?" Ott said.

"Yeah, well, one or the other," Jaworski said.

Crawford saw Ott's silent chuckle.

"Did this also take place twenty-two, twenty-three years ago?" Crawford asked.

Jaworski thought for a second. "More like twenty-five."

Crawford snuck a look at Ott, then his watch. It was five of two. Fifty-five minutes of theories, none of which seemed to add up to much.

"Then there was his granddaughter," Jaworski moved on.

"What about his granddaughter?" Ott asked, stifling a yawn.

"There was real bad blood there," Jaworski said. "Something happened. Don't know what, though."

"Bad blood between Clyde and his granddaughter, you mean?" Crawford asked.

"So I heard," Jaworski said.

"About what?" Crawford asked.

Jaworski went into a thousand-mile stare. Finally, "Sorry, I can't remember exactly."

Crawford looked at his watch again. It was 2:03. "One final question, were you there when a stripper came to Loadholt's house, the night of a poker game?"

Jaworski's expression didn't change. "A stripper?" he said, scratching the back of his head. "I don't know anything about a stripper. Well, there was one at my brother's bachelor party, but that was like...forty-five years ago."

"Mr. Jaworski," Crawford said. "I want to thank you for coming in. You've been very helpful, but we have another interview that was supposed to have begun a few minutes ago."

Jaworski looked disappointed. Like he could have gone on for another couple of hours. Like what the hell was he supposed to do with the rest of his day?

"Glad I could help," Jaworski said getting to his feet. "You boys ever need me again, I'd be happy to come back in and help you solve this sucker."

THE FIRST WORDS OUT OF LEM RICHEY'S MOUTH AS HIS OLD friend, Rob Jaworski, walked out of the station were, "Did the old buzzard talk your ear off?" Richey was the man who owned the Jiffy Lubes and looked to be in his mid-sixties.

"We had an interesting conversation," Crawford said tactfully, leading Richey back to his office where Ott was waiting.

Richey chuckled over an apparent memory of Jaworski after being introduced to Ott. "We had to practically gag him sometimes," he said. "Had this little joke that the reason the dogs ran so fast at his track was to get away from Rob and all his jawboning."

Crawford and Ott laughed politely.

Richey chuckled to himself. "I didn't say it was a good joke," he said. "I used to think that Rob's chatter was a way to distract us in the poker game. You know, so we'd mess up. But maybe I was over-thinking it—" then a sudden frown came across Richey's face. "By the way, I want it understood, no questions about any strippers."

Crawford glanced at Ott, then back at Richey. "Did you talk to Chuck Mitchell, Mr. Richey?"

"Doesn't matter who I spoke to," Richey said. "Is that understood?"

Reluctantly, Crawford nodded.

Unlike his poker friend, Lem Richey didn't have any theories. He just said he was really shocked when he saw the story in the *Morning News* about Loadholt's murder. Said Loadholt was really generous with the booze on poker nights and how he thought the game was pretty much all Loadholt had for a social life anymore. Kept to himself, tended his garden, and watched his Marlins on TV.

Crawford and Ott saw Richey out a little after two thirty then went back to Crawford's office.

"That was a waste of a perfectly good hour and a half," Ott said.

"You don't think our killer was any of Jaworski's suspects?" Crawford said with a smile, sitting at his desk.

Ott laughed and shook his head. "I'd say the priest at my church is more likely to have done it," he said. "I mean, a guy Loadholt busted for road rage somewhere back in the nineteenth century? A dirty cop or was he a contractor? His granddaughter pissed off for some goddamn reason… I mean, are you eff-ing kidding me?"

Crawford smiled and shook his head. "Let's split up Loadholt's past cases," he said. "See if the guy's as squeaky clean as Rutledge remembers him being."

TWELVE

Ted Bundy was more famous than the Crazy Bitch, but not by much. Plus the Crazy Bitch had a big time movie made about her, and all Bundy got was a lame made-for-TV flick. Like her, the lights went out for Bundy at Florida State Prison. The difference was he went out in the clutches of Old Sparky, whereas she took a lethal injection thirteen years later.

Back in 2002, Libbie had driven down to Raiford and met with the Crazy Bitch again. She was pretty near the end of the road on death row but was still chatty. The first thing Libbie asked her was what she did when she first left home.

"Left home?" said the Crazy Bitch. "That makes it sound like I had a choice in the matter. Like I told you before, my grandfather kicked me out of the house at age fifteen, after one of his buddies knocked me up."

"I remember you telling me that," Libbie said. "I'm wondering where you went after you got kicked out?"

"Told you that too. Ended up in the woods behind my house in Michigan turning tricks for beer money. I didn't know where else to go. Eventually ended up getting the hell out of there. Became a pretty decent hitchhiking hooker, also known as a truck-stop whore." She smiled like she was talking about getting straight A's on her report card.

"And at some point you got married, right?"

The Crazy Bitch roared with laughter. "Oh, yeah, that was a fuckin' doozie. I was twenty and the horny old bastard was sixty-nine. You can imagine that was a match made in heaven."

"I'll bet."

"Got annulled after a few weeks," the Crazy Bitch said. "Then I went back on the road. Lived in the back of cars, cheap motels, and jail."

"Jail?"

"Oh, yeah, honey, between drunk driving, armed robbery, obstruction of justice, disturbing the peace—"

"How'd you disturb the peace?"

The Crazy Bitch cackled. "How didn't I? One time I threw a cue ball at a bartender in this dive in Daytona. Another time tossed a plate of grits that had pubic hair in 'em at a waitress. You name it, I disturbed it."

"What else did you do?"

The Crazy Bitch cocked her head. "Why are you so curious?"

"Because I can relate to what you've been through."

The Crazy Bitch looked at Libbie in disbelief.

"Oh, yeah. You can relate, huh?" said the Crazy Bitch. "'Cause you had a kid at fourteen, 'cause you lived in the back of an old Pontiac, 'cause you married a guy fifty years older 'n you?"

"Well, not exactly."

"Not exactly. I'm lookin' at you and I see this righteous young thing—what early twenties?"

"Twenty."

"A twenty-year-old chick with a nice dress and an expensive ring—"

"I ran away from home when I was a kid. Been workin' eighty-hour weeks ever since—"

The Crazy Bitch shook her head so hard it looked like a filling might shake loose. "Well, bully the fuck for you, darlin'."

"I'm sorry, I didn't mean that to sound—"

"Like a holier-than-thou little bitch. Too late, cupcake," the Crazy Bitch said. "You're sitting there judging me, that's what this is all about. 'Cause you're thinkin' I'm the way it coulda gone for you if you didn't work your sweet little ass off, dug yourself out of the big fuckin' hole you were in?"

The Crazy Bitch had pretty much hit the nail on the head. Even though Libbie really was genuinely sympathetic too. "No, that's not it at all," she lied. "I just want to understand."

The Crazy Bitch shook her head, unconvinced. "Understand? Where the fuck's that get you?"

Now desperate to change the subject, Libbie asked, "So what else did you do?" One thing was clear, the Crazy Bitch liked detailing her criminal exploits.

"Like I said, what didn't I? Armed robbery, check-forging, car theft, whatever the fuck I had to, to stay alive."

Libbie nodded. She had successfully gotten the focus off of herself. The guard with the crew cut came up behind her.

"Ten more minutes," he said.

Libbie nodded and turned back to the Crazy Bitch.

"Was there ever a moment when you thought, 'I'm gonna turn it around. I don't give a damn how bad I had it as a kid. I don't care how many bad things happened to me that I didn't deserve—'"

"Okay, cut the shit, will you," said the Crazy Bitch, shaking her head so hard saliva flew. "Just 'cause that's your story doesn't make it mine. No way I was ever going to have a sane, normal life 'cause nobody I knew had a clue what a sane, normal life was. You think I had role models? Think I grew up in the Partridge family?" Suddenly, the Crazy Bitch went into a laughing fit and her whole tone changed. "I remember wondering whether Susan Dey balled her grandfather. I remember wondering why they called it the Partridge family in the first place. Why'd they pick a bird and since they did, why not the Vulture family or the Yellow-bellied Sapsucker family." She laughed her little maniacal laugh again. "I remember wondering whether Susan Dey married that guy with the hat."

Libbie had no clue. "What guy with the hat?"

"You know, Boy George."

"What?" said Libbie, totally lost.

"Susan Dey George, duh?"

Wow, so this is what prison does to you, Libbie thought to herself.

The guard came up behind her and tapped his watch.

That was the last time Libbie spoke to the Crazy Bitch.

A month later—October 9, 2002, at 9:47 a.m. EDT—she died by lethal injection. She declined the last meal that she was entitled to and had a cup of coffee instead. Her last words were, "Yes, I would just like to say I'm sailing with the rock, and I'll be back, like *Independence Day*, with Jesus, June 6, like the movie. Big mother ship and all. I'll be back, I'll be back."

At least so far, she has not been spotted.

THIRTEEN

Ott walked into Crawford's office with a big grin on his face.

Crawford leaned back in his chair and put his hands behind his head. "I can tell you got something good. I'm assuming on Loadholt."

"Correct on both assumptions," Ott said sitting down across from Crawford. "I've got two suspects, both—turns out—of the female persuasion."

"Really?" said Crawford. "Tell me all about it."

"Okay, so the first one happened thirteen years ago," Ott said. "About three years before Loadholt retired at the age of sixty."

"Okay, so he was around fifty-seven."

Ott nodded. "There were a series of home burglaries that took place in houses that were on the ocean."

Crawford nodded. "Like how many?"

"Six over the course of a year, mainly snatching jewelry—necklaces, rings, watches—plus some furs and one time a couple of expensive paintings. Only thing they had was that on two occasions a couple was seen walking on the beach near the house that got hit. Both times it was like nine or ten at night, kind of an unusual hour for a beach stroll, and the witnesses said, in both cases, it was an older guy and a young woman."

"So they were scouts?" Crawford asked. "Looking for a house where no one was home?"

"Good guess," Ott said. "So Loadholt posted some under covers on the beach and also a couple guys on a boat, including himself. The boat would run with no lights and the engine cut, patrolling. One night, report said it was really foggy, one of the under covers on the beach saw a couple go into a house from the beach side. He radioed the boat, which Loadholt happened to be on that night, and waited. Ten minutes later the couple—older guy, younger woman— came running out of the house with full pillowcases in both hands and ran down to a boat that had just pulled up a few feet from shore."

"So Loadholt was nearby in his boat?" Crawford asked.

Ott leaned forward in his chair. "Yeah, and he pulls up—'cause it's all foggy—not far from the other boat, just waiting for the couple to get on, then take 'em down."

"So what happened?"

"Turned out the suspects had a lot faster boat than Loadholt's," Ott said. "The couple got on it, a cop with Loadholt flashed a big light at 'em, while Loadholt, through a bullhorn, told 'em to shut off the engine and put their hands up." Ott took a pull on his water. "So the guy driving the boat suddenly guns it. Turns out it's a Cigarette with a 2,200-horsepower Mercedes engine that the driver races in his spare time. In like three seconds all Loadholt sees is spray. He pulls out his Glock and starts firing, totally blind. Can't see anything but spray."

"Yeah, and?"

"Couple of bullets hit the boat's engine and it dies," Ott said, taking another pull on his water. "Another one hits one of the burglars."

"Jesus, what happened?" Crawford asked.

"Loadholt pulls up to the boat, and the woman's hysterical.

Screaming at Loadholt, 'You killed him, you killed him.'" Ott lowered his voice, "Turns out her father took one right in the head."

"Holy shit," Crawford said. "Was there any kind of disciplinary thing? That's not exactly by-the-book."

Ott shook his head. "No, Loadholt's story was he heard gunshots and returned fire. That the people in the Cigarette were shooting at them. The guys with him backed him up. So the girl gets attempted murder."

Crawford shook his head slowly. "I'm getting the sense Loadholt was kind of a loose cannon," he said. "Literally."

"Yeah, well, wait 'til you hear the next one," Ott said. "But to finish it up, the daughter and the guys on her boat go to trial and the daughter's lawyer points out how there were no guns found on the Cigarette. He's trying to get them to drop the attempted murder charge, reduce it to aggravated burglary. And of course, Loadholt testifies that he saw them tossing guns over the side. Then the daughter gets up and says she and her father never shot a gun in their whole lives. Anyway, at the sentencing, the daughter yells at Loadholt, 'You murdered my father and you're gonna pay. Trust me, we're gonna make sure of that.'"

"'We?'"

"That's what I wanted to know, so I dug around a little more and found out she has a brother down in Miami who supposedly heads this gang that hits banks and jewelry stores. He was actually on that show *America's Most Wanted*, got the nickname, 'the Ghost.' Has a couple murders on his lengthy resume."

Crawford was nodding. "So the obvious question—"

Ott nodded. "If he killed Loadholt, why would he wait thirteen years?"

"Yeah, exactly."

"Okay, so here's the clincher," Ott said. "The daughter, Sonia Reyes, is her name, just got out of Broward jail a month ago"

"No shit," Crawford said, clenching his fist. "Did you happen to check who the judge was?"

"Knowing you'd ask me that, I did," said Ott. "It wasn't Rich Meyer, but a guy named John Pickett."

Crawford looked at his watch. "All right, we gotta track down this Sonia Reyes," he said, getting up.

"I'm already on it," Ott said. "Where you going?"

"Mookie's," Crawford said, referring to a downscale cop bar in West Palm Beach.

"Don't you want to hear about the stripper?" Ott asked. "I saved the best for last."

"Yeah, I do," Crawford said. "But I'm meeting Don Scarpa over there. I want to hear what he has to say about Loadholt. They worked together for a long time. I'll come back here afterwards."

Ott looked at his watch. "You better get there pretty soon; that crusty old bastard's usually in the bag by seven."

"Yeah, but he can still think pretty straight even after six or seven Jim Beams."

ON THE WAY OVER TO MOOKIE'S CRAWFORD GOT A CALL ON HIS cell. 'Alexa Dillon,' according to the display.

"Hello," said Crawford.

"Hi, Charlie," she said. "It's Alexa Dillon, you know, that pesky reporter."

"Pesky and persistent. What's up?"

"I just wanted to know how you're coming on the Clyde Loadholt murder. And, once again, offer to buy you a drink to make up for—"

"Getting sand in my eyes?"

"Well, yeah."

"Sorry, Alexa, I don't drink. I've been a teetotaler since...well, that terrible day back in 2007."

"What happened back in 2007?" She asked, trepidation in her tone.

"Sorry, I...I can't talk about it."

"Okay," she said, "but I didn't think there was a cop in the world who didn't drink."

"Is that one of those stereotypes? Like all reporters are pains in the ass?"

She laughed. "Okay, then, what if I buy you a Coke?"

"All that sugar," Crawford said.

"All right, a bottle of water?"

"Sorry, Alexa, gotta go." Crawford swung into Mookie's parking lot. "Just pulled into my cop bar."

A pause. "So...that was all a big lie?" Alexa asked.

"Nah, just a little fib."

FOURTEEN

It was known as the Donald Bruce Scarpa Honorable Barstool and nobody sat in it except, of course, Don Scarpa. It was down at the end of the bar right under the poster of Clint Eastwood in the role of Dirty Harry, complete with his .44 Magnum hand cannon. In fact, there was a resemblance between Scarpa and the old actor, though Scarpa was twenty years younger than Clint and had a whole lot less hair.

Scarpa had a Marlboro dangling out of his mouth and a fresh Jim Beam and water in one hand. The owner, another ex-cop, Jack Scarsiola, had demanded, cajoled, and pleaded with Scarpa many times not smoke in his establishment, but Scarpa ignored him. On several occasions, Scarsiola had pointed out that Scarpa was in a profession committed to upholding the law—and no smoking in a public establishment was the law. Scarpa, who had been retired for twelve years, had responded in his typically cryptic manner, "Ain't a cop no more, bucko."

"Thanks for taking a break from your busy day to see me," said Crawford slipping into the barstool next to Scarpa.

Scarpa chuckled. "That meant to be humorous?"

"Just givin' you a little shit," Crawford said. "Keeps you on your toes."

"I see," said Scarpa with a wry smile. "So you wanted to ask me about my old buddy, Clyde Loadholt?"

"Yeah," said Crawford, holding up his hand for the bartender. "What can you tell me about him?"

"A ballbuster," Scarpa said. "Made Rutledge seem like a day at the beach. Ran a pretty tight ship, which a lot of people liked."

"Yeah, someone else said that," Crawford said, as the bartender put down a mug of Bud in front of him.

Crawford flicked off the foamy head with a finger and took a long sip. "I'm getting the impression he was the type to shoot first and ask questions later."

Scarpa laughed.

"What?"

"Palm Beach ain't exactly Dodge City," Scarpa said. "Not usually a lot of shooting going on in your little burg."

Crawford nodded. "Yeah, I hear you, but every once in a while," he said. "Like when he shot that guy on a boat who'd been burglarizing houses on the ocean."

Scarpa nodded and thought for a second. "I forgot about that. That was like out of *Miami Vice* or something. Also, there was another thing that happened. Where Loadholt crippled a guy."

Crawford swung his head around to Scarpa. "You're kiddin'. What the hell happened?"

Scarpa lit up another Marlboro with his vintage Zippo. "So I think it was the reason he had to retire two years before mandatory," he said. "See, there was this really public gay couple who Loadholt always seemed to be busting for minor shit. Just didn't like seein' 'em around."

"What do you mean, really public?"

"Well, like kissing in restaurants, I heard. Shit like that. But, you know, harmless shit," Scarpa said. "So what happened was the two of them were walking down Worth Avenue one day, holding hands, and along comes Loadholt."

"Oh, Christ," said Crawford.

"So he tells 'em to knock it off or something."

"Like there's a public ordinance against it," Crawford said, shaking his head.

"Yeah, I know. So apparently they'd been drinking and one of 'em lips off to Loadholt. Tells him to go fuck himself or something. So Loadholt loses it and decks the guy. Starts kickin' the shit out of him, then the other one jumps on his back."

"Jesus, right in the middle of Worth Avenue?"

"Yeah, right in front of Polo, I remember," Scarpa said. "So, long story short, when the guy hit the pavement something happened to his back and he ends up paralyzed."

Crawford was shaking his head very slowly, tempted to ask Scarpa for a cigarette. "That's unbelievable. Why wasn't he fired right away?"

"'Cause he said the guy threatened him," Scarpa said. "Had a pistol in his waistband."

"You're shittin' me? Hardly sounds like a guy—"

"Everybody figured it was a throw-down that Loadholt pulled out of his ankle holster or something," Scarpa said. "Which is exactly what the other guy claimed. That he saw Loadholt stuff it in his buddy's waistband. But, ends up being Loadholt's word against theirs."

"That's incredible," said Crawford, draining his Bud.

"Palm Beach got hit with a five million dollar lawsuit, which it ended up settling. The gay couple, I heard, got the hell out of town."

"Jesus, who can blame 'em."

"You got anything yet on his murder?" Scarpa asked.

"We just came up with a suspect. Ott's been digging around. Up 'til then we didn't have squat. Nothing but a few people probably pretty happy Loadholt's dead," Crawford said. "Like these two guys you're talking about. Pretty unlikely, though, they'd do something so long after it happened."

Scarpa shrugged. "You never know, man."

Crawford got to his feet. "Thanks for fillin' me in, Don. I appreciate it. Gotta head back to the station, hear about a stripper at Loadholt's house."

"Oh, you mean at his poker game?"

"Yeah, you know about that?"

"Fuck, yeah, those games were notorious," Scarpa said. "I heard he'd send his wife over to her sister's whenever they played."

"On the theory that what she didn't know wouldn't hurt her?"

"Something like that."

CRAWFORD GOT BACK TO THE STATION AT 7:30 P.M. OTT AND the woman in dispatch were the only ones there. Ott came into Crawford's office with an apple in his hand and asked what Scarpa had to say about Loadholt.

Crawford filled him in.

"Jesus, Rutledge's beginning to sound like a goddamn saint compared to this guy," Ott said.

"Yeah, I know," Crawford said. "So tell me about the stripper."

Ott put his apple down on Crawford's desk. "Okay, so apparently they found her at Gussie's, a strip club up on 45th Street" Ott said. "You ever heard of it?"

Crawford shook his head.

"That's the right answer, Charlie. Good to know you stay out of dens of iniquity like that," Ott said with a grin. "So she came to Loadholt's house—I guess his wife was away or something."

"Yeah, Scarpa said Loadholt sent her over to her sister's sometimes."

"Just where I'd want to go. Hang out with Mavis the mouth." Ott shook his head. "And by the way, if you're Susie Loadholt, wouldn't that get you a little suspicious? Your husband tellin' you to go see sis so he can get shitfaced and eye-fuck strippers?"

"Eye-fuck?"

Ott nodded. "Yeah, you've never heard that before?"

Crawford shook his head. "No, but it's very colorful, Mort."

Ott snickered. "Anyway, I guess the stripper starts peeling and having a few drinks with the boys."

"Wait, where'd you get all this?"

"The transcript of the trial."

Crawford's mouth dropped.

"Guess I didn't mention that," Ott said, picking up his apple. "There was a trial."

Ott took a bite, chewed, and swallowed.

"You're kidding? And what was the charge?" Crawford asked.

"Rape. She claims she got raped, by Meyer."

Crawford was silent.

"So she went home after leaving Loadholt's. She's all hysterical and traumatized, so her husband calls the cops. Well, obviously that's a joke since Loadholt *is* the cops. Flash forward to the shortest trial in history. I mean, you got a defendant who's a judge and an accuser who's a stripper. Who, of course, the defense attorney makes out to be a hooker. Who you s'pose is gonna win that one? You know how it goes, basically she's the one who ends up getting put on trial."

"Yeah, I've seen that movie a million times," said Crawford, taking a sip of coffee.

"So after the trial, the stripper—"

"How 'bout calling her by her name," Crawford said.

Ott held up his hands. "Jesus, sorry, man. Chelsea McKinnon," he said. "So after the trial, Chelsea's husband gets interviewed by some TV reporter and totally flips out, says something like there's a 'place in hell for animals like them.' Then says, quote-unquote, 'Their day will come, trust me.'"

Ott tossed his apple into Crawford's wastebasket.

"So, sure enough, it did come," said Crawford.

Ott took a peek inside his notebook. "Yeah, five and eight years later."

Crawford nodded. "But I'm having the same reaction I keep having: if it was Chelsea's husband who killed 'em, why'd he wait so long?"

Ott shrugged. "I hear you, people usually cool off over time."

"Okay, so let's split 'em up," Crawford said, draining his coffee. "I'll go talk to Sonia Reyes and then I'll track down the gay couple. You talk to Chelsea and her husband and also see what else you can find out about Loadholt's stellar career."

Ott started shaking his head.

"What?" Crawford asked.

"It's amazing to me that the guy stuck around for as long as he did," Ott said.

"Yeah, 'cept it sounds like he was a master at covering his tracks. Plus, he mighta had the knack Rutledge has."

"And that would be?"

"Sucking up to those in high places."

FIFTEEN

Marla Fluor, Elle T. Graham, Diana Quarle, Beth Jastrow, and Rose Clarke were in a small private, dining room in the back of Cafe L'Argentine, a five-star restaurant on Royal Palm Way.

"So Sandy is off and running," said Elle, the billionaire Silicon Valley entrepreneur.

They were talking about Sandy Lu, the ambitious nail-shop owner.

"Yeah, girl's definitely going places," Diana said. "I got her hooked up with my friend who franchised that chain of Thai restaurants, Tamarind Seed."

"Yum," said Rose Clarke. "I love their food. So Sandy's going into Miami, Jacksonville and Orlando?"

"Tampa, too," Elle said. "It's tough holding her back. She wanted to go wide in all of the Southeast, not just Florida."

Marla laughed. "We tried to explain the concept of baby steps, but she just kept saying, 'I want to be in all fifty states,' in that cute little accent of hers."

"So we told her, all in due time," Elle said.

"What did she say?" Beth asked

"'So, you mean, by next year?'" Elle said and all of them laughed.

"I used to be like that," Diana said. "It takes its toll after a while, though. You're just exhausted all the time"

All five nodded.

Beth took a sip of her wine, then put it down. "Okay, so I want to talk about this woman singer who absolutely killed at Balthazar."

Balthazar was one of the two Vegas casinos that Beth Jastrow had a majority interest in.

Elle Graham frowned. "I don't exactly see us going into show biz. Not exactly our wheelhouse."

"Why not, it could be fun?" Diana said. "I know Oprah's agent. That might be a pretty good start, if she's really that good."

"Trust me, world-class," said Beth.

"What's her name?" Diana asked. "And what kind of singer is she?"

"Name's Lulu Perkins," Beth said. "And I'd say a cross between Sheryl Crowe and, um, Janis Joplin maybe."

"Well, they did pretty well for themselves," Diana said. "Where can we see her?"

"She's got a gig coming up in Atlanta, I think," Beth said.

"A 'gig,' huh?" Diana said. "How very hip of you."

Beth laughed and shrugged. "Hey, that's what you call it."

Rose raised her wine glass. "Well, come on then," she said. "Road trip."

The five clinked glasses.

SIXTEEN

CRAWFORD HAD A DREAM ABOUT HIS OLD GIRLFRIEND, Dominica McCarthy. He'd had a few in the last month. They were at something that resembled a junior prom and he asked her to dance. The problem was the words came out of his mouth really slowly and before he got the whole question out she was dancing with a guy who looked like a young Norm Rutledge with a pink bow tie and baggy white ducks. Being beaten out by Rutledge was about as low as he could go, so he got out of bed and decided to try to erase the memory with a jolt of Dunkin' Donuts—dark, no sugar.

The diminutive Janelle smiled up at Crawford. "The usual, Charlie?"

"No, I'm gonna ix-nay the shot of milk and sugar. Just black, please."

"Ix-nay?"

"Pig Latin," Crawford said. "Maybe they don't teach that in school anymore."

"But you're not ix-naying the two blueberry donuts, right?"

"Never," said Crawford. "Gotta have my health food."

He took his coffee and donuts and settled in with the *Palm Beach*

Morning News, which was, at most, a fifteen-minute read. He had tracked down Sonia Reyes the night before, gotten her phone number and called her. She did not warm to the idea of talking to a cop, but eventually he'd persuaded her to meet at her house in West Palm. Their meeting would take place in...he checked his watch. Oops. Five minutes from now.

SONIA REYES LIVED IN A MODEST RANCH HOUSE THAT HAD electric blue shutters and was dwarfed by a twenty-foot tall Canary Island date palm tree. She answered the door with a scowl and a lop-sided tilt of the head.

"Thank you for seeing me, Ms. Reyes," Crawford said. "I'm Detective Crawford." He was doing his best 'charmin Charlie', which was what Rose Clarke had dubbed it. He was pretty sure Reyes wasn't going for it, though.

"Yes, Detective," said Reyes, "let's get this over with."

She was tall and paper-thin, probably around his age, which was thirty-nine. She had penetrating green eyes and looked as if she might blow away if a stiff breeze kicked up. Not exactly the profile of a partner in a burglary team. Or a killer.

He followed her in to a sun-filled living room that had a lot of heavy furniture and bouquets of flowers everywhere.

"Beautiful flowers," said Crawford.

"They're fake," said Reyes, motioning to a club chair.

Crawford sat down in it. "So Ms. Reyes, I'll get right to the point. As I'm sure you have either read or heard, Police Chief Clyde Loadholt was killed the day before yesterday."

She nodded. "And you think I might have had something to do with it?"

"It's my job to go around and talk to everyone who might have had a motive to kill Loadholt," Crawford said. "And because of his involvement in the death of your father, I needed to talk to you."

"Involvement? Is that your word for it?" Reyes said. "That bastard killed my dad in cold blood. We weren't shooting at them. My dad never shot a gun in his whole life. We were just trying to get away."

Crawford nodded. "I understand," he said. "Ms. Reyes, where can I find your brother? How do I get in touch with him?"

Reyes laughed. "You get on a plane and fly to Mexico City, then go out to the suburbs to a quaint little town called Almoloya de Juarez, then go to Altiplano Federal Penitentiary. That's the same place where El Chapo Guzman escaped from. You didn't do your homework, Detective. My brother's been there four years."

Thanks a lot, Mort.

Crawford had planned to ask Reyes whether she had a boat, thinking it might be the boat on which Loadholt may have gotten killed. But there was no way in hell this woman could have lured Clyde Loadholt onto a boat or anywhere else. Plus, there was no way Loadholt would have had a pang of conscience to go "repair an old wound" for having killed her father.

Crawford got to his feet. "Thank you for your time, Ms. Reyes," he said as she stood up too.

"Just so you know," she said, her eyes flinty and her jaw set, "I intend to go dance on that man's grave just as soon as he's in the ground."

Crawford smiled and nodded, thinking, *Somehow I doubt you'll be the only one.*

SEVENTEEN

CRAWFORD GOT A CALL ON HIS CELL IN THE CAR. HE recognized it as a Connecticut prefix, 203, and thought immediately of his brother. He picked up.

"Hey, Chas, it's your fuck-up brother," Cam Crawford said.

"You mean my *former* fuck-up brother," Crawford said.

There was a long pause. "Nah, 'fraid not," Cam said, sounding grim. "I had a little relapse."

"Oh, shit, what happened?" Crawford asked, pulling over to the side of the road.

Cam laid out the whole sad story in painful detail. He had arranged to be picked up by a limo—without the knowledge or approval of the authorities at Clairmount—in the early morning and headed into New York to attend a breakfast business meeting with an important client. It had gone well but on his way back the sight of one bar after another along Third Avenue, the majority of which he had logged hours in, was too much for Cam's rapidly diminishing willpower. He had asked the limo driver to pull over in front of one establishment that, he fondly remembered, made one of the best martinis in town. And at ten thirty in the morning, he'd ordered one. Then another. Then a third. After that he stopped counting.

He had tried to slip back into Clairmount without anybody noticing, but had gotten caught just as he was about to get to the safety of his bedroom, where he planned to sleep it off.

Now a special meeting was going to be held that night to see whether Cam was going to be kicked out of Clairmount.

Crawford sighed and thought for a moment. "First thing you gotta just get down on your knees and beg," he said. "Tell 'em how much you need the place. And, yeah, how it was a bad slip-up—I would *not* say fuck-up—but it will never happen again. Tell 'em how you're gonna redouble your efforts, work harder than ever, and be able to look back at that moment as the turning point in your life."

"I don't know, Chas," Cam said. "It's a pretty serious offense."

"No, shit, I get that," Crawford said. "But you get booted and you'll be back in the first bar you see."

"Yeah, I know. I probably shouldn't be back out in the real world at this time of my life."

"Damn right. You should be in a goddamn straitjacket," Crawford said. "Oh, hey, I got another idea. Tell 'em about how you were thinking about creating a scholarship or something at Clairmount. Or, how about this? Give 'em a building. You know, in honor of your beloved brother, The Charles A. Crawford Halfway House has a nice ring to it. I'm kidding, but it sure as hell doesn't hurt to remind 'em you're a rich guy. That you want to give back a bunch of money to your alma mater, good ole Clairmount."

"That's not a bad idea," Cam said.

"I know," Crawford said, "but remember, you'd really have to do it."

"Hey, whatever it takes."

EIGHTEEN

CAM HAD A BRAND NEW HAMMER IN HIS TOOL BELT AS HE walked up the steps to the house at 102 South Ocean Boulevard. New work boots too. Like this was his first day on the job. But the job at 102 South Ocean had actually started five weeks before. Beside him, Marco was carrying a red metal toolbox, also brand new, but he had scuffed it up with sand paper and dented it with his hammer so it didn't looked fresh off the rack. If all their tools seemed brand new they wouldn't look like real construction workers.

The third guy, Mel, came up behind them, pulling the 72-inch rolling metal toolbox that they had bought cheap on Ebay. It came with rows of shelves for tools, but Mel had taken them all out so now it was just a big empty box with nothing in it.

Cam had come by a few days earlier and had seen the Butler Brothers sign on the front lawn of the house on South Ocean. He took down the number and got his girlfriend to call it. She got a man named Jason Butler. She told Butler that she and her uncle, owners of the house at 102 South Ocean, were sick with the flu and didn't want to hear a lot of electric saws and nail guns, so could the work crew not come to the house on Friday. She added that her uncle was happy to pay them extra for the downtime. Butler said yes, that was no problem, but they should come on Monday, right? The girlfriend said yes, that should hopefully give them enough time to get over the flu.

Cam knocked on the front door of the house. All three of them were wearing dust masks and caps and about all you could see were their eyes. A Latina woman answered the door, looked them over, then laughed. "You men look like banditos," she said in a lilting Spanish accent.

Cam gave her a big smile. "We're the finish carpenters," he said, "here to work on the guesthouse."

The woman nodded and motioned them inside. She walked through the house with them behind her and opened the French doors that went out to the swimming pool and the guesthouse behind it. She pointed, "Right over there."

"Thanks." Cam went through the door followed by Marco and Mel, with the tall, rolling toolbox. The three went up to the second story of the guesthouse. There was a stack of two by fours, a sawhorse, and several boxes of nails off to one side in the living room.

Cam looked at Marco and smiled, "You know how to saw?"

Marco nodded.

"Well, go for it," Cam said. "Probably a good idea we make a little noise up here."

Two hours later the girl came out to the pool. Cam looked down and saw her as she took off a white terrycloth robe, spread suntan lotion on her body, and lay down on the green slatted chaise longue.

He walked downstairs and past the pool to the main house. He had the dust mask on so the girl couldn't see his face. She saw him and gave him a wave. He waved back.

He opened the French doors to the house and walked in. The

woman walked out of the kitchen when she heard his footsteps. "Can I help you?" she asked.

"I just wondered if I could get some ice," he said. "The water I brought got pretty warm."

She gave him a nod and a smile. "Sure, come on in."

He followed her into the kitchen. "Anybody else here?" he asked casually as he reached down for his hammer.

"No, just me and Lila, the girl out by the pool," she said as she opened the refrigerator door.

He raised the hammer and the handle came crashing down on her head. He didn't give it all he had, fearing it would kill her. He caught her as she fell backwards and lowered her down on the travertine floor. He pulled out the note he had written ahead of time and put it on the floor next to her.

He walked through the house and back out through the French doors. He reached into his pocket and pulled out the roll of duct tape. Noiselessly he walked over to the girl who was lying face down on the chaise longue with headphones on. He pulled out an eight-inch strip of duct tape and, with his teeth, cut it from the roll. Then he came up behind her and, putting one leg over the chaise longue, straddled it quickly and reached down and covered her mouth with the duct tape.

She started to scream, but her voice was muffled. Cam grabbed her arms, pulled them behind her back, and tied them up with another strip of duct tape as Marco and Mel ran out of the guesthouse. Marco had a syringe in one hand. He walked up to the girl, and as Cam held her arm tightly, Marco injected her. Mel, towing the long metal toolbox behind him, came up parallel to the chaise lounge the girl was lying on and opened it. Mel took the girl's arms as Marco took her legs. They lifted her into the rolling toolbox that had plenty of room to spare.

Five minutes later they were crossing the south bridge to West Palm Beach.

NINETEEN

It took a little digging, but Crawford found out that the gay couple, one of whom had been crippled by Clyde Loadholt, were named Johnny Baxter and Ben Silver. Baxter was the crippled one, now in a wheelchair. They had run a little shop over on Dixie Highway in West Palm. Crawford went there and talked to people who ran neighboring shops. The word was they were the nicest guys in the world and would do anything for you. A woman in a clothes shop told Crawford about how after a hurricane had flooded some of the other shops, Silver had gone door to door with a huge shop vacuum and vacuumed up the floodwater in the neighboring stores. That same woman had kept in touch with Baxter and Silver and said they had moved down to Key West.

She gave him Silver's cell number, which Crawford dialed. When Crawford asked Silver where his partner and he had been three nights ago, Silver said that he and Baxter had gone up to Miami to celebrate Baxter's birthday and had spent the night at a hotel there. Crawford called the hotel and found out that, in fact, they had been there on the night of Loadholt's murder.

OTT WENT TO SEE CHELSEA, THE FORMER STRIPPER, NOW A salesperson at the Macy's up at Palm Beach Gardens. Ott suspected that her last job in her old profession might have been at Clyde Loadholt's poker game. It turned out to be Chelsea's day off and though she wasn't thrilled about re-hashing the night at Loadholt's, she agreed to meet Ott with her husband, an out-of-work carpenter.

Pete the carpenter was still seething about the incident and particularly the trial. Chelsea seemed to have done a much better job than him of putting the whole thing behind her. When Ott asked them where they were the night of Loadholt's murder they said they were bingeing on a TV show on Amazon Prime called *Bosch*. Ott perked up when he heard that, knowing the show was about a cop named Harry Bosch, Michael Connelly's tenacious, jazz-loving homicide detective in the Hollywood division of the LA Police Department.

Pete suggested Ott watch it, pick up some pointers maybe. That was a joke, he said.

Ott thanked them and left for a four thirty meeting with Norm Rutledge to discuss the case. A meeting Ott was looking forward to as much as having a tooth pulled with a pair of pliers and no novocaine.

AS HE LOOKED ACROSS THE DESK AT RUTLEDGE, CRAWFORD wondered if a prerequisite for becoming police chief of Palm Beach was that you either be a loose cannon or quasi incompetent. Rutledge's office had always bothered Crawford because on all four walls were pictures of Rutledge and his loving family in a wide assortment of ridiculous poses. The one that took the cake was the family all dressed in their matching brown outfits. There were pictures everywhere, no escaping them: Rutledge, his wife Jean, his two daughters, and his two sons, Normie, Jr., and Brockton. Crawford wondered who would ever name a son after a grimy town in Massachusetts where Rocky Marciano was from anyway? In another picture, Rutledge, his wife, and Brockton knelt on their hands and knees on the bottom, his two daughters above them, then smiling, tow-headed little Normie the cherry on top of the family pyramid. But the thing that bugged Crawford most was the fact that, despite appearing to be the patriarch of the happiest family in America, Norm was a serial cheater.

The designation police chief was actually no more, because six years ago it had been given a new, pasteurized version—Director of Public Safety. Crawford wondered what the hell was wrong with police chief? Director of Public Safety conjured up an image of a man with a whistle in his mouth and a day-glo orange belt ushering blue-haired ladies across the street. Which was something Rutledge would actually have been good at.

Rutledge had started their meeting by railing about how, on its official website, the Palm Beach Police Department—which it was still called—had 2.3 stars, versus West Palm, which had 4 stars, and Palm Beach Gardens, 4.6 stars.

"Are you tellin' me that Palm Beach Gardens is twice as good as us? *Really?*" Rutledge said.

Crawford ignored the question but Ott shrugged and said. "Hey, Norm we're not trying to tell you anything. I mean, who gives a shit? One star, twenty stars, who the fuck cares?"

Crawford laughed his agreement.

Rutledge shook his head. "So where are you guys on Loadholt anyway?" Then he had an afterthought. "And how' bout one of these days you catch the guy in the first forty-eight?"

Ott looked at Crawford and did a quick roll of the eyes. Ott had a habit of challenging Rutledge; Crawford couldn't be bothered.

"Whoa," said Ott. "How many other teams do you know that are five for five? You know what the national clearance rate is? Something like forty percent. Chicago is twenty-eight percent. We're one hundred percent." He paused. "Aren't you glad you brought it up?"

But this time Crawford decided to chime in. "Hey, we'd like to catch 'em in the first five minutes, but it doesn't usually work out that way. What the hell does it matter, the fact is, we catch 'em," he said. "And while we're at it, why didn't you give us the full story on Loadholt?"

"What are you talking about?"

"Oh, I don't know, the fact that a rape allegedly took place at his house, for starters," Crawford said.

"Or the fact that he killed a guy in a pretty hinky burglary take-down," Ott piled on.

"You didn't think any of that was relevant, Norm?" Crawford asked.

Rutledge shook his head dismissively and stared hard at Crawford. "Anybody ever accuse you of something you didn't do, Crawford?" he asked. "Seems to me I remember something about a police brutality charge up in New York."

He was referring to a story in the *Palm Beach Morning News*. The paper's silent owner, a man named Ward Jaynes, later to become a convicted murderer, had browbeat a reporter into planting a story in an effort to discredit and humiliate Crawford.

Crawford's fist tightened and his jaw got rock hard. "That was total bullshit. Every single word of it and you damn well know it."

Rutledge smiled. "Exactly my point," he said. "That story about you was bullshit and so is all this shit about Loadholt."

Ott wasn't buying it. "You might be able to dismiss it like that," he said. "But more and more stories about Loadholt keep coming out of the woodwork. Like that guy he crippled."

Rutledge shook his head and dialed up his best sneer. "I got news for you, Ott," he said, "this is a murder case and Loadholt is the victim, not the perp. And the idea is, just in case you lost your way, to find out who did it. Not to run around dredging up all kinds of shit on a cop with a distinguished thirty-five-year career in law enforcement who's not around to defend himself."

Crawford had to admit it, sometimes Rutledge could sound like the head of the debate team.

Ott started to say something, but Rutledge cut him off. "How 'bout just tellin' me what you got."

After a long pause, Ott detailed his interview with Chelsea McKinnon and her husband; then Crawford proceeded to tell Rutledge about the gay couple who seemed to be in the clear and about Sonia Reyes and her incarcerated brother.

"So that's it?" Rutledge asked.

"We're still digging," Ott said.

"We're looking into a tie-in with Meyer's murder," Crawford said. "The common denominator being the regular poker game at Loadholt's house."

Scrolling on his iPhone, Rutledge looked up. "Yeah, I told you about that game."

"It was way more than a card game," Crawford said.

Rutledge looked up. "Whatever happened there, it went away, just like your brutality charge. I can't believe there was even a trial."

Ott shot a glance at Crawford and then turned back to Rutledge. "If you had a card game at your house, would you send your wife—"

"All right, enough. This isn't about some goddamn card game, it's about a cop killer," Rutledge said. "And whether he was retired or active, it doesn't matter. Whether he had a stripper at his card game, it doesn't matter. Whether he used undue force in that incident ten years ago on Worth Avenue, it doesn't matter. What matters is a cop was killed and we need to take down his killer."

Crawford had to give it to him again. It was one of Rutledge's better speeches.

Crawford sighed. "And that's exactly what we're going to do."

"Yeah, but the question is…when?" Rutledge said looking at his watch. It was two past five. "Well, it's quittin' time. I'd be happy to resume this conversation at O'Herlihy's."

He stood up to go. Despite his little speech, Rutledge seemed much more interested in his first cocktail of the day than Loadholt.

CRAWFORD AND OTT GOT INTO THE CROWN VIC THAT HAD 'Wash Me' scrawled on the back trunk.

Ott turned to Crawford. "Just what I want to do. Go have a drink with that horse's ass at his dipshit bar."

"Yeah, you'd think just once he could stretch it out a few minutes at work. You know, make it to five thirty," Crawford said.

"If he did, he'd miss part of happy hour," said Ott, waving at Bill Nesto, one of the motorcycle cops, as they drove out of the parking lot.

O'Herlihy's was a cop bar. Sort of.

Unlike Mookie's, it didn't have one of those big jars with pickled eggs in it that looked like it could incubate several diseases simultaneously. Unlike Mookie's, it didn't have a dart board or a pool table with ripped green felt in front of one of the corner pockets. Unlike Mookie's, it did have waiters and waitresses instead of just one bartender who was also the owner. Unlike Mookie's, it didn't have an ashtray at the end of the bar so Don Scarpa could smoke illegally at his seat of honor.

The cops who frequented O'Herlihy's were a decidedly more reputable-looking bunch than those who hung out at Mookie's. They sported much less facial hair and had not one tattoo in sight. And the conversations there were generally on more elevated subjects: the latest trends in law enforcement and new, breakthrough technologies as opposed to the bust size of the new girl in the Bicycle Patrol Unit or who was going to win the Gators-Bulldogs game that Saturday.

Crawford's cell phone rang as they pulled into O'Herlihy's. He looked down at it and slid the unlock button. "Well, Alexa, it's been three whole hours since I heard from you."

"Hello, Charlie," she said. "I knew you'd be missing my voice."

"What's up? I'm just about to go into another cop bar," he said.

"Jesus, is that all you do?"

"Pretty much."

"So how about a drink tomorrow night at a *reporters'* bar?"

"So I can field questions from you and your newshound friends?" Ott turned off the car's engine.

"Just me. Come on, it'll be fun," she said.

"Otherwise you're just gonna keep harassing me, right?"

"Pretty much."

Crawford sighed dramatically "Okay," he said.

"Cool," she said. "It's called Jack's, on Congress."

"Okay."

"Seven good?"

"See you then," Crawford said and clicked off.

"Who's that?" Ott asked as they got out of the car.

"Remember that reporter at the Loadholt scene? Dropped her card from the chopper?"

"How could I forget," Ott said. "The hottie."

CRAWFORD AND OTT FELT LIKE DUCKS OUT OF WATER AT O'Herlihy's but were making the best of it. They were at a table with Rutledge, who was having a conversation with the West Palm Police Chief Ron Mendoza, seated one table away.

"So the sensors are mounted on rooftops and telephone poles and can immediately pinpoint the location of the gunshot," Mendoza said. "Then the systems computer triangulates the origin of the gunshots based on how far it is from the sensors. And boom, a uniform can be there in minutes. Oh, and plus, it can tell the difference between a car backfire and a gunshot."

"No kiddin'," said Rutledge. "What's the thing called again?"

"Shotspotter," Mendoza said. "They've been using 'em in California for quite a while now."

"Ah, Norm," Crawford said, waving to get Rutledge's attention. But Rutledge was too engrossed in the Shotspotter.

Crawford's cell phone rang.

He looked at the number but didn't recognize it.

He clicked it. "Crawford."

"Hey, Charlie, it's David Balfour," Crawford could hear panic in his voice. "I've got a bad situation here."

"What is it?" he asked as Rutledge babbled on across the table.

"I can't talk about it on the phone, can you come here? To my house."

"I'm on my way. I'm with my partner," he clicked off, stood up, and turned to Ott. "David Balfour. Something serious."

Crawford stood then Ott followed suit. Crawford didn't even bother to catch Rutledge's attention as he and Ott walked quickly toward the front door.

Crawford turned to Ott when they got outside. "Had enough of this shithole anyway."

"Yeah, totally lacking in atmosphere." Ott said. "Not to mention, no tasty pickled eggs."

TWENTY

CRAWFORD'S CELL PHONE RANG AGAIN AS HE AND OTT CROSSED the bridge over to Palm Beach. It was David Balfour again. Crawford clicked it. "Yeah, David?"

"I was thinking," he was whispering now, "it's a bad idea to drive up to my house. You'll understand why later. So here's what you do: park down at Mellor Park, then walk up the beach and come through my tunnel. You remember where it is, right?"

"Yeah, that bulkhead door on the dune," Crawford said.

Balfour lived at the south end of South Ocean Boulevard. There was a stretch where no houses were directly on the ocean because the road had been built so it separated the houses from the beach. Several of the houses had tunnels that went under South Ocean and came out right on the beach.

"Okay," Crawford said. "We'll be there in ten minutes."

"Thanks, man," said Balfour. "I really appreciate it."

"For my best CI," Crawford said, "anytime."

David Balfour was hardly a confidential informer. He was a fifty-five-year-old man who had inherited a lot of money. But he was also a down-to-earth, good-hearted man who had become a genuine friend of Crawford's. Crawford had met Balfour through Rose Clarke, who had gone out with him briefly, and Balfour had given Crawford information a few times that was helpful in solving murders. So Crawford had designated Balfour as his unofficial CI.

It seemed to give the man purpose.

Ott pulled the Crown Vic into Mellor Park and parked. They got out and walked to the beach. It was a full moon and the stars looked as though they were only a few miles above.

"What do you s'pose this is about?" Ott asked as they walked over a dune.

"No clue," said Crawford, looking out at the lights of a big tanker ship several miles out. "Something pretty serious, I'm guessing. That's it over there." Crawford said, pointing at a white bulkhead door.

They walked up to it and Crawford pulled on the metal door handle. It opened up and light streamed out. Crawford walked down three steps, Ott was right behind him.

"If I was part of that father-daughter burglary team, this would have come in pretty handy," Ott said halfway through the tunnel.

"Yeah, except it's got all kinds of locks at the other end and usually the beach door is locked," Crawford said walking down the tunnel.

"Charlie," came a voice. David Balfour waited at the end of the tunnel.

"Hey, David," said Crawford.

Balfour shook his hand like he hadn't seen him in years then turned to Ott. "Hey, Mort. I really appreciate you guys coming."

"No problem," Ott said.

"So what's goin' on, David?" Crawford asked as the three went up the stairs from Balfour's house's cellar into a corner of his enormous kitchen.

Balfour turned to them. "My niece, Lila, has been kidnapped."

"Oh, Jesus," Crawford said. "Really?"

"Yeah, come on into the living room," Balfour said. "You guys want a drink or something?"

"No, thanks," said Crawford, motioning with his hand, "but let's go back down to the cellar. In case someone's watching the house."

Ott nodded.

"Good idea," Balfour said.

The three of them went back over to the stairway leading to the cellar and went down the stairs. Balfour flicked the light on. The finished basement room had a pool table in it and, Crawford guessed, Balfour's second-string furniture. The centerpiece was a big brown leather sofa, which had some mileage on it, facing two leather chairs. The room had a slightly dank smell and a cluster of cobwebs over in one corner.

"I'm guessing you don't use this much," Crawford said.

"Couple times a year is all," Balfour said.

None of them made a move to sit.

"So start from the beginning," Crawford said.

Crawford knew the backstory about Balfour's niece. How she had lived with him ever since her parents—Balfour's older sister and brother-in-law, Kirk and Kitty Bacon—had been killed in a car accident six months before. The two were on 95 coming home from a dinner party up on Bush Island when a drunk driver in a pickup coming from the opposite direction had jumped the median and plowed into them. Lila was eighteen or nineteen Crawford guessed, and, he seemed to recall, was taking classes at a college in the area. He wasn't sure which one.

Balfour held up his iPhone and Crawford and Ott looked at the screen. It was a picture of a grim-faced Lila holding the day's *Palm Beach Morning News* in front of her—the date clearly recognizable.

Crawford patted Balfour on the shoulder. "We'll get her," he said. "So when did they contact you? When did you know she was missing?"

"I got a call around quarter of six then that text of her with the paper. I left the house around nine this morning, had a meeting with my accountant. That lasted about an hour, then I went to buy some stuff at CVS, after that went to the Poinciana," a country club he belonged to in Palm Beach. "Hit some balls out on the range, had an early lunch and then had a one o'clock tee-time. I got a call on my cell from Valentina right after I teed off," Balfour turned to Ott, "that's my cook. I didn't take it, figured I'd get back to her after I was finished up. Then she called again, I didn't take it the second time. Then, as I said, around quarter of six I got this call that said 'Unknown.' I decided to take it and this guy said he had Lila and wanted three million dollars by Monday at five or he'd..." a long sigh, "kill her."

"What were his exact words?" Crawford asked.

Balfour winced. "Said they'd 'have a little fun with her, torture her then kill her.'"

Ott clenched his teeth, his jaw muscles flexing.

"I love that girl like a daughter," Balfour said. "You guys gotta get her back. I'll pay the damn money."

"We'll get her," Crawford said again. Then he put an arm on Balfour's shoulder. "You know, David, I'm going to have to take this to my boss, who's probably going to bring in the FBI."

Balfour winced like he felt a sharp jolt of pain. "No, please, man, you can't do that. I just want you involved. I know you, I know what you're capable of."

Crawford glanced at Ott. Ott was looking down, but Crawford knew what he was thinking. We'd get our asses handed to us if we didn't go by the book on this.

Balfour sighed and put a hand up to his forehead. "Please, Charlie, I need you to do it. I don't want fifty guys in crew cuts and black suits clusterfucking this thing," he said, his voice querulous. "Put yourselves in my shoes. If you can't do it, I gotta go it alone. I can't lose that girl. I'll give these bastards everything I have."

Ott looked up and narrowed his eyes. "David, you can't do this yourself. You need men who have been down that road. It's just too damn risky otherwise."

Balfour exhaled loudly. "You're a father, right, Mort?"

Ott nodded. "Yes, I have a daughter."

"Okay, so you know how it is," Balfour said.

"What's that, David?"

"How it's not all about you anymore," Balfour said. "How precious someone becomes to you..." A long pause, followed by, "Now imagine the possibility of losing that person."

Crawford could see Ott at a loss for words. A rare phenomenon.

Balfour turned to Crawford, "Look, if anything goes wrong or we don't get her back by the end of Monday, I'll call PBPD myself. I'll say I tried to work it out on my own—big mistake—and fucked up. I won't mention calling you or Mort."

"That's not the point—"

"Charlie, do I have to beg you?" Balfour pleaded.

Crawford glanced over at Ott. Ott nodded imperceptibly.

Crawford exhaled. "Okay, but if we feel that we're losing control of this, or we're in over our heads, we're goin' down the other road."

"Agreed," Balfour said with a smile. "Thank you. Thank you so much."

"Okay, first of all," Crawford said. "I'm assuming you don't have that kind of money just lying around. It's either in a bank account or a stock brokerage, right?"

"Exactly, so I can't get it until Monday."

"Which is good," Ott said. "It buys us some time."

"Yeah, definitely," Crawford said. "Do you know exactly where it happened? Where she was when they took her?"

"So after I got the call, I called Valentina—who was in the hospital."

"Jesus, what happened to her?" Crawford asked.

"She told me three guys showed up a little after I left the house. They were dressed up as carpenters. See, I'm adding on to my guesthouse. They told her they were finish carpenters and she didn't think anything of it. A couple of hours later one of them came into the house, asked her if he could get some ice. So when she went to the refrigerator, he hit her over the head with something. Next thing she knows, she wakes up and they're gone and so is Lila."

"What'd she say they looked like?" Crawford asked. "She give you any kind of a description?"

"That's the problem," Balfour said. "They were wearing those masks that construction guys wear—"

Crawford nodded. "Dust masks."

"Yeah, whatever. So she just said they were three white guys, average height, all wearing baseball caps, couldn't give much of a description."

"Did she call the cops when she came to?" Ott asked, pretty sure she hadn't or they'd have heard about it.

"No, the one who hit her left a note next to her in the kitchen that said something like, 'You call the cops and the girl's dead.' After I spoke to Valentina I went straight home, then got the text."

"Was anyone else at your house today?" Crawford asked.

"Just Valentina," Balfour said, his voice suddenly shaky. "No, wait, the pool guys come in the afternoon."

Crawford could hear the emotion suddenly rise in Balfour's voice as he put a hand up to his forehead.

"What's the name of the construction company that's doing the work on your house, David?" Ott asked.

"Butler Brothers," said Balfour. "The only thing I could think of is maybe the kidnappers intercepted the real construction guys going to my house then pretended they were them. You know, like another part of the crew."

"Who's your main contact there?" Ott asked.

"Jason Butler," Balfour said. "As straight a guy as you'll find."

Balfour gave them Butler's phone number.

Ott wrote the man's name and number down in his notebook.

"When do your landscapers come? And the garbage guys?" Crawford asked.

"Landscapers came yesterday," Balfour said. "Garbage guys same. I can't see them having anything to do with this."

"I'm just thinking somebody else might have seen these guys. Could maybe give us more of a description of them. Or could have seen them getting in or out of a car or truck. Could describe it maybe."

Balfour nodded and gave them the name of the pool, landscape, and garbage companies even though they weren't scheduled to come that day. "Sorry, I don't have their numbers," he said.

"No problem, I can look 'em up," Ott said, writing down the names.

"You've had some time to think, David. Is there anyone at all you can think of who could be involved in this?" Ott asked. "A lot of the time it's someone you know."

"Or someone who knows the victim," Ott added.

"Yeah, I've been thinking about it," Balfour said. "But I really don't have a clue."

"What about Lila? Anyone in her life you might be suspicious of? Someone who could be behind this?"

Balfour thought for a second. "She's been going out with this guy, kind of off and on, since back when my sister was alive."

"Tell us about him," Crawford asked.

"Well, he's a little older, like maybe twenty-three or twenty-four," Balfour said. "I remember my sister telling me she thought the guy was kind of a 'ne'er do well.' Or maybe it was a 'good-for-nothing.'"

"What else?" Crawford asked.

"She told me how he had flunked out of two colleges up north," Balfour said. "Moved down here and was freeloading off his grand-parents who have a house up on Dunbar, I think. Always seemed like a nice enough guy to me. Kind of an affable slacker."

"What's his name?" Ott asked.

"Jamie Ransom," Balfour said.

"Name's appropriate," Ott said.

"Never thought of that," Balfour said.

"Based on what you've said, sounds like a plan like this might be more than he's capable of," Crawford said.

"Yeah, hiring guys, planning it all out," Balfour said, nodding. "It might be."

"Well, we'll check him out anyway," Crawford said.

"Anybody else, David?" Ott asked. "Any other ex-boyfriends or anyone sketchy?"

"She had a few dates with a guy who is the assistant golf pro at the Poinciana," Balfour said. "I forget what his name is."

"What's your gut on him?" Ott asked.

"I like him," Balfour said. "But what do I know? Said like twenty words to the kid in my whole life."

Crawford had been quiet for a while, thinking things over. "The person who called—obviously wasn't Jamie or the golf pro—what did he sound like? Age? Accent? Anything distinctive or unusual?"

"Oh, I meant to tell you," Balfour said. "He was using one of those things that disguises your voice."

Ott nodded. "Yeah, that's an app you can buy."

"Which means it actually could have been Jamie or the golf pro or someone else you know," Crawford said. "Or someone who didn't want you to be able to recognize his voice, in case he got caught."

Ott was nodding. "So how'd the guy leave it?"

"I told him I couldn't get the money until Monday morning and he was pissed. Like he hadn't thought of that. Banks not being open, I mean."

Crawford chewed on that. "Sounds kind of like an amateur," he said. "Then what did he say?"

Balfour shrugged. "He just told me to stay at home and wait for his call on my cell. Don't go anywhere or talk to anyone, he said."

Crawford nodded his head slowly, a plan starting to take shape. "How would you feel about having a houseguest for the weekend?"

"You mean...you?"

"Yup," Crawford said. "Got an extra toothbrush?"

"Whole drawer full."

Crawford nodded. "Good possibility someone might be watching to see if anyone comes or goes here, so I'm just gonna camp out down here for the weekend," Crawford said. "I need you to come down every hour or so, so we can talk about what to do next. Also, if you get a call from the kidnapper, put it on speaker and come down as fast as you can."

"Will do," said Balfour.

Crawford turned to Ott. "I can take the weekend off from Load-holt. I'll be checking in with you from time to time. If you get anything good, let me know."

"On Loadholt, you mean?" Ott asked.

Crawford nodded.

"If you need me to do something, just call," Ott said. "Go somewhere, interview someone, whatever."

Crawford nodded. "Thanks, man," he said, turning to Balfour. "You got a bathroom down here, David?

"Yeah," he pointed to a closed door, "but sorry, no shower."

Crawford grinned. "Guess I'm gonna be good and ripe come Monday morning.

TWENTY-ONE

MARLA FLUOR, ELLE T. GRAHAM, DIANA QUARLE, BETH Jastrow and Rose Clarke had just left the The Tabernacle, a music venue in Atlanta, and were now having drinks at the bar of the Four Seasons Hotel where they were staying.

"I'm not much of a rock n' roll girl, but that chick really *rocked*," said Marla.

"The place was kind of cool too," Diana said. "Not too big, not too small, nice acoustics."

"Yeah," Beth said. "I read Adele played there last year. Bob Dylan, once, way back in the day."

"So what's our game plan?" Elle asked, turning to Beth. "You're kind of the quarterback on this one. What are you thinking?"

"I had a bunch of ideas," Beth said, setting her scotch down on the table. "Diana, you mentioned you know Oprah's agent, so let's set up an intro between Lulu and her. She's got dates at my hotels again a month from now and some other place in a few days." Then, turning to Elle, "What'd you tell me about knowing someone in the record business in LA?"

"Yes, his name is Eddie Buskey. He's the head of something

called Rhino Records, which, I think, is owned by Warner Brothers. Anyway, he told me once he likes to go to clubs and discover up-and-coming artists."

"That would be a fun job," Rose said after a sip of her rosé, "going around and plucking someone out of obscurity. Making 'em a star."

Beth smiled and nodded. "Oh, here she comes now," she said, looking at the woman approaching their table. She was Lulu Perkins, the singer who they had come to see. She was in her mid-twenties and had long, straight blond hair, abundant cleavage, and wore aviators.

"There you are," Beth said to Lulu, holding out her hand. "You were *fan*-tastic."

"Thanks," said Lulu, with a big glowing smile.

"Incredible," Rose said with a nod.

Beth proceeded to introduce Lulu to the four others as she sat down at their table.

"So you liked the show?" Lulu asked.

"Liked it?" Diana said. "Only thing I didn't like was it was too short."

"Yeah, I agree," said Marla. "I could have listened for another hour."

"Well, thanks," Lulu said, looking around the table. "So you ladies are gonna make me a star?"

"No, *you're* gonna make you a star," Beth said. "We're just gonna try to speed up the process a little."

Beth proceeded to tell Lulu about their contacts with Oprah's agent and the man at Rhino Records.

They had two rounds of drinks, then, at around midnight, paid the check, said goodnight to Lulu Perkins, and headed to the elevator. They agreed to meet again and talk in the morning.

"I really like her," said Rose, as she pushed the button for an elevator. "I wish I could pull off that look."

"You mean indoor shades?" Diana asked.

"Yeah," Rose said. "Too Hollywood for me."

The elevator opened and the five got in.

"Hold it, please," came a man's voice as the door was closing.

Rose put her hand up on the door and it opened back up.

"Thanks," the man in his fifties said, looking over the women. "Wow! Look what I stepped into...a *Charlie's Angels* reunion."

Diana rolled her eyes as Rose eyed him disdainfully.

"That was a compliment," the man said, mimicking an air kiss to Rose.

"You really made our night, sir," Rose said.

The man smiled and ogled. He had clearly come from the bar himself. "Man, you're a buncha hotties."

No one responded.

The elevator door opened on the twenty-sixth floor. The women walked out, Beth bringing up the rear.

The man suddenly reached out and grabbed her ass.

In a blink, she whirled and kicked him in the groin then, as he pitched forward, she brought her knee up fast and slammed him under the chin.

The other four women turned and watched in jaw-drop amazement as the man fell to the floor just outside of the elevator.

But Beth Jastrow was not done. She kicked him in the ribs as Rose and Diana grabbed her arms and pulled her back.

The man, groaning, looked up at Beth, terror in his eyes.

"Don't you *ever, ever—*" Beth broke out of the grasp of Rose and Diana and kicked him again, "touch a woman like that again."

TWENTY-TWO

CRAWFORD SUGGESTED THAT BALFOUR GO UP TO LILA'S bedroom and see if her computer and cell phone were there as he and Ott talked things over in the basement. A few minutes later, Balfour came back down with both. Crawford shot him a thumbs-up.

"So, Mort, I'm gonna see what I find in those," he said pointing to the computer and cell phone in Balfour's hands, "then give you a call, probably first thing in the morning. I might need you to do some legwork for me. Go talk to somebody maybe. If I decide it's better for me to be on the street, I'll just come through the tunnel and you can pick me up down in Mellor Park."

Ott nodded. "In the meantime, until I hear from you, I'll just be working Loadholt."

"Yeah, exactly," Crawford said, looking at his watch. It was just past nine. He turned to Balfour. "This'll take a while. I'll call you if we need to talk."

Balfour nodded. "I'll get you some sheets, a pillow, and stuff," pointing at the leather couch. "Looks like that's your bed for the next few nights."

"Hey, I've slept in worse, trust me," Crawford said. "Do me a favor while you're up there, get me a cup of coffee, would you please?"

"I'll do better than that," Balfour said. "I'll bring the whole Keurig thing down here. Got any special flavors you like?"

"Got any Dunkin' Donuts?"

"Think you might be in luck."

OTT LEFT A FEW MINUTES LATER AND CRAWFORD OPENED UP Lila's MacBook Air. She had left it on, which was fortunate, because he didn't need her username and password. He went straight to her emails and immediately felt like a snooping parent. It was quickly apparent that the two people she emailed the most were a woman named Jenny Montgomery and slacker on-again-off-again boyfriend Jamie Ransom. He was surprised she communicated so much by email because his sense was that kids her age did nothing but text. The emails with Montgomery were about everything under the sun. The ones from Ransom were essentially him trying to win her over and the ones from her to him were friendly, chatty, and non-committal. The ratio was approximately two to one, his emails to hers.

One of the things that Ransom mentioned in a number of them was that he was hoping to get into law school. He mentioned Harvard and Yale, with Stetson, in Florida, as a backup. Crawford found that curious, since Balfour had told him that Jamie had flunked out of college twice.

Crawford also found a number of emails to Lila from a professor of hers at Palm Beach Atlantic College. They started off strictly teacher-to-student in tone, but over the course of a month, the professor seemed to get a little more familiar. Crawford spent three hours on Lila's computer, going over her Twitter, Facebook, and Instagram accounts, as well as through her emails. Then he spent an hour on her cell phone. There were a few things on it he couldn't open up.

At the end of it, he felt he knew her almost as well as her uncle did. It was a little past 1:00 a.m. when he stopped. He decided that first thing in the morning he was going to ask Ott to go talk to Jenny Montgomery to see what light she could shed on things.

He took one of the sheets and spread it out on the leather couch, then placed the pillow at one end. Then he went into the small bathroom and brushed his teeth with the toothbrush Balfour had provided him. He went and stripped down to his boxers, climbed into his makeshift bed, and pulled the sheet up over him.

But he didn't get to sleep for over an hour, his brain was churning through and processing everything he had just learned in the past few hours.

He ended up having a lot of strange dreams. In one, he and Dominica and Lila Bacon went skiing together, somewhere out west, Colorado maybe. Lila broke her leg and there was no ski patrol around, so Crawford had to ski down the mountain with Lila on his back. Which was a pretty neat trick, since although Crawford had gone to college in the middle of ski country—Hanover, New Hampshire—he had never skied a day in his life.

TWENTY-THREE

CRAWFORD WOKE UP TO THE SMELL OF BACON AND FIVE minutes later Balfour came down the stairs with a plateful of eggs, bacon, and toast.

Crawford looked up at him and smiled. He had to admit it, it beat the hell out of his blueberry donuts at Dunkin' Donuts.

"Least I could do for making you sleep down here," Balfour said.

"It actually was pretty comfortable," Crawford said, looking at his watch.

It was seven-thirty. "You had any calls yet?" he asked Balfour.

"Not yet," Balfour said, putting the tray down on the coffee table in front of the leather couch. "You find out much on Lila's computer and phone?"

"Plenty," Crawford said. "I feel like I know her now like she was my own niece."

"You'd make a good uncle, Charlie."

"Thanks," Crawford said. "I'm going to call Ott. I want to have him talk to Lila's friend Jenny Montgomery, see if she can give us some help."

"Good idea," Balfour said. "Jenny is her best friend. Probably knows more about Lila than us uncles do."

Crawford chuckled. "Do you know a professor of Lila's named Arthur Sandusky?" he asked, taking a bite of toast.

Balfour sat down in the chair opposite the couch. "Yes, I think he's her college advisor. Marketing professor, I'm pretty sure."

"Marketing?"

"Yeah, Lila wants to go into the advertising business. Up in your old stomping grounds, New York."

Crawford got up off of the couch and put his pants on over his boxers. He was feeling less than professional discussing a case in his underwear, sitting on his makeshift bed. "It seemed as though in the course of a month's worth of emails the guy's tone went from professorial to...let's just say, a little friendlier."

Balfour shrugged. "I don't really know anything about the guy."

Crawford picked up Lila's computer. "Well, so listen to this: 'Lila, I think you've got a big career ahead of you in advertising. Don't hesitate to ask for my help. I'm happy to be of assistance in any way possible. Best, Professor Sandusky.' Then, like, three weeks later: 'L, You make the class something I so look forward to. I always wonder what chic outfit you'll show up in! xxx, Arthur.'"

"Jesus, I see what you mean," Balfour said, shaking his head. "That's really creepy."

Crawford nodded.

Then he finished off the piece of toast and picked up the shirt Balfour had left for him on a blue club chair. It was a green silk shirt with a multi-colored peacock on the breast pocket.

It was a long way from standard-issue cop wear.

Probably cost about a month's salary, Crawford thought, seeing the Maus & Hoffman label, a pricey shop on Worth Avenue. "So I was thinking about why a kidnapper would have picked Lila."

"Yes. And?"

"Well, don't take this the wrong way, but why wouldn't you pick the kid of someone—no offense—who was *really, really, really* rich?

You know, billionaire rich. Who could easily come up with the ransom money."

"No offense taken," Balfour said then took a sip of coffee. "I agree. Why screw around with someone who's just a little bit rich."

Crawford picked the plate up and put it in his lap. "Anyway, I'm still going with the kidnapper being either someone you know or someone Lila knows."

"Makes sense to me," Balfour said.

Earlier Crawford had flashed to a scenario, which he was not about to share with Balfour. It was a disturbing phenomenon that had probably been around forever. There were certain kinds of men who —if they couldn't have the women they wanted—would in the end, destroy them. He could think of more than a few cases that he had seen close up. He knew a cop up in New York—in fact, they had been pretty good friends—whose wife had kicked him out because, basically, the guy never came home. Then she started seeing another man. The cop pleaded with her to get back together with him and when she said no, he strangled her to death.

Crawford knew too little at this point to suspect this was a possibility in this case, but had uneasy feelings about both Jamie Ransom and Arthur Sandusky.

TWENTY-FOUR

CRAWFORD CALLED OTT AT THE STATION AT A LITTLE PAST eight.

"How was it sleeping in a ten-million-dollar house?" Ott asked, sounding fully caffeinated.

"Lemme tell you, his basement beats the hell out of the master suite of my palace any day of the week," Crawford said, taking a swig of his Dunkin' Donuts coffee.

"So what did you find out from Lila's computer and phone?" Ott asked.

"Ninety percent girl stuff, ten percent...very interesting."

Crawford proceeded to tell Ott about the Jamie Ransom and Arthur Sandusky emails, along with the ones back and forth to Jenny Montgomery. They agreed that Ott would go interview Jenny Montgomery. Ott was going to look into Ransom and Sandusky, but not interview them. Crawford and Ott feared that questioning them would tip their hand that they were regarding them as possible suspects, and thus jeopardize Lila's life.

Crawford had hung up with Ott and was pouring a second cup of

Dunkin' Donuts into his mug when he heard David Balfour come charging down the stairs.

"Hey, Charlie," he said before he got into the room. "I got a call, a real short one, didn't even have a chance to get down here," he was clearly amped up. "The voice sounded like it might be someone I know."

Crawford turned to Balfour, mug in hand. "Who?"

"He was still using that voice distortion thing," Balfour said, "but I noticed an accent, a Spanish accent."

"So who do you think it might have been?"

"Valentina's husband, Luis, is a guy who can't hold down a job," Balfour said. "In the last year alone he's been a waiter, a bartender, my driver, and guess what? A construction worker."

"Wait a sec," Crawford said. "Hasn't Valentina been with you for, like, forever?"

"Yeah, she has, and she'd never have anything to do with this. No way in hell," Balfour said, shaking his head. "But she and Luis are kind of estranged at the moment and he's always strapped for cash. Hits me up from time to time, makes me swear I'll never tell Valentina."

"Where's all the money go?" Crawford asked.

"Guy's got a gambling problem," Balfour said. "Meaning he spends more time at the Seminole Hard Rock down in Hollywood than at home. Valentina took me aside one day and told me about it. I feel so bad for her 'cause she works her ass off. Not just for me but others on the side."

Crawford nodded. "You said he was your driver?"

Balfour took a quick belt of coffee then looked a little sheepish. "On those nights when I know I'm going to have a few more than I should," he said. "When I don't want your brothers in blue spotting me weaving down South County Road, I call up Luis."

"Very wise," Crawford said. "So what's he like? I mean, could you see him carrying through with something like this?"

"Not really," Balfour said. "But, you know how it is, sometimes desperate men do desperate things. I mean maybe he's in way over his head."

Crawford nodded.

He was thinking about loan sharks. How desperate they could make a man feel.

TWENTY-FIVE

OTT CALLED JENNY MONTGOMERY AND TOLD HER HE'D LIKE TO speak to her as soon as possible about her friend, Lila Bacon.

"Is she okay?" Jenny asked immediately.

"Yes," said Ott without further explanation. Jenny said her first class at Palm Beach Atlantic wasn't until one in the afternoon, so Ott made a date to meet her at ten-thirty. She lived in a small rented house that she shared with another young woman on Washington Street in West Palm Beach.

Sitting in her cramped living room, Ott remembered the array of dumps he'd lived in through college. Women's places were always way neater and had a lot fewer beer cans and cheap liquor bottles on every available surface. Jenny was wearing a t-shirt, blue jeans, and flip-flops, a pretty young woman with no make-up.

"I appreciate you seeing me," Ott said. "As I said, Lila's fine, but I need to ask you some questions."

"I called her after I got your call," Jenny said, "and didn't get her. You sure she's okay?"

Ott nodded. "But I need you to promise you won't mention this conversation to anyone," he said. "Not a word, okay?"

She nodded.

"And please, don't try to call her again," Ott said. "You'll just have to take my word for it, it's better this way."

She nodded again.

"Thank you," Ott said. "So if you would, first tell me about relationships Lila had with men."

After he spoke, Ott realized that it sounded a little abrupt. A little too quick out of the gate.

Lila frowned like the subject of her friend's boyfriends was the last thing she wanted to talk about. She looked away and cleared her throat. "Well, she had quite a few guy friends."

It was a start. "Could you give me a few names?"

Jenny scrunched up her eyes. "Um, there's this one guy Jamie. It's kind of like...I never know the status of their relationship from one day to the next. He's pretty persistent, if you know what I mean. The type of guy who always gives her stuff. You know, flowers and stuff. She likes him, but..."

"But what?"

"He wants it to be more serious than she does. I mean, he's older, so I think he's thinking of like...marrying her." Her lips tightened like she couldn't think of anything much worse.

"And she isn't ready for that?"

"No, I mean, she's nineteen, a sophomore in college," Jenny said. "I don't think the idea of dropping out and making babies is of much interest to Lila."

"But she hasn't actually broken it off with him, has she?"

Jenny started twirling a strand of her brown hair. "Lila isn't so great at saying no. She's always so sensitive about not hurting guys' feelings. I told her that could get her in trouble, but..."

"What about, do you know a professor of hers named Arthur Sandusky?" Ott asked.

Jenny's head snapped back. "How do you know about him?"

"Her uncle."

Jenny nodded. "I guess it's not all that uncommon."

"What's isn't?"

"You know, professors hitting on their students," she said. "Thank God it's never happened to me."

"So that's what happened?"

"Him hitting on her?" Lila asked.

Ott nodded.

"Yeah, I mean, she would never have been the one to initiate it," Jenny said.

"So just how far did it go?" Ott asked.

Jenny's face got red. "You mean...? No, definitely not. The guy just wouldn't leave her alone. Same as Jamie, I guess. Except more so actually. To the point where he kind of turned into a stalker. Lila told me he followed her home to her uncle's one time."

Ott was busy taking notes.

"I think he did something, or said something maybe, that really creeped her out. She finally told him to leave her alone," Jenny said. "Said she had a boyfriend. But I think he was like really obsessed. I think she finally just dropped out of his class. He was her advisor too. So now she's in the process of trying to get another one."

Ott looked up from his note taking. "Wow, that's a pretty drastic step."

"Yeah, no kidding," Jenny said. "I think she really liked the class too."

"That's too bad," Ott said. "So back to Jamie Ransom, are they still seeing each other?"

"Like I said, off and on."

"And Jamie is planning to go to law school. Do you think that's... to impress Lila maybe?"

"I'm sure it is," Jenny said. "But he's moved on to something new."

Ott looked up from taking notes. "You mean, not going to law school?"

Jenny nodded.

"Really? Like what?"

"He went to some seminar—Lila told me—about flipping houses. You know, make a million in a month or whatever."

Ott chuckled.

"So he told Lila he was going to make a fortune in Palm Beach real estate," Jenny said. "He just needed to get his grandfather to lend him a little money, learn some stuff about construction, and he'd be off to the races."

Ott looked up again, riveted. "'Learn some stuff about construction.' Is that what he told Lila he was going to do?"

"Yeah, he told her he knew a guy who was a carpenter. He asked the guy if he could be his assistant or something for a while." Jenny shook her head and smiled. "Even to me that sounded a little, um, naïve. You know, like go pound a few nails for a week, and boom, you know all about construction. I mean, *really?*"

Ott nodded. "What about...what do you know about a golf pro?"

Jenny didn't react at first. "Oh, him," she said. "Yeah, I think he works at some club in Palm Beach."

"Okay, and what's he seem like to you?"

Jenny shrugged. "Nice guy. I don't know him that well," she said. "They aren't really going out anymore is my take."

"Has Lila been going out with anyone else on a regular basis, to your knowledge?"

"Nah, that's pretty much it," Jenny's eyes cruised the room then came back to Ott. "I'd put her in the 'still looking' category."

TWENTY-SIX

OTT WALKED INTO THE STATION HOUSE AND THE RECEPTIONIST, Bettina—don't call me Betty—caught his eye. "Gentleman over there wants to talk to either you or Charlie," she said, pointing.

Ott looked over at a man reading a magazine. Both the magazine and the man had a lot of mileage on them. It was Rob Jaworski from Clyde Loadholt's poker group. The guy who talked a lot. Ott toyed with the idea of sneaking back to his cubicle, avoiding him altogether. But then he decided he didn't want to have to keep ducking him. Might as well get it over with.

"Mr. Jaworski," Ott said, walking over to him. "What can I do for you, sir?"

"Hello, Detective," Jaworski said, looking up and smiling. "Just wanted to see if I could help you some more on Clyde's murder."

Rather than go all the way back to his cubicle, Ott sat down next to Jaworski.

"I can use all the help I can get," Ott said. "Whatcha got?"

"Well, remember I told you last time there was real bad blood between Clyde and his granddaughter?"

"Yeah, sure do."

Jaworski put the magazine down on a side table.

"I remembered something else," Jaworski said. "Clyde telling me once she threatened to kill him."

Ott watched two motorcycle cops walk in and give him a wave. "So you're saying it was way more than just bad blood. And did Clyde take it as a serious threat? I mean, you know how kids get pissed off and say crazy things. Like they've got no governor."

Jaworski looked out a window then slowly came back to Ott. "I know what you mean. I can't honestly remember how seriously Clyde took it, Detective. It was a long time ago."

Ott chose to suddenly remember an appointment he didn't actually have. "Well, thank you again for stopping by with that information, Mr. Jaworski," he looked down at his watch. 10:25. "I've gotta go jump on a conference call at ten thirty."

Jaworski looked like he had no idea what a conference call was.

Ott stood.

"Oh, okay, so, you mean...we're done?" Jaworski asked.

"Yes, sir, I think we've about covered it," said Ott. "I appreciate you coming in. I think I can take it from here."

As if right on cue, Ott's phone rang. It was Crawford. "Oh, there's my call now," Ott said.

Jaworski nodded and walked away.

"Hey, Charlie," Ott said, dropping his voice. "Perfect timing."

"What do you mean?"

Ott watched Rob Jaworski walk out the front door of the station and go south on County Road.

"Remember the old guy in Loadholt's poker game with all the theories?"

"Yeah? Jaworski?"

"Well, he stopped by to have another chat. I had to tell him I was expecting a conference call and ring-a-ding-ding, right on cue, there you were."

Crawford filled in Ott on Luis Arragon, Valentina's husband, and

Ott did the same with what Jenny Montgomery had said about Jamie Ransom and Arthur Sandusky.

"So we've got two carpenters," Crawford said. "Luis Arragon and Jamie Ransom."

"I know," Ott said. "Two carpenters and a stalker."

"Sandusky, you mean."

"Yeah," Ott said. "And if he followed Lila to Balfour's place, he knows David's rich. A guy who can come up with three mil."

"Yeah, but all three of them know that." Crawford said. "What's your gut after talking to the girl?"

Ott started walking toward the elevator to go to his office. "Sandusky, I got no clue. Just don't know enough about him. Jamie Ransom, I'm still not sure he's up to the job. Plus, he's all about getting the girl. And he seems to think the way to do that is convince her he's somebody—a guy going to law school first, now a guy who's gonna make millions flipping houses."

"So from what you heard from Montgomery, you don't think he's capable of it?"

"Not really," Ott said. "But let's just say for the moment he did do it. Hired these guys to go to Balfour's house and kidnap Lila. And let's assume Lila never sees Ransom while she's being held and has no reason to suspect he's got anything to do with it. So then, let's say, Balfour pays the money and Lila is returned..."

"Okay."

"So what's Ransom gonna say to Lila?"

"What do you mean?"

"I mean is he gonna say, 'Hey, guess what? I just flipped a house and made three million bucks. Will you take me seriously now? Oh, and hey, while we're at it, let's get married?'"

Crawford didn't say anything for a few moments. "I hear ya, probably doesn't add up. Sandusky then?"

"Shit, Charlie, it's hard to say. But seems like Sandusky's probably more qualified to pull it off," Ott said. "Montgomery mentioned he did something to quote, creep out Lila."

"But she didn't say what?"

"No, I asked, but I don't think she knew exactly," Ott said. "Whatever it was, though, it was enough to get Lila to quit his class and want to get a new advisor."

"Really?" Crawford said. "We've gotta find out what it was. I'm gonna take another look at Lila's cell phone. I went through it pretty fast. Couple things I couldn't open."

"Okay, and I'll do an FCIS and a DAVID search on both Luis Arragon and Sandusky."

"Sounds good," Crawford said. "Then we'll talk again."

TWENTY-SEVEN

The Mentors were on the fantail deck of Beth Jastrow's 146-foot Feadship. The sun had just gone down and there was a light breeze on the starlit night.

"Lulu thinks Eddie is going to sign her," Elle said. "It's in the lawyers' hands now."

Eddie Buskey was Elle T. Graham's friend at Rhino Records.

"Wow, that was fast," Diana said.

"Eddie loved her," Elle said.

"'New Rhino recording artist, Lulu Perkins,'" Beth said. "That ought to help fill up seats in my casinos for the two weeks she'll be playing them."

"Probably going to have full houses, I would imagine," Elle said.

A man in a white jacket and black bow tie came back to the aft deck with a bottle of champagne and refilled all of their glasses.

Rose said, "Thank you, James," then, "So who's next?"

Marla set her champagne glass down on a mahogany table. "How would you ladies feel about a politician?"

"After the big check I wrote Hilary," said Elle, "I'm kind of gun shy."

The others laughed. "I hear you," Marla said. "But let me just tell you about her. Her name is Laura Dominguez—"

"Oh, yeah, down in Miami, right?" Rose said.

"Yes," Marla said. "She's a Democratic councilwoman there. Last election she got seventy-six percent of the vote. She was a protégé of Marco Rubio before switching parties. Very smart, charismatic, photogenic, and she's after Neil Griscom's seat in the senate."

"Good," Rose said. "That guy's old and on cruise control. I'd love to see her fight it out with him."

Beth stood up. "Gotta pee," she said. "Champagne just goes right through me."

Marla turned to Beth. "I'd like to get Laura up here to meet with us. You guys in?"

"I'm in," Beth said, walking inside.

"I think it's a great idea," Diana said.

"Hey, speaking of fights," Rose said lowering her voice. "I'd put Beth up against Muhammad Ali any day."

Marla and Elle laughed. Diana didn't get it at first. Then, "Oh, you mean, that little incident in the elevator."

"Yeah," Rose said. "Girl's maybe got a little anger issue."

"Hey," Elle said. "As long as she's on our side."

The waiter with the champagne came back out again. No takers this time.

"And let me just say," Marla said. "This is a pretty damn nice spot to have our meetings."

Beth walked back out. "I miss anything?"

"Nah," said Rose. "We were just saying how much we like your boat."

TWENTY-EIGHT

CRAWFORD WAS GOING THROUGH LILA BACON'S iPHONE AGAIN when he saw the Snapchat he had first noticed the night before. What he hadn't noticed before was that it was from Arthur Sandusky—at one thirty in the morning. Being oblivious to most things technological, Crawford at least knew that Snapchat was an app where you could send and receive photos, which would then disappear in ten seconds. He was dying to know just what kind of photo Arthur Sandusky would have sent to Lila at one thirty in the morning.

He called West Palm Beach chief, Ron Mendoza, the man who had been telling Norm Rutledge all about the latest police technology the other night.

"Hey, Ron, it's Charlie Crawford," he said. "So you being Mr. Tech Wizard, I've got a question for you."

"Fire away, Charlie," Mendoza said.

"Okay, let's say I get a Snapchat from somebody and it's gone in ten seconds."

"You actually set a timer for how long until it disappears."

"Okay, good to know," Crawford said. "But let's say that, after it's gone, like maybe the next day, I want to take another look at the photo. Is there any way I can? You know, retrieve it?"

"It's called a snap, by the way," Mendoza said. "And, yes, it's a piece of cake."

"Really?"

"Yeah, nothing to it."

"You made my day," Crawford said. "How the hell do I do it?"

Mendoza walked him through it.

Finally, after he followed all of Mendoza's instructions, he clicked the snap.

And God, it was not pretty.

It was a full-length shot of a naked and smiling Arthur Sandusky. He had to be drunk, Crawford concluded, seeing the half-filled wine glass in his hand.

The guy was double-chinned, triple-gutted, and had flaccid albino skin.

Not to mention, Crawford thought, the man was one sick bastard.

Crawford put the iPhone down on the table in front of him and just thought for a few minutes.

He had met a shrink at Ultima, his gym in West Palm Beach. The guy could bench almost as much as Ott, who could do his weight plus fifty pounds. Phil Ulrich was outgoing, friendly, and had a hail-fellow-well-met personality—the antithesis of the stereotypical New York City shrink. Crawford had called and asked him a shrink question once before and still had the man in his contacts. He dialed him on his cell.

"Hello."

"Hey, Phil, it's Charlie Crawford," he said. "Got a patient stretched out on your couch there?"

Ulrich laughed "Hey, Charlie. Nope. Someone just left. I'm writing up some notes."

"Can I take five minutes of your time?"

"Sure, that'll be...nine dollars and thirty three cents, but you can buy me a can of FitAid instead." That was a drink sold at the gym.

"So, I've got a hypothetical question: a college professor develops an interest in a young woman in his class, a really beautiful girl. She doesn't encourage it, but then it like ramps up, turns into an obsession on his part. The guy's calling her and emailing her all the time; then he starts stalking her. Finally, he sends her one of those Snapchat things—"

"Yeah, a snap."

"Of him...naked," Crawford said. "And this ain't like some buff guy in the gym."

"Hardly matters," Ulrich said. "The guy's clearly got a serious problem."

"So, the girl who was just mildly freaked out before is now totally freaked."

"Who can blame her?"

"My question is, what is the next move a guy like this makes?"

Ulrich exhaled long and loud. "Jesus, I don't know, Charlie. That's an impossible question to answer."

"I know it is," Crawford said. "But, in your experience, does he ratchet it up? Possibly get violent with her, or does he just quietly go away after a while?"

"'I don't know' is not the answer you want to hear, but it's the only honest—"

"Girl's the niece of a friend of mine. I—"

"Is she all right?"

"I don't know."

Ulrich was silent for a few moments. "Honestly, Charlie, I'd say that's the profile of a guy who went from zero to sixty, then eighty, and might keep his foot on the accelerator. But there's no way to say with any real certainty. First thing I'd do is check, see if he's got any history."

"We're on that now," Crawford said.

"Unofficially, it doesn't sound to me as if he's just going to 'quietly go away.'"

Crawford sighed. "All right, Phil, thanks for your help. I understand it's not like anybody can predict what a guy like this is gonna do next."

"Exactly," Ulrich said. "Good luck, Charlie. Hope it works out okay. See you down at the gym."

"Thanks, man."

He dialed Ott's number. "You got anything on Sandusky yet?"

"I was just gonna call you," Ott said. "Guy's a real beauty. Turns out four years ago he got fired from his job at University of North Carolina, Chapel Hill."

"Why?"

"Sexual harassment," Ott said. "Charges filed by two students. And get this: one was a girl, one was a guy. Then, when they went to arrest him, they get him for possession of an unlicensed firearm too. He claimed there were a series of burglaries in his neighborhood."

"Wonder how the hell he got the job at Florida Atlantic?"

"Somebody did a shitty background check would be my guess," Ott said. "Eventually UNC dropped the charges. Probably didn't want it publicized. It was right around the time of that incident at Duke with the lacrosse players."

"Good job, man."

"Oh, and also, you asked me to check up on Sonia Reyes's brother. The guy in the Mexican jail?"

"Yeah, and?"

"Turns out Hector Reyes has been out of prison for six months," Ott said. "So either he didn't tell his sister or she was lying to you."

Crawford didn't have to think about that for long. "I'd go with the latter."

"So I sniffed around the Miami area," Ott said. "Got a little help from a detective down there and guess what?"

"What?"

"Hector apparently took a little fishing trip recently, ended up at Palm Harbor Marina a while ago."

"Which is where?"

"400 North Flagler, West Palm."

"No shit."

"I think we should pay him a visit," Ott said.

"I agree, but Sandusky's my top priority right now," Crawford said. "I think he might be our guy. Particularly after what you found out."

"What do you want to do?"

"I called Palm Beach Atlantic," Crawford said. "Arthur Sandusky teaches a class on Saturday. How would you feel about auditing it?"

"Sure. What's the course?"

"It's called Marketing in a Mega Media World."

"Oh, yeah," Ott said. "Right up my alley."

"I'm thinking you and the prof have a little after-class chat," Crawford said.

"Done," said Ott.

"So back to Hector Reyes," Crawford said, "maybe we pay him a visit before you go to class."

"Gonna be a busy day, huh?" said Ott. "When do you want me to pick you up?"

"How 'bout we meet at Mellor Park in fifteen minutes."

"See you then."

CRAWFORD AND OTT WERE ON THEIR WAY TO THE PALM Harbor Marina.

"Hector's boat is called *The Ghost*," Ott said. "It's a 53-foot Rybovich, if you know what that is."

"I don't know shit about boats," Crawford said.

Ott shrugged. "I know less than you. Never did any boating on the Cuyahoga River. Too damn polluted."

On the way over to pick up Crawford, Ott had spoken to Kelly Poe, the harbormaster of Palm Harbor Marina, who told him exactly where *The Ghost* was moored. Ott drove up Flagler and pulled into a parking lot in front of the marina.

They hopped out and walked to the southernmost dock. *The Ghost* was supposed to be the next to last one on the right. They started walking faster as they saw a boat pull away from the dock at that location.

Then Crawford started running. He spotted the name on the hull of the moving boat. Sure enough, *The Ghost,* and below it, *Miami, Florida.*

He turned back to Ott. "That's it," he shouted. They both started running at full speed.

Then, after going about twenty yards, Crawford jumped down into a boat right next to *The Ghost's* just vacated berth, where a middle-aged couple with coffee mugs in their hands were sitting in deck chairs. The startled couple looked up at him in shock.

"What the hell?" the man said.

Crawford already had his ID out as Ott thudded down onto the boat's deck not three feet from the woman.

"We're detectives, Palm Beach Police. We need to commandeer your boat. We'll reimburse—" Crawford saw the key to the right of the wheel and walked over and turned it. The engine started up and had a nice, powerful rumble to it.

The owner still had a full-blown '*this can't really be happening*' look on his face.

"Won't take long," Ott tried to assure him. "We'll have you back at the dock in a jiffy."

The man's expression didn't change. "Where are we going?" he asked.

"We need to talk to the owner of that boat," Ott said, pointing at *The Ghost* off in the distance, as Crawford turned past the end of the dock and slid the boat's throttle forward.

"About what?" the owner asked.

The fewer details the better, thought Ott. "Something that

happened last week," then he had a second thought. "Would you folks mind going into the cabin?"

He was imagining the possibility of shots being fired.

"Okay," said the owner. "Come on, honey."

The woman looked to be still absorbing the shock of seeing a two-hundred-thirty-pound, quasi-bald man drop from out of the sky.

"Come on, honey," the man said again. "They want us inside."

She shook her head. "Thought you gave the orders on this ship, Sam."

He shrugged and without another word they went inside.

Crawford had the boat going full throttle and they were catching up with *The Ghost*.

Ott unholstered his Glock and took a few steps over to Crawford.

"Good idea," Crawford said. "Getting them inside."

The Ghost was a football field away. Crawford unholstered his Sig Sauer semi.

Ott spotted a bullhorn stowed behind the front seats. He handed it to Crawford. "So you don't need to yell."

Crawford smiled and took it. "Thanks."

He eased back on the throttle as they pulled up to *The Ghost* then raised the bullhorn. "Hector Reyes, Palm Beach Police, we need to talk to you."

A short man up on the bridge, wearing a tan baseball cap and Oakley's, turned and had an expression of being both confused and put upon. "What the hell do you want?" he shouted back.

"We want to come aboard," Crawford said, pulling up next to *The Ghost*. "Ask you a few questions."

Reyes scowled.

Four men came out of the cabin. None of them seemed to be armed, but Crawford didn't want to take any chances. He raised his Sig Sauer and Ott did the same with his Glock.

The four men looked as though they had never had guns pointed at them before.

"Jesus, what the hell's this?" one of them said in a frightened tone.

"You four," Crawford said. "Walk up to the front of the boat."

"It's called the bow," Reyes said, then shaking his head. "You know, these men are paying good money to go after tuna, not be ordered around by a couple Palm Beach cops."

Crawford had a sinking feeling. "This is a..."

"Charter boat," said Reyes.

Crawford heard Ott sigh his, 'oh shit' sigh.

"Where were you last Thursday night, Hector?" Crawford asked, shading his eyes from the sun.

"I don't see why it's any of your goddamn business," Reyes said. "But are you talking about the night my old friend, Clyde Loadholt, got capped?"

"Yeah, exactly," Crawford said, a little voice telling him he wasn't going to like the answer.

"Well, first of all, a bar in Nassau, then a restaurant in Nassau, then a fleabag of a motel just outside of Nassau," Reyes said, reaching into his back pocket and pulling out his wallet. "Care to see a few receipts...Detective?"

Ott walked over to the side of the boast, got up on the gunwale, then jumped down into *The Ghost*.

Reyes showed him two receipts. Both were from last Thursday. Ott turned to Crawford and nodded his head.

"Okay with you if we go catch some tuna now?" Reyes said to Crawford with a sneer. "Oh, by the way, Detective. Love the shirt. That what they got you guys wearing these days? Green silk shirts with little flamingos on 'em."

Crawford shook his head. "It's a peacock."

TWENTY-NINE

CRAWFORD AND OTT SCRAPED UP EIGHTY-FIVE DOLLARS AND gave it to the couple who owned the boat. Sam and his wife seemed to think it was a pretty fair price for twenty minutes of boat rental and probably wouldn't have minded if Crawford and Ott took it out on a regular basis.

On the ride back to Mellor Park, Crawford filled in Ott about the snap of Arthur Sandusky. Ott shook his head disgustedly and reminded Crawford what Jenny Montgomery had said about Sandusky 'creeping out' Lila. This was definitely what it was. Ott said he figured a third of his teachers back at his alma mater had something a little "hinky" about them.

Five minutes later, Ott dropped Crawford at Mellor Park and said he was going to see what else he could get on Sandusky, then go back and research more of Clyde Loadholt's past cases. He said he wanted to be absolutely sure he hadn't missed anything.

Crawford went through the tunnel to David Balfour's house and found Balfour in his basement waiting for him. Before Balfour could say anything, Crawford said, "Hey, David, I just wondered if you had another shirt, maybe like a plain old t-shirt or something?"

"T-shirt, huh?" Balfour said. "I'm not really a t-shirt kind of guy. How 'bout a nice, simple polo shirt. No alligator, no club logo—"

"Perfect."

"I'll get you one, but first I gotta tell you about my call."

"From the kidnapper?"

Balfour nodded. "It was the same guy again. Spanish accent. Could be Luis, but I couldn't tell for sure," he said. "Anyway, he was really pissed off and said, 'I told you not to go to the cops.' Then said I'd better 'call 'em off or say goodbye to Lila.'"

Balfour started to choke up. Crawford put his hand on his shoulder. "David, you gotta realize they can make threats, but bottom line it's all about them getting the money. And that's not gonna happen unless they deliver Lila."

Balfour nodded. "Yeah, I know, but—"

"Which means one of two things," Crawford said. "Either it was a bluff to see if you'd admit you were in contact with us, or someone knew Ott talked to Jenny Montgomery."

"I told him I hadn't talked to anyone," Balfour said. "I mean, I said it really emphatically too."

"So, like I said, they were just bluffing or somehow they found out about Ott and Jenny," Crawford said. "I know Ott and there's no way anybody'd know he talked to Jenny, except Jenny."

Balfour put his hand up to his chin. "So do you think she could be involved?"

Crawford shrugged. "I don't know. You know her, do you?"

Balfour sighed and shook his head. "I really can't see it. But how else would the guy who called know you guys were on the case?"

Crawford shrugged. "That's the question."

His cell phone rang.

"Yeah, Mort."

Ott got right to the point. "I was doing a search on DAVID for Clyde Loadholt and got a hit from way back in 1996. Seems like Loadholt's neighbors—on both sides of his house—phoned in a report of gunshots fired in his backyard."

"You're kidding."

"No, so the responding officers go there and it turns out Loadholt's seventeen-year-old granddaughter had a gun and was shooting at him. Ended up hitting him once in the wrist, but finally he wrestled the gun away from her just as the guys got there."

"Jesus," Crawford said. "Just like Jaworski said. There definitely was bad blood between Loadholt and his granddaughter."

"Yeah, but what could have been so bad that it escalated up to something like that?"

"I don't know," Crawford said. "But it's worth you taking a drive back to Susie Loadholt's house to try to find out."

"I was thinking the same thing," Ott said. "Find out where the granddaughter is too."

"Yeah, definitely."

"Okay," Ott said. "I'll let you know what I come up with."

OTT WAS IN SUSIE LOADHOLT'S LIVING ROOM. IT SEEMED LIKE Susie and her sister Mavis were a package, you didn't get one without the other. Ott wished he had brought along duct tape for Mavis's mouth.

"Girl was hell on wheels," Mavis had just volunteered.

Susie wasn't disagreeing with her sister. "Yeah, she and Clyde seemed to go at it all the time."

"What happened to her parents, Mrs. Loadholt?" Ott asked.

Susie looked at Mavis. Mavis looked grim.

"Well, her father just up and left one day. Megan, my daughter, never heard from him again."

Mavis exhaled loudly. "Guy was a good-for-nothing bum. She was better off without him."

Again, Susie didn't disagree with her. "So then Megan had her own problems. Wasn't really up to taking care of anyone, including herself. Ended up we took in Elizabeth Jeanne. Adopted her."

"Bad decision," Mavis muttered under her breath.

"She was always a handful," Susie said.

"So what happened? Where is she now?" Ott asked. "Elizabeth Jeanne."

Susie shrugged. "I don't know," her voice was so low it was almost inaudible. "She ran away. And just like her father, we never heard from her again."

"When did she run away?" Ott asked.

"Right after that incident with the gun you were asking about," Susie said. "A few days after she graduated from high school."

"Good thing she took off," said Mavis, "or else she might have killed Clyde."

"So you have no idea where she went? Or where she is now?" Ott asked.

Susie shook her head. "Nope. None. We tried really hard to find her. Even with all of Clyde's resources in law enforcement, but there was no trace."

Mavis cocked her head. "You sure Clyde tried that hard?"

"'Course he did," Susie said, but it wasn't the strongest affirmation Ott had ever heard.

"What about Elizabeth Jeanne's mother, Megan?" Ott asked. "Where is she?"

Susie frowned. "Up in Hobe Sound. This house in a development off of Route 1. She got remarried."

"Another bum," Mavis volunteered.

Susie turned to her sister. "At least he didn't take off on her."

"Yet," said Mavis.

Ott got Megan's address in Hobe Sound, thanked the two women, and got to his feet.

He drove straight up to Hobe Sound and found Megan Sullivan outside her house with a dog that had one eye. Megan was expecting him because Susie had called and said he'd be coming. She wasn't able to offer any more information about the whereabouts of her daughter. It was a short conversation and Ott was back in his car ten minutes after getting there.

He called Crawford and filled him in.

"Can't say I've run across a lot of granddaughters taking pot shots at grandpa," Crawford said.

"I know," Ott said. "Not so sure I want to be one now."

Ott was referring to the fact that he had a married daughter who, he suspected, was trying to get pregnant.

"You don't have a lot of say in the matter," Crawford said.

"Do I ever?" Ott gave a half-hearted laugh. "So where do we go with this? Looks like another dead end. Plus I'm not sure I see Elizabeth Jeanne—who'd be in her late thirties now, *if* she's alive—as being prime perp material. Violent nature or not."

"Yeah, I know," Crawford said. "Coming back twenty-one years later to finish off the job she started in the backyard...seems pretty unlikely."

"Okay, so if she's out, Hector Reyes and his sister are out, the gay couple is out," said a frustrated Ott, "and the stripper Chelsea and her husband are out, who the hell's in?"

"Slow down, Mort, they all *seem* out," Crawford said. "Which doesn't mean they definitely are."

"I don't know, all their alibis were pretty tight," Ott said.

"Not Elizabeth Jeanne's," Crawford said.

"Wherever the hell she may be," Ott said dubiously, looking at his watch. It was twelve forty. Twenty minutes to Professor Sandusky's class. "All right, Charlie, gotta cut you loose now. Got a class to get to."

"Take good notes, bro."

THIRTY

CRAWFORD DIALED ALEXA DILLON'S NUMBER. THE REPORTER
answered right away.

"You're not going to cancel out on me, are you, Charlie?"

"I'm afraid I am," he said. "I'm sorry, but let's do a rain check.
Something came up and I gotta work."

"Understood," she said. "Something on Clyde Loadholt?"

"I can't say," Crawford said.

"C'mon, Charlie, you blow me off," she said, "how 'bout throwing
me a bone?"

"Sorry."

"Just a little tidbit?"

"Sorry."

It was her turn for a dramatic sigh. "O-kay," she said, "but definitely a rain check, right?"

"Yes."

OTT WALKED INTO THE CLASSROOM AT 1:01.

Arthur Sandusky eyed him like he was a Martian.

"Auditing," Ott said. He walked past him briskly to the back of the room and sat at a desk. He had always been a back-of-the-room kind of student. He looked up. Sandusky was still eyeing him suspiciously. Ott smiled back.

Sandusky shot a somewhat forced smile back at him then started in on his lecture.

Ott thought it was actually pretty interesting as he wondered what the likelihood of a man who was knee deep in a kidnapping plot would be doing delivering a marketing lecture like it was just another day. Unlikely was the word that came to mind. A word he and Crawford had been using a little too often lately.

Nevertheless, there were a few things that pointed to Sandusky as possibly being the man behind the kidnapping.

A girl a few seats ahead of Ott kept looking back at him. Shooting him furtive glances. He realized that it was not that she was finding him cute, or that she was smitten with a fifty-one-year-old, slightly overweight, hair-challenged man, but that she was wondering just what the hell he was doing there. The big thing Ott noticed was that most students spent the majority of their time texting away on their cell phones rather than taking notes. He wondered whether it was like that now at his alma mater. Arthur Sandusky was actually an authoritative, engaging speaker and, Ott figured, the class's subject was way more interesting than something like calculus. In his head, Ott rehearsed what he was going to say to Sandusky at the end of class.

He waited until all the other students had left. Sandusky picked up his North Face book bag and started toward the door.

"Great lecture, professor," Ott said, raising his voice.

Sandusky turned to him. "Thank you," he said, then cocking his head. "Who are you, anyway?"

Ott walked up to him. "Your second worst nightmare," he said. "Second only to those cops who arrested you up in North Carolina."

That knocked what little color there was out of Sandusky's face. He had a caged look, as if he were considering making a run for it.

"I'm a friend of Lila Bacon." Ott said.

Sandusky got blinky and started to shake a little.

"Got a question for you," Ott said. "Is that what you professors do these days: make students drop your classes and go looking for new advisors?"

Sandusky exhaled and looked down. "I...I've called her to try to get her back."

Ott took a step closer to Sandusky and rose up on his toes to get eye-to-eye. "Are you fucking kidding me?" he said, getting in Sandusky's face. "You think anybody who got a snap like that would want to come back and get advised by a scumbag like you?"

Sandusky's eyes darted around like he was looking for a hole to dive into.

"I have another question," Ott's vitriol had kicked up a notch. "Where were you yesterday, and what exactly were you doing?"

Sandusky looked up. "As a matter-of-fact, I was up in New York City. Flew back late last night. I was at a seminar called Empower 17 all Thursday and Friday."

Ott frowned. "And you've got receipts and ticket stubs to prove it?"

Sandusky was already reaching into his back pocket. "I don't have a ticket stub for the flight, but you can check. I've got receipts for breakfast and dinner yesterday."

He pulled out his wallet, reached in, pulled out two receipts, and handed them to Ott. The first one was for a lunch place in the east thirties of Manhattan. The second one was from an IHOP on Third Avenue. The total, including tip, was twenty-two dollars and fourteen cents.

"How many people is this for?" Ott asked, holding up the receipt.

"Just me," Sandusky said with a shrug. "Hey, it was New York City."

THIRTY-ONE

CRAWFORD HAD JUST GOTTEN A CALL FROM OTT, WHO TOLD HIM in so many words that Arthur Sandusky was not their man. Ott had confirmed that Sandusky had taken a Jet Blue flight up to JFK airport at 6:00 a.m. on Thursday morning and returned to West Palm Beach airport at 11:55 on Friday night. He had also checked Sandusky's calls on his cell phone and there were none to, or from, anyone in the West Palm/Palm Beach area. If he had been involved in a kidnapping, Ott was certain there would've been calls to his accomplices, unless he used a burner phone. But no, Ott was absolutely certain, a burner wouldn't even have been in Sandusky's vocabulary.

Crawford was sitting on the couch in the basement of David Balfour's house, having just hung up with Ott. With Sandusky out and Jamie Ransom highly unlikely, that left Luis Arragon as the leading suspect.

Crawford dialed Balfour's number.

Balfour picked up after the first ring. "Yeah, Charlie?"

"Can you come down here?"

"Sure, be right there," Balfour said. And a minute later he came down the steps.

For a guy who was always perfectly coiffed and turned out, he was unshaven and looked haggard.

"What's up, Charlie?"

"So I had an idea," Crawford said. "Can you give Luis Arragon a call and tell him you need him tonight? That you're planning on going out and having one too many."

"Sure. What are you thinking?"

"I'm thinking you spend some time with him, have a conversation or two, find out what he's been up to the last few days."

"So you mean, see if he's got an alibi or not?"

"Yeah, exactly. Only problem is, if Luis is our guy, he's gonna think it a little strange you going out bar-hopping the night after your niece got kidnapped."

Balfour nodded.

"Which is why I came up with a cover story," Crawford said. "You need to act all worried and stressed out. Not your usual self. That's what he'd expect, if he's behind this thing."

Balfour nodded. "Well, I *am* all worried and stressed out, don't need to fake it," he said. "So I make it seem like I'm goin' out 'cause the pressure got to me? Needed a couple of shooters, right?"

"Yeah, exactly," said Crawford, "and you can even say to him, when you first get in the car, something like, 'Luis, I might be getting an important call and I'll need to take it in privacy. So if a call comes in, I want you to pull over and I'll get out and take it.'"

Balfour was nodding. "Sounds good," he said. "Want me to call him now?"

Crawford nodded. "Where are you thinking of going?"

"Cucina Dell'Arte," Balfour said. "Bartender there makes stiff drinks. The way I'm feeling, I'm gonna need a double or two."

THIRTY-TWO

THE MENTORS, THREE-FIFTHS OF THEM ANYWAY, WERE SITTING in Rose Clarke's living room having cocktails. Marla Fluor and Elle T. Graham were also in attendance. Diana Quarle was up in New York working on a big deal to acquire a retail competitor. Beth Jastrow had flown off in her private jet to put out a fire at one of her Las Vegas casinos. Both would return to Palm Beach for the weekend.

At their last meeting, on Beth's boat, Marla had proposed that they put their collective weight behind Laura Dominguez, the Miami politician, and Beth had sung the praises of a twenty-four-year-old author named A. Carol Owurson who had just written her first novel.

Dominguez was scheduled to come and meet with the five on the weekend. Beth had said she was sure Owurson's book would be a blockbuster if they got behind it. The other four agreed that they would read it just as fast as they could.

"I have a lot of respect for Beth's taste," Rose said, "I mean, witness Lulu Perkins"—the singer who they had gone to hear in Atlanta—"but if this woman's so good, wouldn't she have an agent?"

"Not necessarily," Marla said. "I understand it's really tough to get one these days. The question is, what did we think of the book?"

The three looked around at each other.

"It's pretty dark, that's for sure," Elle said. "They call it 'dystopian,' right?"

Rose and Marla nodded.

"Yeah, I actually looked that up," Rose said, reading from a piece of paper. "'A society characterized by human misery, as in squalor, oppression, disease, and overcrowding.'"

Elle laughed, "She's got all that in the book, except overcrowding."

The other two laughed. "Gotta say," Rose said, "it kind of bummed me out. I mean, what a rotten life she had. Can you imagine growing up in that household?"

"I'd kill myself," Elle said.

"She tried that once, remember?" Marla said.

"I'd succeed," Elle said.

"What'd you think of the ending?" Elle asked.

All three thought for a few moments.

"I actually thought it was kind of...hopeful," Marla said. "Like she had a chance to turn things around."

"You did?" Elle said. "I thought she was doomed."

Marla exhaled loudly. "Question is, do we believe in the girl enough that we go and put our muscle behind her? Help get her an agent who gets her a publisher who sells a million copies of the damn thing?"

"Part of me says, even though I didn't love the book, that we go with Beth's gut," Rose said.

"Yeah, she's been spot-on before," Marla said.

"So is that a yes?" Elle asked.

"Why don't we do what we've done with everyone else, meet her face to face," Rose said.

"But where's she live?" Elle asked.

"I think up in Michigan somewhere," Rose said. "Where Beth's from."

"Beth's from Michigan?" Diana asked.

"Yeah, originally," Rose said. "Why?"

"I don't know. I just thought she was originally from around here somewhere," Diana said.

"Yes, I know what you mean," Marla said. "Never really heard much of a Michigan accent."

"What in God's name is a Michigan accent?" Rose asked.

"Well, I had this friend in college from there. She said stuff like, 'Where at?' and practically every question ended in a preposition. Another thing, she called that white stuff from cows 'melk.'"

"Melk?" Elle said.

Marla nodded.

"Minnesota people say that too," Rose said.

"Oh, really," Marla said.

"Okay," Elle said. "I'll call Beth. She can ask—whatever she calls herself, A. Carol or just plain Carol—to meet with us."

Marla and Rose nodded. "We can all kick in for the flight," said Marla.

"Sounds like a plan," Rose said.

THIRTY-THREE

AFTER FIVE MINUTES IN THE CAR WITH LUIS, DAVID BALFOUR had pretty much eliminated him as having any participation in any capacity in his niece's kidnapping. Luis was driving Balfour's BMW and telling Balfour about how the night before—Friday—had started out so promising down at the Seminole Hard Rock Casino in Hollywood.

"So I hit the jackpot on a progressive slot machine fifteen minutes after I got there. Good for two hunner and eighty bucks,"—should have hopped right in your car and headed home, thought Balfour —"then I went to the blackjack table and walked away up another hunner or so."

Balfour had heard a few of Luis' hard-luck stories before. Something told him this one ended like the others. Badly.

"So then I went to this place and watched these wackos do karaoke for an hour or so," Luis said as he drove up County Road.

"How was that?" Balfour asked.

"Lame, man," Luis said. "Really lame. Probably had a few more drinks there than I shoulda," he went on. "Real strong margaritas. Ever had a Texas margarita, Mr. B?"

"No, what is that?" Balfour asked, thinking he had drunk everything under the sun.

"Cointreau, Triple Sec, lime juice and a *sheet-load* of Tequila," Luis said, shaking his head. "After two of those I got lost trying to find the men's room. Wandered into the kitchen unzipping my fly. Ay caramba, it was ugly, Mr. B."

"Sounds like it," Balfour said, chuckling. "Then, I'm guessing, you went back to the tables."

Luis exhaled long and loud as he pulled up in front of Cucina Dell'Arte.

"Yeah, what a mistake," Luis said ruefully, shaking his head. "Craps...now I unna-stan why they call it that."

Balfour grabbed for the door handle, knowing the end of the story. "So you lost it all, huh?"

Luis nodded sheepishly.

Inside Cucina Dell'Arte, Balfour ordered a drink and dialed Crawford's number.

"Luis is not our man, Charlie," Balfour said. "Spent last night getting drunk at Seminole Hard Rock, losing all his money. Poor Valentina. Came back at three in the morning with two cents in his pocket."

"Okay," Crawford said with a sigh. "So no way he'd be in the middle of a kidnapping carrying on like that?"

"No way in hell," Balfour said.

"So what are you going to do?"

"Have a quick drink and come back home," Balfour said.

"Okay, see you in a little while."

"I'll cook you something to eat. You must be starving," Balfour said. "Make you a salad and my famous spaghetti Bolognese."

"Good?"

"Good? Like you died and went to heaven."

It was pretty damn good, Crawford had to admit. As was the bottle of Chardonnay he shared with Balfour.

Crawford was weighing whether to have a second helping when a phone call interrupted his meal. He didn't recognize the caller, but excused himself from the table and picked up.

It was from the owner of a shop on Dixie. When Crawford had gone around inquiring about the gay couple, one of whom Clyde Loadholt had crippled, he had left his card with a sales clerk and asked her to ask the shop's owner to call him. That had been two days ago. Better late than never, Crawford figured. The owner was named Chris Penna.

"Thanks for getting back to me, Mr. Penna," Crawford said. "I was trying to track down two fellas who had a shop near you on Dixie. Johnny Baxter and Ben Silver. Live down in the Keys now. But I actually got in touch with them yesterday."

"Oh, yeah," Penna said. "So they called when they were up here?"

"Here? No, they'd been at a hotel down in Miami."

Penna paused, like he wasn't sure whether he was telling him too much. "Well, actually they were up here."

Crawford straightened up in the leather couch. "What day was that?"

"They came up last Thursday."

The day Loadholt was killed.

Crawford started tapping his foot on the carpet.

"Are they still here, do you know?"

"I think so," Penna said. "When they come up, they usually stay about a week. Catch up with old friends and all."

"And do you know where they usually stay?"

"Yes, at the Flagler," Penna said. "They love the place 'cause of the shows."

"Shows?"

"They told me they saw Liza there once," Penna said. "I think either Tommy Tune or Mary Wilson is there now."

Then Crawford remembered hearing that the Flagler Hotel had cabaret shows, which attracted name performers. He guessed Liza might be Liza Minnelli and he was pretty sure Mary Wilson was one of the original Supremes. She had to be up there in age. Liza too.

"Did you see Johnny and Ben when they were here on Thursday, Mr. Penna?"

"Yeah, that's how I know they were in town."

"What time of day was it?"

"Right before I closed up," Penna said.

"So that would be?"

"Just before six."

Crawford started to tap on the table next to him. "And do you have any idea where they were going from there?"

Penna exhaled. "Why do you—"

"Mr. Penna, please, where were they going after your shop?"

"Uh, Johnny said something about a friend on a boat."

Crawford's foot tapped faster. "Where was the boat?"

"At a marina, I think, but I don't know which one," Penna said. "I'm not real comfortable telling you any more, Detective. I mean, these guys are my friends, I don't want to—"

"Thank you, Mr. Penna, you've been very helpful," Crawford said, "I appreciate it."

Crawford hung up then got up and started to pace. Then he dialed Ott.

"Yeah, Charlie?" Ott answered.

He told him about his conversation with Chris Penna.

"But what would prompt these guys after ten years to want to kill Loadholt?"

"That's always been our question. After so long. Maybe there's nothing there but why would they lie? Claim they were down in Miami?"

As they pondered that question, Crawford told Ott about having ruled out Luis Arragon.

"Oh, hey, by the way," Ott said, "I ran a search on Elizabeth Jeanne Loadholt on FCIS and had quite a few hits, back like twenty-some-odd years ago."

"Tell me."

"They were from right after the time she ran away from Load-holt's house," Ott said. "First one was for shoplifting."

"Jesus, they still got shit like that in the system that far back?"

"Hey, goes back to Ponce De Leon," Ott said.

"What'd he do?"

Ott laughed. "So then—like two months after that—she steps up in class: prostitution. Up in Jacksonville. She just got a slap on the wrist for both of those. But two months later she gets caught with some dude named Duane Lanier holding up a liquor store."

"No shit. Armed?"

"Yeah," Ott said. "They both had Saturday night specials. So apparently Duane's got a pretty long sheet and the cops there were dying to put him away," he said. "So basically she turns state's witness and testifies against him. Says he threatened to kill her unless she went along with it. So she ends up with a suspended sentence, basically just gets time served, and then they cut her loose."

"What next?"

"Nada. That appears to be the end of the budding criminal career of Elizabeth Jeanne Loadholt. Nothing after that. Either went straight, died, or just never got caught again."

Crawford didn't say anything for a few seconds. Then, "Goin' back to Ben Silver and Johnny Baxter—"

"Yeah?"

Crawford looked at his watch. It was nine thirty. "What are you up to tonight, Mort?"

"Watching Harry Bosch on Amazon Prime."

"You s'pose I could tear you away from that if I bought you a couple of drinks? I'm feeling a little cooped up here."

"Where you thinkin'?"

"How would you feel about...a gay bar?"

THIRTY-FOUR

HIS BAR REFERENCE GOT CRAWFORD THINKING ABOUT HIS
brother Cam. He had gotten a call from him and the good news was
that Cam was still at Clairmount, thanks, at least in part, to his
generous contribution to the Founders Fund. Crawford didn't ask,
but assumed that the check Cam had stroked probably had at least
five zeros in it. What the hell? It would have gone to booze and drugs
otherwise.

Cam extolled the virtues of AA and the doctors and staff at Clairmount then assured his brother that this time he really was going to
make it.

Crawford was holding his breath.

CRAWFORD FELT PRETTY CERTAIN THAT BALFOUR WOULDN'T BE
hearing from the kidnappers that night. What would they have to
say? Everything had been laid out, except where the drop would be
and Crawford figured they'd tell Balfour that at the very last minute.

The Flagler Hotel was on South County Road just down from

Worth Avenue and had a bar that did a brisk business with the gay community in and around Palm Beach. Crawford figured the time to go was after the show at the Monarch Room. He checked and found out that it was, in fact, Mary Wilson who was playing there from nine to eleven. He guessed that after the show was over many of its attendees would cruise over to the adjacent Shadow Lounge.

So Ott picked Crawford up at ten thirty at Mellor Park then they drove up to the Flagler, hoping to get a couple of barstools before the place filled up. They were in luck.

"I wouldn't have minded hearing Mary Wilson," Crawford said. "A third of the Supremes is way better than just about one of anything else."

"I'm with ya," Ott said. "Even though I was more a Martha & the Vandellas guy."

"Hey, she was great too. Still out there doin' shows, I hear," Crawford said, raising his hand to the bartender. "But the Supremes had way more hits."

"I'll give you that," Ott said, as the bartender approached.

"A Yuengling, please," Ott said. "And a Bud for my...bud."

The bartender didn't look amused or impressed with their plebian selections. The Shadow Room was more of a martini kind of place.

Ott smiled at Crawford. "I thought that was pretty good," he said. *"A Bud for my bud."*

Crawford shook his head. "You've used it before."

"I have?" Ott said. "Well, then next time I'll just say, 'a Bud for my asshole friend here.'"

Crawford shook his head and looked around the room. There were definitely a lot of guys there. Well-dressed, stylish, and mostly older, Crawford guessed they were probably some of the most successful men in the community. They looked like guys who could be anything: doctors, lawyers, bankers, architects...he bet there were a few, too, who were in the arts. Movies, TV, the theater. A lot of them were old enough to be retired.

"There's a guy over there checkin' you out, Charlie," Ott said, under his breath. "Guy in the beige jacket."

Crawford looked around and saw the guy, who smiled at him.

Crawford smiled back.

"So whaddaya want to talk about, Charlie?"

Crawford laughed. "That's not usually something you have a problem with, Mort. Making conversation."

"I'm just feeling a little uncomfortable, Charlie," Ott said, taking a sip of his newly-arrived Yuengling.

"What are you talking about?"

"Well, I've never been to a gay bar before."

"Your loss," Crawford said.

Ott's eyes got big. "You have?"

"Shit, yeah," Crawford said, lifting his glass, but not taking a sip. "Before I was into girls."

Ott made a scoffing noise. "No, seriously."

"I'm tellin' ya, been to quite a few up in New York."

"Really?"

"Yeah, with a date—of the female persuasion," Crawford said. "She had a lot of guy friends who were gay. Told me they're way funnier than straight guys. Nicer too."

"Oh, yeah?"

"Plus the food was really good at this one place."

Ott clinked Crawford's glass. "You know, Charlie, you're a pretty versatile guy."

"Well, thanks, Mort," Crawford said.

Ott stood up. "And on that note, I'm gonna hit the head."

Crawford nodded.

Ott had been gone for only about a minute, when a guy came up to him. He was probably in his mid-forties, had a nice tan and an expensive gray suit.

"Hi," he said. "Don't think I've seen you in here before. Name's Ty. I rent that barstool over there."

Crawford laughed. "Hi, Ty, Charlie," he said. "First time I've been here. Nice place."

"Yeah, it is."

"You live here?" Ty said. "Or just visiting?"

"Live here," Crawford said, gesturing with his head. "West Palm actually."

Ty nodded.

"Question for you," Crawford said.

"Shoot."

"You wouldn't happen to know a couple guys named Johnny Baxter and Ben Silver, would you?"

"Hell, yeah, they're here a lot," Ty said. "Live down in Key West now. But I think they miss it up here."

"Have you seen them tonight, by any chance?" Crawford asked as he saw Ott pick his way through the crowd.

"No, I haven't," Ty said. "But I know they're staying here. At the hotel."

Ott came up and sat down. He nodded at Ty. "How ya doin'?" he said. "Mort."

"Ty."

"I asked Ty if he had seen Johnny and Ben," Crawford said.

"Oh, yeah," Ott said to Ty. "We're hopin' they're gonna show up."

"They always do," Ty said, then standing. "Well, nice to have met you guys."

"Same here," Crawford said and Ott nodded as Ty walked away.

"Think he thought I queered his action...so to speak," Ott whispered.

"Don't be an asshole, Mort. Guy was just being friendly."

Ott rolled his eyes. "Uh-huh," he said. "Probably wondering what a hottie like you is doing with an old shlub like me."

Crawford frowned, shook his head and lowered his voice. "Are you an intolerant gay-basher in addition to all your other charming qualities?"

Ott put up his hands like he was afraid of being spanked. "Shit, Charlie, I was just kidding around."

Crawford's frown suddenly changed to the look of a bird dog spotting its prey, as he saw a man in a wheelchair come in with and another man.

"There they are," Crawford said, flicking his head. "Talking to Ty."

Ty pointed to Crawford and Ott.

Johnny Baxter and Ben Silver looked over at them.

"Absolutely no clue who we are," Crawford said, as Baxter and Silver started coming toward them.

Silver was the first one to get to them. "Hey, guys," he said, cocking his head. "Do we know you?"

Crawford smiled. "We spoke on the phone once," he said. "I'm Detective Crawford and he's my partner, Detective Ott."

Baxter and Silver looked as though they had just gotten a whiff of rotten eggs.

"Oh," Silver said, like he was thinking of bolting.

"I know," Ott said. "Kind of a buzz kill."

"How 'bout we buy you guys a drink?" Crawford asked.

Silver raised the drink in his hand.

"Well, then, the one after that," Crawford said.

"What is it you want?" Silver said, then with a chuckle. "You fellas look like fish out of water, by the way."

Crawford looked around and saw an empty table. "How 'bout we sit down over there," he said. "Tell me what you're drinkin.'"

Silver glanced at Baxter, who shrugged. "I'll have a Tanqueray martini," Silver said.

"Same," Baxter said.

Crawford flagged the bartender down and ordered four more drinks.

"I'll bring 'em over," Ott said.

"Thanks, Mort," Crawford said, walking toward the table, with Silver right behind him and Baxter lagging back in his wheelchair.

The three got to the table and Ott followed them with the drinks a few moments later.

Silver raised his martini glass and leaned forward toward Crawford and Ott. "To that bastard Clyde Loadholt, not being around anymore to make people's lives miserable."

"Hear, hear," said Baxter, raising his glass and clinking it with Silver.

"So you knew why we wanted to talk to you," Crawford said.

"What else could it be?" Silver said.

"And, yes, we were here when it happened, and, no, we didn't do it," Silver said. "As much as we couldn't stand that sadistic cretin."

"A man who owns a shop over near your old one said you were going to a boat the night Loadholt was killed," Crawford said.

"Yeah, Chris told me he told you," Silver said. "We were there from six thirty 'til the next morning. You can ask the other two staying there."

"What are their names?" Ott asked pulling out his pad.

"Len Barrow and Darcy Cole," Silver said.

"Is Darcy a...woman?"

"Yes, Detective," Silver said. "We've been known to consort with the occasional heterosexual couple."

Baxter laughed.

"So why did you say you were at that hotel in Miami?"

Silver eyed Baxter then turned to Crawford. "'Cause we planned to be," he said. "Then, last minute, Darcy called and asked us up to Palm Beach for my birthday."

Sliver shrugged. "Why not, we figured," he said. "Never got around to canceling the hotel reservation. Then when you called, after I read about Loadholt's murder, and you said you were a cop... well, I knew what you were calling about."

Crawford thought a moment then nodded. "Okay, we're gonna need to speak to your friends."

"Be my guest," Silver said, and Baxter nodded.

"Hey, look," Crawford said. "If it's any consolation, we didn't even know Loadholt. And obviously we don't condone what he did—"

"Condone it?" Silver said, his voice turned into a low growl. "He crippled Johnny, for chrissake. Clyde Loadholt was a sick fuck and a gay-bashing asshole who got exactly what he deserved. Only problem is it took someone 'til he was almost dead to do the job."

"So where was your friend's boat?" Ott asked.

"Up in Jupiter," Silver said. "I forget the name of the marina."

"And your friends can vouch for the fact—"

"That we never left it," Silver said, nodding.

"Hey, look," Baxter said. "I don't know about you, Ben," turning to Silver, "but I haven't wasted one second thinking about that guy in the last ten years." Silver nodded. "Why would we waste our time on a shithead like that?"

Baxter finished off his martini.

Crawford put his hand out to Baxter. "Thanks," he said. "Appreciate you sitting down with us."

Baxter shook it and smiled. "Wish guys like you were around twelve years ago."

Then Ott shook his hand as Crawford shook Silver's.

"You may not believe it," Ott said, "but most of the men in the department are pretty good guys."

"Glad to hear it," Silver said, standing up.

Crawford heard a loud crash and looked over to the far side of the bar.

A well-dressed man with a shaved head in his fifties threw a wild, roundhouse punch at a man in a blue blazer with a fashionably short ponytail. His fist smacked into the side of the man's head. Then a younger man stepped between them, trying to separate them. But the shaved-headed man shoved him out of the way and took two steps forward, his arms raised.

Crawford took off like a shot, Ott right behind him.

As Crawford rounded one side of the bar he saw the man with the ponytail take a swing but miss by a good foot.

Crawford tackled the shaved-headed man, bear-hugged him, and drove him back several feet. Ott grabbed the man with the ponytail and pulled him away.

"What the hell's goin' on here?" Ott yelled at the ponytailed man.

A third man—short, young, handsome—came over to Ott and the man he was restraining.

"That jerk had his hands all over me," the man said, pointing at shaved-head. "Peter was just trying to stop him."

Peter was apparently the man Ott was holding. "Guy's always pulling shit like that," Peter said, gesturing with his head to the shaved-headed man.

"All right, all right," Crawford said. "We're cops. You've got a choice. Either you go home or come down to our station."

"Let me go," said the man with the shaved head, struggling to break out of Crawford's grasp.

Crawford released his bear hug. "Home, right?"

The man nodded and started walking quickly out of the Shadow Lounge.

The bartender waved at Crawford. Crawford walked over to him. "That's not the first time he's pulled something like that," the bartender said. "I asked him to leave once before. Peter and Bob were just minding their own business."

"Thanks," Crawford said, then walking over to Ott, who was still holding onto Peter. "You can let him go." Then to Peter and Bob, "You guys are free to stay."

"Thanks," said Bob, the younger one. "That guy wouldn't leave me alone. Peter was just—"

Crawford nodded. "I know. Come on, Mort."

"Thanks," Peter said.

Crawford and Ott walked back to the table where Silver and Baxter were still sitting.

Sliver shook his head and smiled. "That was a first," he said to Crawford.

Crawford smiled. "Doesn't strike me as a place that has a lot of barroom brawls."

"I've certainly never seen one here before," Silver said.

"Well, thanks again," Crawford said. "Nice to have met you guys."

Ott nodded at them.

Crawford and Ott walked out.

Out front, Ott gave the valet the ticket stub and turned to Crawford. "That was an experience," he said. "Not much different from any straight bar."

"What do you mean?"

"Well, you know, some random guy tries to horn in on another guy's date, the date gets pissed, words are exchanged, it escalates and next thing you know, one of 'em starts swingin'."

THIRTY-FIVE

THE MENTORS WERE MEETING AT MARLA FLUOR'S MODERN house at the corner of Dunbar and the ocean.

None of them would admit it but there was an unspoken competition between all of them about whose was the better house. Why would they be any different from rich, highly successful men, who, since the beginning of time, were always trying to one-up each other? The bigger house, the bigger boat, the bigger bank account, the bigger...well, the list goes on.

It was nip-an-tuck between the top two, but Marla's was probably the winner based on the artwork in hers. A noted curator from Sotheby's, who had been through her house, estimated that she had over two hundred million dollars in paintings covering her walls. That would put Elle in second place. She had a distinctive old Maurice Fatio house, which had won the Residential Architect Design Award in 2014 and the RIBA award in 2015. The decorating, though, was a little on the dowdy side featuring a lot of old, out-of-style brown furniture— highboys and the like—which perhaps reflected Elle's conservative New Hampshire upbringing.

Rose, they all agreed, had the nicest view, with three hundred feet on the ocean. But Rose's house was only four thousand square feet—the size of Marla's guesthouse. Rose, however, found that her house was actually about a thousand square feet more than what she needed. And she was more into comfort and casual than size and dazzle.

Marla's house approached flashy, but didn't quite cross the line. Starting with her art collection, full of big and loud Pop Art—Warhol, Rosenquist, Lichtenstein, Oldenburg and Hockney—which made walking into her living room unprepared almost an assault on the senses. Some of her pictures were so big she needed every inch of her sixteen-foot high walls. Someone had observed that Marla's house had "every nouveau riche bell and whistle there was"—but made the person she said it to promise she'd never be quoted.

Diana was smart. She had entrusted the design of her house to Timmy Greer, the New York decorator and successor to Mario Buatta, who specialized in restrained, WASPY, good taste. One could tell that all her extravagant furnishings cost a fortune, but it was not something that she was shouting from the rooftop. What nobody knew was that Diana had quietly campaigned a friend at *Architectural Digest* to shoot her house for the cover of the Christmas edition in 2015 a few years back.

Beth had flown in that afternoon and was explaining why the author she was so excited about couldn't come down to Palm Beach to meet with them. "First of all, she lives way up in the upper peninsula of Michigan. In like some cabin with no electricity and an outhouse—"

Diana groaned. "Seriously? An outhouse?"

"Yeah," Beth said. "I don't even think she's got a car."

"They don't have Uber in Michigan?"

Beth laughed. "Uber snowmobiles maybe."

"What's her name again?" Elle asked.

"Carol Owurson," Beth said.

"What is that...Swedish?" Elle asked.

"Yeah, Swedish, Finnish, I'm not sure," Beth said.

"So is she like the female equivalent of J.D. Salinger?" Elle asked. "Living like a hermit up in Vermont?"

"New Hampshire," Diana said. "And he's not living there anymore."

"He moved?" Elle asked.

"He died," Diana said.

"Oh, sorry."

"So I'd say we all hop in my jet and go see her," Beth said, "but I doubt we'd all fit into her little cabin."

"I don't want to sound spoiled," Diana said, "but I just can't see peeing in an outhouse."

"So, unlike with Lulu Perkins, I guess we're just gonna have to make a decision based on the book," Beth said.

"So I guess if the book came out, she'd never go on Oprah," Diana said.

"If Oprah wanted her," Beth said. "Trust me, I'd fly the jet up there to pick her up."

"You know what I've been hearing?" Diana said. "Dystopian novels are all the rage since carrot top won the election."

Rose laughed. "Carrot top, huh?"

Diana smiled.

"I heard that too," Marla said.

"So what are we waiting for?" asked Beth.

Diana threw up her hands. "Let's sign her up."

THIRTY-SIX

CRAWFORD CAME THROUGH THE TUNNEL FROM THE BEACH AT eleven fifteen and Balfour was waiting for him, sitting in one of the leather chairs.

Crawford had told Balfour earlier that he was going out for an hour or two, but not where he was going.

"So where'd you go, Charlie?" Balfour asked.

"It's kind of a long story," Crawford said. "Anything new here?"

"Something just dawned on me," Balfour said. "The assistant pro at the Poinciana is Spanish. Accent and all. And I remembered his name. It's Camilo."

Crawford sat down opposite Balfour and leaned close to him. "So he took out Lila a few times?"

"Yeah, like a couple of months back. Maybe three," Balfour said. "My sense was that it didn't really go anywhere."

Crawford started wondering how they could talk to the assistant pro without tipping him off that he had just become a possible suspect.

"I keep thinking," Balfour said, "that chances are it is someone who knows Lila. Otherwise, like we said before, why wouldn't they kidnap a billionaire's kid? I mean, I'm on the lower end of the net-worth spectrum here."

Crawford smiled. "Yeah, but it's all relative. Maybe the lower end in Palm Beach, but probably in the top one percent of the whole country."

"I guess you're right," Balfour said, tapping his fingers on the table. "Charlie, I want to make it absolutely clear, I'm fully prepared to pay that money and never see it again to get Lila back. You got that, right?"

"Loud and clear," Crawford said. "Getting her back is top priority."

They talked a little bit more then Balfour went back upstairs. It was eleven forty. Crawford went and brushed his teeth, spread the two sheets and comforter over the leather couch and climbed in between the sheets and fell asleep right away.

His cell phone woke him up at seven thirty. It was Ott.

"Fucking asshole, Rutledge," Ott croaked.

"What'd he do this time?" Crawford asked.

"Said he couldn't find your cell phone number, so he called me."

"Better you than me, " Crawford said. "What'd he want?"

"So he starts out, 'You and your boyfriend are making me proud again, I see.' I go, 'What the hell are you talking about, Norm?' He says, 'Duking it out in some gay bar.'"

Crawford groaned. "How the hell'd he find out about that so quick?"

"I asked him," Ott said. "Asshole just said, 'I have my sources,' in that smug way of his. So I told him we were there workin' the case. Not 'duking it out,' but breaking up two guys who *were*."

"And he said?"

"'First that fight in Mookie's last year, now this,'" Ott said. "Then he goes, 'If I'm not mistaken, you guys have a murder you're s'posed to be workin' on. Guy by the name of Clyde Loadholt. Not screwin' around in gay bars.'"

"What a jackass. What did you say?"

"Told him that's what we were doing there, workin' on Loadholt," Ott said. "And the dipshit starts laughing like a hyena and goes, 'Maybe it's time you and Charlie came out of the closet.'"

"What a dick."

"What is it you always say, Charlie?"

Crawford thought for a second. "Oh, you mean, upper one percentile of world-class assholes?"

"Yeah," Ott said. "I think that about captures it. Hey, by the way, I had to give him your number, so I wouldn't answer your phone."

Crawford heard the beep of call waiting and looked at his display. "There he is now," Crawford said, "Mr. Upper One Percentile."

CRAWFORD COULD SMELL THE BACON AGAIN AND TEN MINUTES later Balfour came down to the basement with a tray. On it was a plate of eggs, bacon, toast, a glass of orange juice, and the newspaper.

"I only know how to make one breakfast," Balfour said.

"I could get used to this," Crawford said.

"I'll expect a nice tip when you check out," Balfour said. "I was just about to call the Poinciana golf shop, see whether Camilo's going to be in today, but they don't open until eight."

It was quarter of eight. Crawford ate his breakfast as Balfour read the newspaper.

At exactly eight, Balfour dialed his cell on speaker.

The voice answered, "Larry Hobart." He was the golf pro.

"Hey, Larry, it's David Balfour, I'm thinking about a lesson today. Does, ah, Camilo have any time available?"

"Sorry," Hobart said, "but he called in Friday morning and said he had a really bad flu. I told him to take a few days off, that me and Ted could cover for him. What time were you thinking of, Mr. Balfour?"

"Either of you got anything available this morning?"

Hobart didn't say anything for a moment. "I'm checking the

book," he paused. "Yeah, looks like Ted had a cancellation. Eleven work for you?"

"Sure, that's good," Balfour said. "I'll be there."

He hung up and gave Crawford a look.

Crawford nodded slowly. "I wonder if maybe he was moonlighting as a carpenter day before yesterday."

"So you heard it all," Balfour said. "Maybe I can find out something from the other pro."

"You mean, more than just how to putt better."

Balfour smiled and nodded as Crawford wrote out a line of questioning for Balfour to use with Ted.

BALFOUR WALKED UP TO THE PRACTICE TEE AT THE POINCIANA. Ted—short, stocky, mid-twenties, ultra-clean-cut—gave Balfour a quick wave and a smile as he approached. Balfour had heard that Ted was a born-again Christian.

"Hey, Mr. Balfour."

"Hey, Ted."

Ted had Balfour's golf bag propped up on a stand on the practice tee. "So what do you want to work on today?"

"Wedge and low irons," Balfour said. "Then chipping, if we've got any time left."

"You got it," Ted said, pulling Balfour's fifty-six-degree wedge out of his big leather bag.

After ten minutes of wedge shots and listening to Ted's suggestions, Balfour shifted gears, trying out his three-iron.

"So Larry said Camilo was out with the flu?"

"Yeah, picked up something, I guess," Ted said then he told Balfour to try to keep his left arm straighter on his back swing.

Balfour hit a few balls. They went a little farther than usual.

"Camilo's been out on a few dates with my niece," Balfour said, looking up at Ted. "'Course she doesn't tell me anything about her love life. They still seeing each other, you know?"

"Me and Camilo are actually pretty good friends," Ted said, pulling a four-iron out of Balfour's bag, and lowering his voice. "Way I heard it from him—and you didn't hear this from me, right?"

"Yeah, yeah, we're off the record here," Balfour said, taking the four-iron and handing Ted the three-iron.

"He told me that Lila wasn't really interested in him, or there was another guy in the picture, maybe it was. So I think they just had the two or three dates like two months ago," Ted said. "But he'd kill me if he knew I was—"

Balfour put his hands up and smiled. "What? Does it look like I'm wearing a wire or something?"

Ted laughed.

"So that was the end of it?" Balfour asked.

"Well, yeah, except—"

"Except what?" Balfour said, addressing the ball with the four-iron.

Ted laughed. "She *really* doesn't tell you anything, does she?" he said, watching Balfour take a long, slow backswing. "So Camilo met Lila's friend, Jenny, on one of the dates with Lila and now they're hot and heavy."

Balfour shanked the ball into the Poinciana parking lot.

THIRTY-SEVEN

AFTER THE LESSON, TED ACCEPTED BALFOUR'S OFFER TO BUY him an early lunch at the snack bar.

Hamburgers and fries had just been delivered to their table.

"So you're like a minus two, right?" Balfour asked.

"Minus three actually," Ted said, which meant he averaged three strokes less than par every time he played eighteen holes. So if par was seventy-two, he typically shot a sixty-nine.

"Man, what I'd give," Crawford said, shaking his head. "So I heard a couple of members were going to sponsor you to try your luck on the Web.com Tour?"

"Yeah, which was really nice," Ted said. "But it's such a grind and I really don't think I'm as good as most of the other guys out there. I was on the junior tour, played with a bunch of those guys, and I'll be honest, Mr. Balfour, I think I'd starve."

Balfour laughed. "What about Camilo, he have any higher aspirations. Go on tour maybe?" he asked as casually as he could.

Ted exhaled. "He actually was on one of them for a season," he said. "Poor bastard—" Ted held up his hands. "I'm sorry for cursing, Mr. Balfour."

Balfour shook his head and smiled. "Relax, Ted, I've heard the word before."

"I apologize," Ted said. "So anyway, all Camilo got out of the tour was a big pile of debt. Plus the poor guy's got a ton of college loans, and he told me his family back in Argentina is really poor. He tries to help 'em out and send 'em money, but..."

Balfour nodded. "That's too bad."

"Tell you the truth," Ted said, "I'm really surprised he's not here. Flu or no flu. We both kinda count on the lessons. The salary's kinda—"

Balfour was on the Golf Committee. "Yeah, I know," he said. "The money's in the lessons."

"Anyway, I'm talking too much," Ted said. "So you think the lesson helped?"

Balfour nodded eagerly. "Damn right it did. You have no idea," he said. "You saw the before and after. After you told me what I was doing wrong, I was hitting it pretty good."

"Yeah, you definitely were," Ted laughed. "Except..."

"Except what?" Balfour said then he smiled broadly. "Oh, you mean, that four-iron I launched into the parking lot. Just hope it didn't hit someone's Bentley."

THIRTY-EIGHT

AFTER BALFOUR FILLED IN CRAWFORD ABOUT WHAT HE HAD just learned about Camilo Vega, Crawford had to make a tough decision.

He needed to get search warrants for both Jenny Montgomery and Camilo Vega's houses, but it was impossible to go to a judge and get warrants for a case that didn't exist. He decided he needed to have a conversation with Norm Rutledge.

Problem was he knew Sunday was Rutledge's church-followed-by-bowling-with-the-family-day. He called him anyway. He got Rutledge's voicemail and left a message. "Norm, this is urgent. Call me right away."

To his surprise, Rutledge called back in fifteen minutes.

"Better be good, Crawford," Rutledge started out.

Crawford imagined him tying up his size thirteen red and blue bowling shoes.

"A guy I know came to me on Friday night and said his niece had been kidnapped. I told him I'd need to report it to you and you'd probably need to bring in the FBI. He said, forget it, he didn't want to risk having a million people involved, he'd do it himself."

"That was a really bad idea," Rutledge said.

"Yeah, well anyway, flash forward to this morning," Crawford said. "He knows who did it and where his niece is being held."

"How'd he find out?" Rutledge asked.

"Doesn't matter," Crawford said. "But's he's absolutely sure. So he's saying either he's gonna take care of it himself—"

"Are you kidding? Fucking amateur hour, you mean?"

"Or me and Ott do it."

A long pause. Crawford imagined Rutledge pulling on his bowling glove.

"There's no choice," Rutledge said finally.

"I know."

"Well, don't fuck it up."

"I'm gonna need to get a warrant."

"Yeah, fine," Rutledge said. "Judge Hendricks is your best bet on Sunday."

Crawford called Ott right away and asked him to get search warrants from Judge Hendricks for both Jenny Montgomery's house on Washington Street and Camilo Vega's house on Gregory Street. Balfour had given him Vega's address since as a member of the Golf Committee, he had access to the golf pro's phone numbers and home addresses.

"Whaddaya talkin' about?" Ott asked predictably. "How do we get search warrants for a case that doesn't exist?"

"I just had a little talk with Norm," Crawford said. "Told him a little about it."

Ott thought for a second. "'Little' being the operative word, right?"

"Exactly."

A few minutes later Crawford had an afterthought and called Ott back and asked him to also get the okay to plant a listening device. An hour later Ott phoned him and said he had them and would come right over and pick up Crawford.

"Sounds like she's pretty guilty to me," Ott said as they drove to

Jenny Montgomery's house after Crawford told him about Balfour's conversation with Ted.

They arrived to find a car in her driveway. It was the same car as when Ott had visited last time. A white Toyota Corolla.

Crawford turned to Ott as he parked on the street. "Let's just ask her about Sandusky to make her think that's what we're focusing on," he said.

"Good idea," Ott said. "She can tell her friend Camilo the cops are barkin' up the wrong tree."

Crawford nodded as they got out of the Caprice, went up to the porch, and hit the buzzer.

A few moments later Jenny Montgomery came to the door. She shaded her eyes as she looked up at Crawford and Ott.

"Hi, Ms. Montgomery," Ott said. "I was in the neighborhood with my partner, and we just have a few more questions. This is Detective Crawford."

"Hi, Ms. Montgomery," Crawford said. "Mind if we come in?"

"Hello," Jenny said, nervously. "But I...I really don't have time right now. I've got to be somewhere."

Crawford got the sense that she didn't want them to come inside.

Crawford dialed up a big smile. "Promise, just take a few minutes."

"Why can't we just talk right here?"

"Well, if it wouldn't be too big an imposition," Crawford said. "Could I just use the facilities?"

How could she say no?

"Okay, but really, I have to make this fast," she said.

She turned and pushed the door open. Then to Crawford, "Right past the kitchen on the right."

"Thank you very much," Crawford said as Jenny sat down at the small dining room table.

Ott stayed on his feet. "Did Professor Sandusky and Lila ever go on a date, Jenny?"

Jenny shook her head. "No way, Lila had absolutely no interest in that guy."

Crawford came into the dining area and looked at Ott. "You asking her about Sandusky?"

Ott nodded.

"In the last few days," Crawford turned to Jenny, "do you know whether she's seen him?"

"I have no idea," Jenny said, "'cause I haven't seen her or talked to her in a few days."

Crawford nodded. "Okay, that's all we need to know," he said, walking toward the front door. "Told you it wouldn't take long. Thanks for your time."

"Yes, thanks again," Ott said following Crawford.

"You're welcome," Jenny said.

Crawford and Ott walked out the door and over to their car.

"Confirmation," Crawford said getting in the car. "There was a tool belt in a corner of the living room. Jenny doesn't strike me as a girl who'd be strapping one on."

"So Camilo dropped it off for some reason after they took Lila," Ott said.

"Yeah, looked like he spends time here. Men's razor and two tooth brushes."

———————

THEY WENT DIRECTLY TO CAMILO VEGA'S HOUSE. CRAWFORD'S guess was he probably rented it. They drove past number 121 Gregory, noting a car in front of the house on the street but none in the driveway.

Crawford took out a pair of headphones from his jacket.

"Whatcha got there?"

"Oh, guess I forgot to mention, I planted a bug in her living room."

Ott high-fived him. "Thought you were just using the facilities?"

"Yeah, well, turned out I didn't have to go."

Crawford opened the glove compartment, reached in, and pulled out a pair of binoculars.

Ott had pulled over at the end of the block. Camilo Vega's house was mid-block. "Get a little closer, will ya," Crawford said, putting the binoculars up to his eyes.

Ott drove closer. "Anything?" he asked.

"The curtains are all drawn," Crawford said.

"Too nice a day to be living in a cave," Ott said.

Crawford nodded. "Why don't we go around back," he said. "Go down to the block one street south of here. Check things out from that side."

Ott nodded and drove down to Flagler, took a right, then took another right onto Phillips Street, and drove halfway down the block.

Crawford pointed at a house that had several old, yellowed newspapers on the porch and a bunch of flyers shoved into a screen door. "That house is right behind Vega's. Nobody's living there."

Ott pulled up in front of it. "Definitely not," he said, pointing. "One of those lock box things realtors use."

Crawford nodded and opened the Caprice's door. "I'm gonna go around back," he said. "Make like I'm a buyer, scoping the place out. Stay here, okay?"

Ott nodded. "Get one of those flyers under the mat."

Crawford nodded, walked up to the porch and got a flyer then went around one side of the house.

Studying the flyer, he walked around the house then positioned himself off to one side so he could check out Camilo Vega's house.

On the two windows on the back of the Vega house he saw something that a safe neighborhood like this wouldn't seem to warrant. Both windows had bars on them: five vertical bars and three horizontal ones on each window. They looked brand new, clearly recent additions to the house. No doubt designed to keep someone in, rather than keep someone out. If Crawford was holding a person captive in the house, he would have done the exact same thing.

He walked back around the house, content that this was where Lila Bacon had spent the last forty-eight hours.

He walked over to the Caprice and opened the car door and got in.

"So?" Ott asked.

"She's in there," Crawford said, putting on the headphones.

They talked about how to get in Vega's house and rejected their first two plans as too dangerous. Then Crawford held up his hand as he heard Jenny Montgomery's voice in his headphones.

"Hey, Cam, just had a little visit from two Palm Beach cops,'" she said, clearly on her house phone. "Looks like they think it's the professor."

A pause, then Jenny laughed. "I know," she said. "Oh, also, I booked our tickets. Talk soon."

Ott shot Crawford a thumbs-up. "Oughta make our boy inside feel nice and safe."

Crawford nodded as he watched a mailman deliver a stack of mail across the street.

"Guy's about your size, isn't he, Mort?" Crawford said, pointing to the mailman.

THIS TIME, CRAWFORD AND OTT SCRAPED UP SIXTY-FIVE BUCKS. Like the couple whose boat they had requisitioned yesterday, the mailman seemed happy with that. He was in the back seat of the Caprice stripping down. He handed his shirt to Ott. It was a blue, short-sleeved shirt with a patch on the left breast. Ott noticed it was a little sweat stained, but put it on anyway. Next came a blue baseball cap with the same U.S. postal service logo on it. Then came the bag that the postman had emptied of its contents. And finally, the blue shorts, with a thin black belt.

Crawford glanced over at Ott. "Get to show off those sexy legs of yours, Mort."

Ott smiled and mouthed, *Fuck off.*

Ott clothed in the mailman's attire, they discussed how they were going to play it.

They decided Ott was going to go to the front door, saying he had a box that didn't fit in the mailbox. Then he was going to reach in and pull out his Glock and shove whoever was at the door back inside.

At the same time, Crawford was going to smash through the door in the back of the house. He remembered it was a metal door, but his experience with doors was that if he got a running start and threw his two hundred pounds into it he could knock it off it's hinges.

The only question was how he'd know when Ott was making his move. They talked about getting backup, but realized that the more bodies crawling around the neighborhood, the higher the chance Vega would be tipped off. Not to mention this was not even an official case. Based on what little they knew about Vega, it didn't seem like his profile indicated he was the type to hurt Lila. Though when someone panics, Crawford pointed out, you never knew.

They finally decided that Ott would call Crawford on his cell right before going up to Vega's house, then put the live phone in his mailbag. Crawford would then hear the whole conversation between Ott and whoever answered the door. At the same time Ott made his move, Crawford would make his.

As for the mailman, Chet, his instructions were just to stay in the back of the car, take a well-deserved break, and think about how he was going to spend his sixty-five bucks.

OTT HAD JUST CALLED CRAWFORD AS HE WALKED DOWN THE sidewalk. He put his Samsung in the mailbag. The only thing that was off about his mailman costume was his old pair of Earth Shoes. The mailman had looked at them, shaken his head, and laughed. Like they were a disgrace to the profession.

"Hear me, Charlie?" Ott asked, almost at the house.

"Loud and clear," Crawford said, his voice coming through the phone's speaker inside the bag.

"I'm going up to the house now."

"Copy," Crawford said.

Ott rang the doorbell.

He waited. A man with a mustache and bad skin opened the door a crack.

"What's up?" he said.

"Got a package I couldn't fit in your mailbox."

"Just leave it on the porch," the man said and started to close the door.

Ott drew his Glock and, with the pistol in hand, threw his weight into the door shouting, "Showtime, Charlie!"

The door slammed into the man so hard it knocked him to the floor.

Ott took a few quick steps and pressed his foot down on the man's neck. "Where's the girl?" he shouted.

The man didn't answer.

He pressed harder. The man made a choking sound. "Bedroom in back on the left," he managed.

Ott took his foot off his neck. "You go anywhere and the snipers outside have orders to shoot to kill."

Then Ott had a second thought. He quickly cuffed the right hand of the man to the door handle set. He wasn't going to go anywhere.

Ott ran down a short hallway to the bedrooms in back.

Crawford had knocked the back door off its hinges and was in the back bedroom with his Sig Sauer trained on a man in shorts and a t-shirt. The man had a kitchen knife up to Lila Bacon's throat.

Lila looked terrified. Her eyes were red and puffy as if she hadn't slept. Her lower lip was trembling.

"Let her go, Camilo," Crawford said. "There's no way you're getting out of here."

Ott stepped into the room, Glock trained between Camilo's eyes. "We've got snipers on all four sides."

"So drop the knife and this ends well," Crawford said. "You go outside and our guys will take you out before you can move that knife."

"Cam, please," Lila said. "Do as they say."

Camilo's leaden eyes looked as though his heart was no longer in it. "What will happen to me?" he asked in a defeated monotone.

"If you put down the knife and let Lila walk away," Crawford said, "good chance, maybe just false imprisonment."

"They've treated me very well," Lila volunteered.

"That goes a long way," Crawford said. "Let her go or you're a dead man. Now!"

"But what will I get?" Camilo said.

"Whatever you get beats a bullet in your head," Crawford said. "'Cause that's how it ends unless you put that damn thing down *right now*."

"*Now*, Camilo," Ott shouted.

Camilo tossed the knife on the carpeted floor and released his grip on Lila.

She ran across the bedroom to Crawford and Ott.

Ott reached into his mailbag and pulled out handcuffs. "Turn around," he said to Camilo.

Camilo did as he was told. Ott cuffed him.

"You all right?" Crawford smiled at Lila, patting her on the shoulder.

She nodded but tears were rolling down her cheeks. "Thank you so much. I was so scared. Thank you, thank you, thank you."

Crawford nodded and handed her his cell. "Give your uncle a call. He's going to be very happy to hear from you."

CRAWFORD AND OTT DEPOSITED CAMILO VEGA AND HIS accomplice, Marco, in a cell at 345 South County Road, then went and arrested Jenny Montgomery. After extensive questioning, it seemed that Jenny was the mastermind behind the kidnapping. She had told Camilo how rich Lila was. How her parents had left her twenty million dollars. Jenny said how unfair it was that Camilo's and her parents were so poor and how she and Camilo had barely enough to pay rent.

She had gradually worn Camilo down until he finally agreed to Jenny's kidnap plan. After Camilo and his friends went to David Balfour's house and kidnapped her, Jenny told Camilo they were going to have to kill her after they got the money since Lila knew they were behind it.

Camilo said he could never do that. That last thing he was, he said, was a killer. Jenny told him the alternative was to have the police one step behind them, how they'd always have to be looking back over their shoulders. Camilo said they could move to Argentina. Jenny told him how naïve he was, they would still come after them there. Camilo explained that his parents lived in a remote village in the Andes.

Jenny looked at him and laughed mockingly. Did he really expect her to live in some godforsaken village up in the mountains, she asked? Live like peasants with three million dollars under their mattress? No, they had to kill her and bury her body.

CRAWFORD AND OTT DROVE LILA HOME. OUT OF HABIT, OTT started in the direction of Mellor Park.

"Where you going, Mort?" Crawford asked him.

"Oh, yeah," Ott said. "Guess I can drive in the driveway now."

Crawford nodded.

Balfour came running up to the car. Ott was in the back seat, having traded in his mailman's outfit for his brown polyester pants and white rayon shirt—a fashion statement perhaps on the wrong side of Cleveland. Crawford was driving and Lila was in the passenger seat, a grin from ear to ear.

Her uncle grabbed her door and pulled it open. She hopped out and he enveloped her in a smothering hug. Neither one said anything for a long time. He just rocked her back and forth. Crawford couldn't have pried them apart with a crowbar.

Finally, Balfour said. "Oh, God, I am so happy to see you, honey."

"So glad to be back, Uncle David."

Then Balfour turned to Crawford and Ott. "You guys...you guys are the best," he said and threw his arms around Crawford, slapping him on the back with his hands. "Thank you, Charlie, thank you *so* much."

"You're welcome," Crawford said.

Then Balfour released him and gave Ott a hug. "Thank you, Mort, I'll never forget this."

"You're welcome," Ott said.

"Never knew you were such a big hugger," Crawford said.

Balfour laughed and put an arm around Lila's shoulder. "Never had such a good reason to hug anyone before."

THIRTY-NINE

CRAWFORD GOT TO THE STATION AT SEVEN THIRTY ON MONDAY morning. He had a lot of paperwork to do on the kidnapping. He had called Norm Rutledge on Sunday afternoon and gave him a blow-by-blow of the whole thing. Instead of saying 'good job' or something complimentary, Rutledge had jumped in with a series of questions: 'Why didn't you get backup?' 'Why didn't you put me in the loop earlier?' Even, 'Why didn't you go back to the station to get a battering ram, to make sure you could knock down that door?'

Je-sus! *Really?*

Crawford answered all his questions very patiently, as he silently wished that he and Ott had just pretended the whole thing never happened and they never reported it. Which he might have done except he needed the warrants. Though if they had gone that route, Rutledge might wonder why there were two young men and a woman in the station's basement jail.

At eight o'clock, Crawford called Susie Loadholt.

"Mrs. Loadholt, I hope I'm not calling too early but I have a few questions about your granddaughter."

"Don't worry, I've been up for hours," Susie Loadholt said. "Ask away."

"First of all, did she graduate from high school?"

"Of course she did," Loadholt said, sounding offended.

"What high school and what year?" Crawford asked.

"Forest Hill Community High School," Loadholt said. "Class of '97."

"And do you happen to remember—I know it was a long time ago —but do you remember the names of her best friends back then?"

Mrs. Loadholt didn't say anything for a few moments. Then offered, "I remember a few. There was Martha McClellan. And Jessie Williams. Then there was one with a funny name...Arria or Ariel, something like that. You know what, I have her yearbook up in her old room. I can take a look at it."

"That would be really helpful. I appreciate it."

"No problem," she said. "What else?"

Crawford heard a voice in the background say, "Who're you talking to?"

Mavis. Of course. The last thing he wanted was for her to get in on the act.

"Just one last question: Those women, some of them probably got married. Would you happen to know any of their married names?"

Silence again. Then, "Only one I know is Martha McClellan," Loadholt said. "She married a man named Raymond. Bill Raymond. He was a local newscaster."

Crawford wrote the name down.

"Thank you, that's very helpful," Crawford said. "If you would give me a call with the other women's names, I would appreciate it."

"You bet, Detective," she said and hung up.

Crawford didn't have any other suspects left. So he figured he might as well pursue the granddaughter as far as it would go.

Susie Loadholt called back a half hour later and said she had done some "detective work"—she got a big chuckle out of saying that

—and found out that Arria's last name was Ware and she had married her high school sweetheart, David Abernathy.

Crawford thanked her and called the high school at a little past nine. He asked for an office staffer, and added, 'the one with the most seniority, please.' Then when he was connected he identified himself, and asked the woman for any information she had on Arria Abernathy, Martha Raymond or Jessica Williams, class of '97. Phone numbers, emails, addresses, whatever she had. He also asked her for anything the school had on Elizabeth Jeanne Loadholt.

The woman said she'd look into it and call Crawford back.

Crawford thanked her and hung up as Ott walked in.

"Mornin', Charlie," he said and sat down facing Crawford.

"Hey," Crawford said.

"Whatcha up to?"

"Trying to track down Elizabeth Jeanne Loadholt."

Ott nodded. "She's about all we got left."

"So nothing else has jumped out at you from Loadholt's past cases?" Crawford asked.

"No, the guy had those three bad incidents in his forty-year career," Ott said. "Some might say that's not too bad a record."

Crawford shook his head and rolled his eyes. "Yeah, well, compared to what?" he said. "I mean, if you or I had just one of those things up in Cleveland or New York, we'd be done."

"Yeah, but as we said before, Loadholt was pretty much the master of the cover-up," Ott said. "Throw-downs, getting other cops to lie for him, the guy was good."

Crawford's iPhone rang. He looked at the display. "Gotta take this," he said. "Hello."

It was the staffer at Forest Hill Community High School.

She explained that Arria Abernathy lived up in Glen Ellen, Illinois, and gave him her phone number. Jessie Williams's whereabouts were unknown and Martha Raymond still lived in West Palm Beach. He took her number as well.

Crawford called Martha Raymond right away.

Crawford put it on speaker and it rang three times.

"Hello," said a voice.

"Mrs. Raymond?"

"Yes."

"Hi, my name is Detective Crawford," he said. "Palm Beach Police Department. I'm calling about an old classmate of yours, Elizabeth Jeanne Loadholt."

"Oh, yes," Raymond said. "I read that her grandfather got killed. I would have called her but don't have her number. What did you want to know?"

"Well, so you haven't kept in touch with her?" Crawford asked.

"I did for a while," Raymond said. "Poor girl had a tough go of it after she graduated."

"I know," Crawford said, "but you lost track of her, or what?"

"Yeah, I did," Raymond said. "Until our fifteenth."

Crawford thought for a second. "Fifteenth? Oh, you mean fifteenth reunion?"

"Yes, exactly," Raymond said. "Which was pretty memorable."

"How so?"

"Well, for starters, Liz showed up in a white limo about a mile long."

Ott sat up straight in his chair.

"Really?" Crawford said. "What else?"

"And she was wearing jewelry worth more than my house," Raymond said. "And her clothes. A Chanel suit and Manolo Blahnik shoes, which I'd never even heard of, but another girl clued me in."

"Sounds like she was trying to make an impression," Crawford said.

"Trying...and succeeding," Raymond said. "It was almost like she had gone away and become a movie star or something."

Ott moved closer. "Mrs. Raymond, this is Detective Ott, Detective Crawford's partner. Did you happen to find out what Ms. Loadholt did for a living?"

"To get so rich, you mean?"

"Yes," Ott answered.

"Or maybe she married a rich man?" Crawford asked.

"She didn't talk about it. Somebody asked, I remember, what she did. She mentioned that she had been married, 'for like fifteen minutes,' I remember her saying."

"So that was all you remember?" Crawford asked.

"Yes," Raymond said. "She was kind of mysterious about the whole thing."

"But she was alone, right?" Ott asked. "No one with her?"

"Yes, all alone in that big monster limo."

"And how did she introduce herself?"

"Same as when we were in high school," Raymond said. "Elizabeth Jeanne Loadholt."

"Thank you, Mrs. Raymond," Crawford said. "You've been very helpful."

"Yes, and if you happen to have any contact with Ms. Loadholt," Ott said, "please call us."

"Okay," said Raymond, "but that's not gonna happen. She lives in a completely different universe than me. Goodbye, detectives."

Crawford clicked off and looked at Ott. "Woman's got my attention now," he said.

Ott nodded. "Big time."

FORTY

ALL FIVE MEMBERS OF THE MENTORS WERE ON BOARD BETH Jastrow's yacht, bobbing out in the ocean ten miles from Palm Beach. It was a pleasant night in the mid-seventies with a gentle breeze and a full moon.

"She says she's on a tear trying to finish up her second book and can't make it down here now," Beth told the group.

Diana Quarle cocked her head, looking first at Rose Clarke then at Beth. "Does she realize what we're capable of doing for her?"

"Yeah, or is she one of those authors who's perfectly content to sell seventeen copies to family and friends?" asked Rose.

"Why's she being so difficult?" Marla asked Beth.

"Whoa, whoa, whoa," Beth said, putting up her hands, "don't shoot the messenger. I'm just telling you what she told me."

"I know, but did you tell her how much we can help her?" Diana repeated her question.

"Yes, of course, I used Lulu Perkins as an example," Beth said. "What more could I do?"

"Nothing," Rose said. "It's just hard to believe that she wouldn't be more..."

"Receptive?" Diana said.

Rose nodded.

"I don't know what to tell you," Beth said. "Can we talk about someone else?"

The other four nodded.

"I want to propose someone who would be only too happy to come meet with us," Elle said. "Even if she had to walk the whole way."

The others laughed. "Okay, let's hear about her," Marla said.

"Okay, her name is Helen Baker and she lives somewhere in Georgia—"

"That's not too far a walk," Diana said.

Elle laughed. "And she's designed, and has a patent for, a full-sized kayak that weighs only five pounds that she can make for just two hundred bucks."

"Five pounds. How is that possible?" Marla asked.

"Good question," Elle said, "but one of the photos she sent me was of the kayak on a scale. And sure enough, five pounds. She claims it's really durable too. Indestructible, she said."

"Sounds like a can't-lose," Rose said. "Just take it to L.L. Bean and what's that other chain..."

"Gander Mountain," Diana said. "And there's another one called Bass Pro, I think it is."

Rose eyed Diana, impressed. "How do you know about these places?"

"Had a boyfriend who was a hunter and all 'round outdoorsy guy," Diana said. "Liked to go camping, sleep under the stars. It didn't last long, 'cause I hated that shit."

"Yeah, give me a bed with thousand-count Egyptian cotton sheets any day," Rose said.

"Amen, sister."

CRAWFORD AND OTT HAD DECIDED TO GO TALK TO CLYDE Loadholt's daughter again. They planned to just show up, say they had some business in Hobe Sound, where she lived.

Ott pulled up to the house where he had gone two days before and there was Megan Sullivan sitting outside her house smoking a cigarette, the one-eyed dog sitting at her feet.

They got out and walked over to her. She didn't look thrilled to see them and stubbed out the cigarette on the ground next to dozens of other ones.

"Hello, Mrs. Sullivan," Ott said, "this is my partner Detective Crawford. We were in the area and decided to stop by."

She shaded her eyes and looked up at Crawford, then back at Ott. "What can I do for you?"

"You mind if we sit down, Mrs. Sullivan?" Crawford asked.

There were two rickety looking rusted aluminum chairs with green canvas seats and backs facing her.

"Help yourself," she said, pointing.

"I think I'll stand," said Ott eyeing the chairs skeptically as Crawford sat in one. "So, first thing, Mrs. Sullivan, do you have any pictures of your daughter, Elizabeth Jeanne? Maybe in a scrapbook or something?"

"Yes, I'm pretty sure I do," she said. "I have her high school yearbook too."

"Oh, you do? Great," Ott said. "Would you mind if we borrowed it for a few days? The photos too. We'll bring 'em back, I promise."

Sullivan stood up. "I'll go get 'em for you."

"Thanks," Crawford said. "We really appreciate it."

Sullivan went into the house.

"Her eyes don't exactly light up when she starts talking about her kid," Crawford said.

Ott nodded.

"I'll bet she didn't hear from her when she came back for the reunion," Crawford said.

Ott nodded. "Bet you're right," he said as Megan Sullivan came out with a book and some loose photos.

She handed the book to Crawford and the photos to Ott.

The first thing that was obvious was that a smile was not Elizabeth Jeanne Loadholt's natural default. In all of the pictures she had the same downcast look. It reminded Crawford of a TV commercial he had seen recently. It was for the ASPCA. Picture after picture of dogs who looked like they had masters who beat them. It was a pitch for people to send them money so something could be done about it. Crawford had written a check for a hundred dollars and taken it out to his mailbox at ten o'clock that night.

Elizabeth Jeanne Loadholt looked like one of those dogs. Like it was not just sadness, but fear as well. Fear that she had to be on her toes to avoid the next beating.

Ott turned to her page in the yearbook. Her expression was even more morose looking, particularly in contrast to the girl beneath her who had an ear-to-ear grin.

Crawford looked up at Megan Sullivan.

"So Mrs. Sullivan, do you know who Martha McClellan is?"

"Of course, my daughter's old high school friend," Sullivan said. "Haven't seen her for years."

"Well, she saw your daughter about four years ago," Crawford said. "It was at Elizabeth Jeanne's fifteenth high school reunion."

"Is that right?"

Crawford nodded. "She seemed to think your daughter had become quite successful. You know, she wore nice clothes, jewelry, and stuff. Did you see her when she was here for her reunion?"

"No, I haven't seen her since she ran away from my dad's house."

Crawford and Ott studied her closely for a tell—a twitch, not making eye contact, something.

But her expression hadn't changed.

"Why do you suppose she didn't—" Ott started.

"Because, Detective, we had a lousy family life," Sullivan blurted.

Ott shifted his weight from one foot to the other. "I can relate," Ott said. "I didn't have the best one either—"

"Trust me, it was way better than ours," Sullivan said.

"Can you tell us a little bit more about it, Mrs. Sullivan?" Crawford asked, doing his best 'casual Charlie'.

Megan Sullivan shot him a hard, cold stare. "Do you think my daughter killed my father?"

"We are trying to find your father's killer," Crawford said. "Whoever it may have been."

"My father was a monster," Sullivan said. "The world is better off without him."

Crawford and Ott just let that hang in the air for a while.

"Just out of curiosity, Mrs. Sullivan, what happened to your dog?" Ott asked finally.

Sullivan actually laughed. "No, he didn't do that."

"I didn't mean to imply—"

"My father molested me," she inhaled deeply, "and he molested my daughter. Now, I have nothing more to say on the subject and would appreciate it if you would go away and leave me alone."

FORTY-ONE

CRAWFORD AND OTT WERE AT MOOKIE'S. SOMETIMES THEY'D go there in the middle of the day for a beer, then go back to the station afterwards. They found it could be a good place to talk over a case because it lacked the distraction of a hovering and badgering Norm Rutledge and phones that were constantly ringing.

They had their go-to beers in front of them on coasters: Crawford a Bud, Ott a Yuengling.

"So we know she had a temper and somehow got her hands on a gun," Crawford said. "I'm talking about that incident in the backyard."

Ott nodded. "Yeah, potentially lethal combo," he said. "Plus there was that liquor store hold-up. A gun there too."

Crawford nodded. "Yup." He said. "The question is, once again, if she did it, why would it have remained dormant for twenty years?"

"Yeah, I know," Ott said. "If she's living somewhere—a thousand miles away for all we know—with all her expensive jewelry and big ass limo, what would prompt her to come back and pop gramps?"

Crawford shrugged and took a pull on his beer.

Crawford's cell phone rang. He looked down at the number, deciding whether to answer it.

"Hello," Crawford answered.

"Hel-lo, Charlie," she said. "It's your persistent friend."

"Hi, Alexa. What's up?"

"So it's Monday, how 'bout dinner tomorrow?" she said. "You can't be going to cop bars every single night."

"Sorry, think I'm gonna be working late tomorrow."

"On Loadholt?"

"Yeah."

"What if I told you I dug up something good on it?"

"Like what?"

"You have to have dinner with me to find out."

"So, where do you want to go?" he asked.

"How 'bout...there's a nice little Cuban place down on South Dixie."

"Havana, yeah, know it well," Crawford said. "How 'bout I pick you up at eight?"

Alexa told Crawford where she lived and they said goodbye.

"The helicopter girl, huh?" Ott said. "Buzzing overhead again."

Crawford nodded. "Says she got something on Loadholt."

"That's maybe half of it."

"What do you mean?"

"You know what I mean," Ott said. "Another woman who's fallen for the Crawford..." Ott shrugged, "whatever-the-hell-it-is."

Crawford drained his beer. "Oh, Christ, put a lid on it, will ya."

"Gwendolyn Hyde, Lil Fonseca, Dominica McCarthy, Rose Clarke, the list goes on."

"Enough." Crawford shook his head and scowled. "Back to Loadholt's granddaughter. We gotta track her down, wherever she is. I'm thinking we get back to Martha Raymond or one of the other women at her fifteenth reunion and find out where she stayed when she was here. Try to get her home address from a hotel she was staying at."

"Good idea," Ott said. "Or maybe get her license plate from one of the photos."

Crawford nodded. "The reunion is definitely the key. Someone who was there has to know something about the woman. I also need to call that one up in Illinois too."

Ott called back the high school office and got the names and phone numbers of everyone who had attended the fifteenth reunion, class of '97.

He was given a hundred and twenty-two names and numbers. Theoretically, Crawford and he would split them up and make the calls, but Ott knew there was no way in hell Crawford was going to call sixty-one people. Six maybe, but the man had an attention span that was shorter than his list of girlfriends was long.

He knew exactly what Crawford was going to do. He was going to con Bettina—don't call me Betty—at the stations front desk to make a bunch of calls for him. Write out several questions for her to ask and butter her up, tell her that her help may be critical to solving a case. Tell her he needed someone who was dogged and determined to dig around and get crucial answers.

Ott knew his partner only too well.

And sure enough, that's exactly what Crawford did.

Ott looked over Bettina's shoulder as she started to go down Crawford's list of questions for classmates who had attended the reunion:

1. Do you happen to know where Elizabeth Jeanne Loadholt stayed while she was in West Palm Beach for her reunion? At a hotel? With a friend?

2. Did she happen to mention where she presently lives?

3. Can you, by any chance, show us any photos that she was in?

4. Did you see the license plate of her limousine or remember what state it was from?

Ott walked back to his office, shaking his head. Then he started calling up the best hotels in Palm Beach and West Palm Beach, figuring it was unlikely that someone with a mile-long limo would be staying at a fleabag. He had struck out with The Breakers, the Chesterfield, the Flagler, and the Four Seasons. It was time-consuming getting them to check back four years into their records. He called another five hotels, told them Loadholt's name and the dates of the reunion and asked them to call him back if they found out she was staying there.

MEANWHILE, BETTINA GOT WHAT SEEMED LIKE A PROMISING hit with a woman named Terry Parsons. Parsons referred to herself as the "unofficial photographer" of the reunion. She said she had taken, literally, hundreds of photos of the event. Bettina went into Crawford's office to tell him about Parsons and gave him her phone number.

Crawford called Parsons right away. It turned out she lived up in Palm Beach Gardens. He asked if he could come right over. She said that was fine and gave him her address. She lived in a nice development off of PGA Boulevard.

She offered him a glass of water and they sat down at her dining room table, where she had laid out the reunion pictures.

The only problem was there was not one of Elizabeth Jeanne Loadholt.

"I can't believe it," Parsons said, looking through them a second time. "It's almost like she was avoiding the camera..." Which was exactly what Crawford was thinking. "I mean, I went out of my way to get shots of everyone."

She then pointed to one where a woman in a white skirt was looking away. Like she had turned from the camera at the very last second. "I think that's her," Parsons said. "I remember her wearing that skirt."

Even Crawford could tell it was an expensive designer dress.

They spent another fifteen minutes looking through the photos, but there was definitely none of Elizabeth Jeanne Loadholt.

OTT HAD NO LUCK WITH THE OTHER HOTELS. BUT OF THE SIXTY-one classmates he tried to contact, a woman finally called him back with something that seemed to have potential.

"I'm looking at a picture of Elizabeth Jeanne's limo," the woman said with a laugh. "Some of us at the reunion nicknamed her Limo Liz."

Ott got the woman's address and said he'd be right over.

He hit her buzzer, ramped up with anticipation.

She opened the door and had the photo in her hand.

She handed it to him. He looked at the long, white limo parked next to a black VW. It had to be at least four times as long as the Bug.

He looked at the license plate. It was a Louisiana plate, with Sportsman's Paradise at the bottom and the vanity plate, H#1.

"I have a copy of it," said the woman, whose name was Linda Stroh. "You can have this one."

"Thank you very much," Ott said. "This is very helpful. I don't suppose you'd know what H#1 stands for?"

"Sorry," she said. "No clue."

He thanked her again and, amped up, dialed the Louisiana Department of Motor Vehicles as soon as he got back to the office. Twenty minutes later he knew who the limo was registered to: Harrah's New Orleans, a hotel and casino at 228 Poydras Street in New Orleans.

FORTY-TWO

OTT WALKED INTO CRAWFORD'S OFFICE WITH A BIG GRIN ON HIS face.

Crawford looked up at him. "I know that look anywhere," he said. "You just struck oil, didn't you?"

"Yup," Ott said, plunking himself down in the chair opposite Crawford. "More like gold. The big, white limo that Elizabeth Jeanne Loadholt came to her reunion in is registered to Harrah's Hotel & Casino in New Orleans."

"What the hell would—"

"Then it gets a little murky," Ott said. "I spoke to the General Manager there, who's been there ten years, and he has no idea who Elizabeth Jeanne Loadholt is. He told me they use the limo for high rollers. You know pick 'em up at the airport, have it at their disposal if they want to go somewhere. But the guy hadn't heard of her, so I guess she wasn't a high roller."

"Unless she went by another name," Crawford rapped his desk and stood up. "We gotta go to New Orleans and check it out."

"Exactly what I was thinking."

"Can we drive there?" Crawford asked.

"It's ten to eleven hours."

"Let's book a flight."

Ott's grin got bigger. "Done. We leave in an hour and forty-five minutes."

THEY HAD A SHORT CONVERSATION—THEIR FAVORITE KIND— with Norm Rutledge. They told him that their prime suspect in the Loadholt murder might be in New Orleans and they wanted to go there and bring her back.

Her, said Rutledge.

Yeah, Loadholt's granddaughter, said Crawford.

Rutledge cocked his head and looked dubious. "Sure that's a good way to spend the department's time and money?"

Another thing about Rutledge, the man was cheap.

Crawford put the hammer down. "So, let me get this straight, Norm, you don't want us to catch Loadholt's killer because of an eight hundred dollar airfare?"

Then Rutledge said, 'Well, why can't just one of you go?"

"You gotta be kiddin' me," Crawford said in a tone reserved for five-star morons.

THEY BOUGHT TOOTHBRUSHES, TOOTHPASTE, RAZOR BLADES AND shaving cream in the airport. So now they were up to eight hundred twenty-five dollars.

Then Crawford made a call on his cell.

"Alexa, I am really sorry, but—"

"Oh, God, not again," Alexa Dillon said. "Why don't you just tell me you have no intention of ever—"

"I'm at the airport going to New Orleans—"

"Oh, goodie, can I come? Mardi Gras is just three months off."

"Alexa, if you'd just let me finish a sentence."

"But all your sentences have bad news in them."

Crawford chuckled. "Hey, I'm not moving to New Orleans, I'm going there on business, probably for a few days," he said. "So as soon as I get back, we'll go out for dinner."

"Okay, Charlie," she said. "I hear the announcements in the background. Go do what you gotta do. Don't miss your flight."

"Thanks," Crawford said. "I'll be in touch when I get back."

He hung up.

Ott looked at his ticket. "Oh, I forgot to tell you: there are no direct flights. We've got a stop in Cleveland."

Crawford frowned. "West Palm all the way up to Cleveland, then back down to New Orleans? Can't be," he said, taking out his ticket for a look.

"Says right here, CLT," Ott said, pointing. "What else could it be?"

"Since when is there a T in Cleveland?" Crawford asked as a pair of Jet Blue flight attendants approached. "Excuse me, what does CLT stand for?"

"Charlotte," one said.

"Thank you," Crawford said.

"Too bad," Ott said with a sigh. "I was gonna get my old Cleveland cop buddies to come to the airport and meet the great legend I work with."

FORTY-THREE

THE FLIGHT BETWEEN CHARLOTTE AND NEW ORLEANS WAS bumpy, enough to cause Ott to grab Crawford's arm at one point.

Crawford patted his hand. "Relax, we're gonna make it, Mort."

Other than that, the five-and-a-half-hours they spent in the air passed uneventfully. At the airport in New Orleans, they rented a Chevy Cruze from Enterprise.

As was their usual custom, Ott would drive while Crawford made phone calls and served as navigator.

"You know what I want to do while we're here in the Big Easy?" Ott said.

"What's that, Mort?"

"I want to go meet Dave Robicheaux and Clete Purcell," Ott said.

Crawford chuckled. "You do know they're fictional characters."

"Maybe go out to Bayou Teche and pet Tripod too," Ott went on.

Ott's favorite author was James Lee Burke, who wrote a crime series set in New Orleans. His heroes, anti-heroes was probably more like it, were two detectives named Dave Robicheaux and Clete Purcell. Violent, prone to alcoholism and vigilante-like actions, the two were fanatically loyal to each other. Robicheaux had a three-legged pet raccoon named Tripod.

Crawford had another thought on the subject. "Besides, Robicheaux works out at some place called New Iberia, not New Orleans."

"Yeah, I know, I looked it up, it's about two hours west."

"So you want to drive out there, walk into New Iberia PD, and ask to see Dave, is that it?"

Ott shook his head and chuckled. "I know they're not real, Charlie. I just wish they were," he said. "Guys are *baad* dudes."

While they made their way through the city, Crawford called the general manager of Harrah's.

"Mr. Eaton, I'm Charlie Crawford, Palm Beach, Florida, Police Department," Crawford said. "My partner, Mort Ott, spoke to you earlier today."

"Oh, yeah, how ya doin'?" said the general manager.

"We wondered if we could come talk to you," Crawford said. "We just got into town."

"Yes, sure, I'll be here 'til six, come on by," Eaton said. "You've got the address, right?"

"I do," Crawford said. "See you in fifteen, twenty minutes." He clicked off.

"What do you s'pose the Big Easy means anyway?" Ott asked.

"I don't know, Mort," Crawford said with a sigh. "Why don't, every once in a while, you just ask normal questions. You know like, 'Do I go straight? Or turn right?'"

The light changed where they were stopped. Ott looked over at Crawford. "Well?"

TED EATON HAD A LARGE, CLUTTERED OFFICE ON THE SECOND floor of Harrah's. He had no window, so Crawford assumed rooms with windows were reserved for paying customers. Eaton sported a thin mustache, the kind favored by movie actors in the 1940s and wore a burgundy blazer with a gold name bar that said, 'Ted.'

Crawford had just shown Eaton the picture of the limo and explained that it had transported a woman named Elizabeth Jeanne Loadholt to her fifteenth reunion at Forest Hill Community High School in West Palm Beach, Florida.

"Which would have made her around thirty-three years old at the time," Crawford said, handing Eaton the yearbook picture Megan Sullivan had given them. "So 'bout thirty-seven today."

"Holy shit," Eaton said, pulling the picture close.

Then he clicked a button on his phone. "Rusty, come in here, will ya."

A few seconds later a short man with almost no neck and hair that was transitioning from orange to orange-gray walked in.

"This is Rusty Bolton, assistant manager," Eaton said, waving him over. "Take a look at this sweet-looking, little high school girl."

Rusty walked around Eaton's desk and looked at the photo.

Rusty laughed. "Before she grew up to be the queen of the ball-busters," he said. "Who'd she kill this time?"

Crawford and Ott's eyes got big.

"Just kiddin'," Rusty said. "Woman's just a real hardass."

"Who is she?" Crawford asked.

Eaton turned to Rusty, "These fellas are detectives from Florida."

"Lisa Troy," Rusty said. "Used to work here."

"Matter-of-fact," Eaton said, "this used to be her office."

"She was general manager?" Crawford asked.

"Uh-huh, when she was real young too," Eaton said. "Thirty-two or so."

"So where is she now?" Ott asked.

Eaton glanced at Rusty. "Macau, right?"

Rusty nodded. "Last I knew."

"Macau, as in that place off of China?" Ott asked.

"Yeah, across the river from Hong Kong, to be exact," Rusty said.

"She got a big offer from a place over there two years ago," Eaton said.

"Place called Starworld," Rusty added.

"A casino?" Crawford asked.

"Yeah, owned by these two Chinese brothers, I think," Eaton said. "I heard she got equity in it."

"What's that?" Ott asked.

"Meaning she got a piece of the action," Eaton said.

"One percent of a place like that and you're set for life," Rusty added. "Macau's way bigger than Vegas."

Eaton turned to Rusty. "Remember how Humboldt made her sign a non-compete?"

Rusty nodded.

"Ah, can you explain that, please?" Crawford asked.

"Yeah, sure. Lisa's contract was up for renewal three years ago," Eaton said, "and our CEO made her sign something that said if she left Harrah's she couldn't take a job at a rival casino anywhere in the U.S. for ten years."

Rusty smiled. "Nothing about Macau, though."

"And the scuttlebutt is," Eaton said, "she upped the gross over there by twenty percent in the first year alone."

"No doubt about it," Rusty added, "girl knows how to run a casino."

Crawford looked over at Ott, whose expression matched Crawford's own look of disappointment. He wasn't thrilled about limping back to Palm Beach with his tail between his legs. Having to tell Rutledge their prime suspect could be ten thousand miles away.

"So as far as you know that's where she still is? In Macau?" Crawford asked Eaton.

"Far as I know," said Eaton. "Why would she come back when she's got such a sweet deal over there?"

"So there's nothing, nothing at all that you can think of, of a business nature, that would bring her back here?" Ott asked

Eaton glanced over at Rusty. Rusty shrugged.

"Wasn't there something about those Chinese guys looking to buy a hotel in Vegas?" Eaton asked.

"Yeah, I did hear something," Rusty said. "I'm not sure what happened, though."

Crawford looked at Ott and shrugged. "Well," he said, standing up. "Thanks for your time, fellas. Not exactly the ending we were hoping for, but we appreciate the information."

"Yeah, thanks," Ott said.

Then they all shook hands.

"You guys might just want to stick around," Eaton said. "I'll comp you on our show tonight. Got a really good singer named Lulu Perkins."

FORTY-FOUR

ON THE WAY TO THE NEW ORLEANS AIRPORT, CRAWFORD
called Alexa Dillon.

"Got done sooner than I expected," he said. "So I'm good for
tomorrow night, if it still works for you."

He was dying to know what she had on Loadholt.

"Sure does," Alexa said, excited. "You'll pick me up?"

"Yup. In my chariot. A gold Camry."

CRAWFORD TURNED TO OTT ON THE PLANE. "I REALLY THOUGHT
we were gonna find her there," he said.

"I know," Ott said. "I was sure we'd be headed back with our
killer in cuffs. What do we do now?"

Crawford thought for a moment then shrugged. "I really don't
know," he said.

And, for once, he really didn't.

But as part of his routine follow-up, he decided to try to track down Lisa Troy, Elizabeth Jeanne Loadholt, or whatever her new name might be, in Macau. He was thinking it was possible, though hardly likely, that she had flown halfway around the world and back again, all to kill her grandfather.

CRAWFORD AND ALEXA DILLON HAD BARELY SAT DOWN WHEN he asked her what her Clyde Loadholt scoop was.

"You're not much for foreplay, I see," Alexa said.

He had been told that before. Rose had said it a few times. How he'd just dive right in.

"Sorry," he said. "Guilty as charged."

The waiter came up to the table and they ordered drinks. Then Crawford asked her how she had ended up in West Palm as a reporter at the *Palm Beach Morning News*.

It actually turned out to be a pretty interesting story. She was the illegitimate daughter of a bass player in an obscure rock band. Though she didn't use the word, her mother was a groupie from Oklahoma City who had ended up in England in the late '80s. Her mother stayed over there and Alexa spent her childhood in Wales after her mother settled down and became a barmaid in a Swansea pub.

Then Alexa told him she had been "discovered"—she did the air quote thing with her fingers—by a scout for Elite modeling agency when she was in New York for her eighteenth birthday. She scrolled down on her iPhone and showed Crawford a cover she had done for *InStyle* magazine back in 2008, when she had blond hair.

Looking at her brown straight hair, Crawford said. "I like your natural color better."

"Thanks," she said. "You know how it is, every girl's gotta be a blond for at least fifteen minutes."

"So how old were you then?" He was trying to do the math.

"When I did the cover?"

He nodded.

"Twenty-five," she said. "On the old side of a model's shelf life. Plus I didn't really like the life. Except the money, of course."

Crawford drained his first mojito.

"You know, you coulda been a model," Alexa said.

Crawford laughed. "Yeah, right," he said, shaking his head. "I was right smack in the middle of New York City for fourteen years and nobody ever discovered me."

"How old were you when you started out there?" Alexa asked.

"Twenty-three. I was there until I was thirty-seven," Crawford said. "Fourteen long years. Most of them good. The last two...not so good."

"Why?"

"Umm, my marriage broke up, for one thing. I guess you could say I burned out," Crawford said. "Staring down at dead bodies on the streets of New York gets old."

She took a sip of her rosé. "But that's what you do here?"

"Yeah, but there aren't as many here," Crawford said. "Plus they have nice tans."

She laughed. "Not Clyde Loadholt."

Crawford laughed. "True," he raised his hand to the waiter. "So back to you, you were too old to hobble down the runway at age twenty-five?"

"Nah, I decided to go to journalism school instead."

"That's a big switch," Crawford said. "Where?"

"Northwestern."

"That's about the best, right?" Then to the waiter. "Two more, please."

"It was good," Alexa said. "Brutal winters out there, though."

"So how'd you end up here?" Crawford asked.

"They offered me a job and I grabbed it," Alexa said. "Been here ever since."

Okay, he figured, that was enough foreplay. "So tell me about Loadholt?"

"Sure," she said, putting her hand on his. "Since you've been such a good boy and listened to me talk about things you probably have no interest in—"

"That's not true."

"Anyway," Alexa said, leaning closer to share her scoop. "Loadholt's granddaughter took a couple of potshots at him in his backyard."

Crawford laughed. "That's it?"

Alexa nodded. "I thought that was pretty good."

"It is, but I already knew it," he said.

She looked disappointed. "So...I suppose you want to go home now?"

Crawford shook his head. "No, I'm having a nice time."

After reading over the menu, they ordered dinner.

Crawford had enchiladas con camarones and Alexa the arroz con pollo.

Then they talked some more. Alexa complained about her boss and Crawford complained about his. She suggested they switch.

Then she started to ask him questions on the subject that always made him cringe. About his first, and thus far only, marriage. He said he still got a card from her on his birthday, but that was about it. He tried to put the spotlight back on Alexa, asking about boyfriends and/or marriages. She said that at age thirty-three she still hadn't met the right guy. A couple of guys for short hauls, she said, but no keeper for life.

Yeah, he had had a few of those too, he said.

"Recently?" she asked.

And then damned if he didn't launch in on the subject of Dominica McCarthy. Those damn mojitos! He actually caught himself from saying she was maybe a keeper—even though he might have been thinking it.

"So you really like this woman, huh?" Alexa asked. "And she works in the same building as you? How does that work?"

He told her that at the moment it wasn't working at all. Fact was, they barely spoke. Except on the occasional job together.

"Well, then," she said, "you ought to do something about that."

"Like what?" Crawford asked lamely.

"What the hell do you think? Don't let her get away."

FORTY-FIVE

HE ACTUALLY DID STOP AFTER TWO MOJITOS BUT THEN THEY shared a bottle of wine. So it wasn't a three aspirin, ice-bag-on-the-head, suck-down-a-quart-of-Tropicana-in-a-single-gulp hangover, but he could still feel it as he rolled into the office at eight the next morning.

He had decided on the drive in that he was going to revisit something he had already done before. Earlier he had checked with security at Emerald Dunes, the gated community where Rich Meyer had been killed, to see if they kept tapes of people coming and going out of the front gate. He knew that was standard practice at many places. The head of security told him that they didn't have tapes going back that far, so Crawford asked him if maybe the Jupiter Police had requested them at the time of Meyer's murder. The man didn't know so Crawford spoke to one of the detectives on the Meyer case, who told him he was pretty sure there were tapes in the cold case file. And sure enough, in a battered, brown cardboard box there were nine tapes. He still felt Meyer and Loadholt were connected. He had found out that Emerald Dunes, where Meyer lived at the time of his death, was a place where a lot of retirees lived, many people sixty and older, therefore the shooter, who Shirley Meyer said was in his twenties or thirties, should stand out.

Then he had another thought and walked downstairs to where the four members of CSEU—Crime Scene Evidence Unit—were headquartered. The first member he saw was Bayard Jones on the phone, the second was Dominica McCarthy, looking into a microscope.

He came up behind her. "Let me guess, DNA off of a perp's toothbrush?"

Dominica looked up and smiled. Known as either the "cute" or "hot" CSEU, Dominica had striking emerald green eyes, sharp, high cheekbones, thick dark hair, and a body everyone agreed was way above average.

"Hello, Charlie," she said. "Good guess but not even close. Hair sample from that B & E on Everglades Island."

Crawford shrugged. "So," he said, trying to sound all business, "can I borrow you for something on the Loadholt homicide?"

"Right now?"

"Well, as soon as you're available," he said.

"Give me ten minutes," she said.

He nodded. "I'll be on the tape machine," he said. "Pick up a cup of office rotgut and join me."

HE HAD BEEN WATCHING THE TAPES OF CARS DRIVING IN AND out of Emerald Dunes. It was of cars coming and going two hours before Meyer's murder and two hours after.

Dominica McCarthy came up behind him with a bottle of water.

"Not real big on the office rotgut," she said.

He got up and pulled over another chair.

"Thanks," she said. "So what are we doing, Charlie?"

"This is a tape from back when a guy named Judge Meyer got killed," he said. "Shows cars going in and out of the development where he lived and where the homicide took place. Two hours before and two hours after TOD." Time of death.

"Okay," she said. "Roll it."

Crawford hit a switch.

THEY HAD BEEN ON THE MACHINE FOR ABOUT FORTY-FIVE minutes now.

"I'd say it's a toss-up between white Buick LaCrosses and silver Cadillac CTSes, with a few gray Lexuses thrown in."

While they watched, Crawford filled her in on the case. The early suspects who had not panned out. Them looking into Elizabeth Jeanne Loadholt's high school reunion. Their trip up to New Orleans.

"So what are you working on?" Crawford asked, making conversation.

"Well, as you know, we came up empty on Loadholt," Dominica said.

"Because the ocean washed everything away?" Crawford said.

"The ocean and the little fishies," Dominica said. "So mainly I've been on that string of burglaries."

"Getting anywhere?" Crawford asked.

"I think so," Dominica said. "Looks like it was an inside job on one. I'm not sure they're all related."

They went back to watching cars come through the Emerald Dunes gate for another fifteen minutes.

"Kind of like watching grass grow," Crawford said.

Dominica smiled and cocked her head to one side. "Why did you get me up here, Charlie? This isn't exactly what us CSI I's do."

"I wanted another set of eyes on it," Crawford said.

"And Ott's old, bloodshot ones wouldn't do, huh?"

Crawford laughed and looked at this watch. "It's lunch time and I'm buying."

"Green's?" she asked.

"You know me, I'm a creature of habit. Dunkin' Donuts for break-fast, Green's for lunch—"

"And Marie Callender's chicken parm in the microwave for dinner."

"Yup," Crawford said. "Some would call it gourmet cuisine."

Dominica chuckled. "You mean someone like Ott."

FORTY-SIX

BEING THE CREATURE OF HABIT HE WAS, CRAWFORD ORDERED the hamburger at Green's.

Being a big eater, Dominica ordered a bowl of clam chowder, chicken Caesar salad and chocolate ice cream for dessert.

"Doesn't that clash?" Crawford asked. "Something from the sea and something from a scrawny bird."

Dominica laughed. "It might, but I have it all the time, so let it clash."

Crawford tilted back in his chair. "I've missed your snappy banter."

"And I've missed your...*less*-than-snappy banter," she said.

Crawford chuckled. "I got a call from David Balfour. He asked me to go out waterskiing then have dinner on his boat afterward. Want to come?"

"I didn't know you and David were all buddy-buddy?"

"I wouldn't say we're exactly *buddy-buddy*," he said. "It's partly payback for a favor I did for him."

Dominica leaned closer. "But...last time I checked, Charlie, we weren't going out anymore."

Crawford nodded. "We weren't. But I'd like to change that."

"Oh, I see. And is that a unilateral decision?"

"Of course not," Crawford said. "You need to be on board with it."

"To use a boat analogy."

"Yeah, exactly," Crawford said. "Come on, it'd be fun. Plus, I'd get to see you in a bathing suit again..."

Dominica smiled. "Oh, so that's what this is about."

"Well, partly."

She smiled. "Where'd you learn how to water ski anyway? Living in New York City."

"On the East River, dodging garbage barges," Crawford said. "Hey, I didn't always live in New York City, you know."

Dominica nodded. "That's right, a Connecticut boy."

"Uh-huh."

Their orders came and they both dug in.

"Just when did you decide you wanted to go out with me again?" Dominica asked, putting her soupspoon down.

"When I was on a date," he said.

"I see." She was nodding again. "Well, it just so happens I have no romantic entanglements at the moment, so I would be happy to accept your kind invitation," Dominica said. "When are we talking?"

"Saturday."

"Which gives you plenty of time to change your mind," Dominica said, digging back in to her clam chowder.

"That's not gonna happen," he said. "Can you wear that green and white bikini, please?"

"Charlie, I've got news for you," Dominica said. "You've gotta be crazy to wear a bikini waterskiing."

"So...be crazy."

"Sorry, it's going to be my black one-piece."

Crawford snapped his fingers. "Damn."

Dominica laughed. "Eat your hamburger, will you."

Crawford did as he was told. In mid-bite he looked up and saw Rose Clarke come through the front door.

The woman had an incredible walk. Smooth and flowing, with a certain swagger and confidence. She came up to their table. Rose and Dominica were friends and many would say the two best-looking women in Palm Beach.

"Hello boys and girls," she said, looking at Dominica, "So back together again. Palm Beach's dream couple."

Dominica looked up and smiled. "How 'bout just a couple of cops having lunch together?"

"No sale," Rose said. "And besides, are you CSU people really cops?"

"CSEUs," Dominica corrected her.

"Well, they're CSUs on TV."

"That's Hollywood, Rose."

Crawford's eyes were going back and forth between them like he was watching a ping-pong match.

"Care to join us?" Crawford asked when they paused.

"Thanks, but I got a customer lunch," Rose said, then leaning down and dropping her voice. "He's only looking to spend two or three million or I'd take him somewhere a little more upscale."

CRAWFORD AND DOMINICA WENT BACK TO THE STATION AND got on the tape machine again.

For twenty minutes, they watched the procession of cars with elderly men and women at the wheel.

Then a yellow sports car with a distinctive teal green stripe and a young woman at the wheel rolled up.

"What's wrong with this picture?" Dominica asked. "Looks too young for this crowd."

Crawford paused the machine. He wasn't much of a car guy but knew it was an expensive sports car. Something from the Ferrari or Maserati family, he thought.

He looked more closely at the driver. Then he leaned even closer.

There was no question about it. It was Elizabeth Jeanne Loadholt.

FORTY-SEVEN

"Well, I'll be damned," Crawford said.

"What?"

"That's our killer," Crawford said. "Clyde Loadholt's grand-daughter."

"You're kidding."

"Nope," Crawford said. "Her name is Elizabeth Jeanne Loadholt, or whatever she's going by these days."

Then he told Dominica about how Shirley Meyer, the judge's widow, had said the killer was short and had what sounded like a boy's voice.

Crawford said Loadholt must have slipped on the nylon stocking somewhere between the front entrance where she got caught on tape and when she showed up at Meyer's condo.

Dominica nodded. "So all you need to do is find her, huh?"

Crawford sighed and gave her more details about his trip to New Orleans with Ott. And how Elizabeth Loadholt was suspected of living in Macau and may have fled back there after killing Loadholt.

"Looks like you and Ott got another road trip," said Dominica.

"Somehow I don't think that's in the budget."

CRAWFORD CALLED OTT, WHO WAS AWAY FROM THE STATION, and told him what he had found.

Ott's mood went from high to low in the course of five seconds. Jazzed up by the confirmation of their killer's ID, followed by the realization that she might be ten thousand miles away.

Crawford was back in his office, going through a stack of 9x12-inch color glossies taken by the police department helicopter on the day after Loadholt's murder. They were of the Palm Beach Marina and four other marinas across the Intracoastal in West Palm Beach. Crawford had asked for them to be shot by the police department photographer after Susie Loadholt made the comment about Clyde going to someone's boat to "repair an old wound."

In the back of his mind he seemed to remember seeing a bright yellow sports car with a stripe when he'd looked at the photos a few days before. Back when yellow sports cars were of no significance.

Crawford couldn't get over the size of some of the yachts as he scanned the glossies. In one he saw two women sunbathing in the nude, clearly not bothered by the hovering helicopter as one of them was waving up at it. In another he saw a man with a golf club in his hand, who seemed to be hitting drives at some unseen target out on the Intracoastal. In another he saw...he bolted out of his chair and ran down to Ott's cubicle.

"Look at this," he said, pointing excitedly at the yellow sports car with a teal stripe. "It's her car."

Unlike Crawford, Ott *was* a car guy. "It's an Aston Martin Vanquish," he said. "Where's this?"

"Palm Beach Marina," Crawford said.

Ott bolted out of his chair. "Well, let's go, man."

They went out the rear of the station and got into a Caprice and made the short drive from the stationhouse to the Palm Beach Marina.

They drove around the parking lot, then got out and walked it from end to end. There was no yellow Aston Martin Vanquish anywhere. Then, glossy in hand, they asked a few people they came across if they'd seen it. One woman said she remembered seeing the car but had no idea who its owner was. Another man thought that its owner also owned a yacht called the *Lady Moura*.

When Crawford and Ott tried to get on the *Lady Moura* they were rebuffed by two large, well-dressed black men with shaved heads.

Crawford and Ott flashed ID and one of the men said to wait on the dock. A few minutes later a man in a thobe, who looked to be Middle Eastern, walked off the boat and came up to them.

"May I help you?" he said in perfect English.

"Yes," Crawford said, holding up the picture of the yellow sports car, "is this your car, sir?"

The man looked at it, then he frowned, as if the photo was of a big steaming turd.

"Please," he said, thrusting the picture back at Crawford, obviously insulted. "My car is a Lamborghini Veneno."

Then he turned and walked up his boat's gangplank.

"A Lamborghini Veneno?" Crawford shrugged.

"Yeah, goes for about four mil," Ott said. "If you can find one."

They spent another hour walking and talking to anybody they could find. But they came up empty. A few people had seen the car but nobody knew who it belonged to. Crawford said to Ott he was going to arrange for a round-the-clock stakeout of the marina parking lot, so if the car showed up they would get word right away.

"It's a good sign the car was there the day after Loadholt got killed," Crawford said on the way back to the station.

"Why's that?" Ott asked.

"What if it was at the airport instead?" Crawford said.

Ott thought for a second, shrugged. "Not that she couldn't have taken a cab."

CRAWFORD HADN'T RULED OUT THE POSSIBILITY THAT Elizabeth Jeanne Loadholt had flown back to Macau. After returning from New Orleans, before finding the tape, he had rung up a pretty hefty phone bill trying to track her down at the Starworld Hotel in Macao where, he had confirmed, she was the general manager. And still going by the name Lisa Troy. But if she was there, she was certainly in no hurry to call him back. He had left four messages and gotten no return call.

Finally, he took a different tack with his latest voicemail. "Ms. Troy, I will be flying to Macau this Thursday and, along with three officers of the PSP,"—which he'd looked up and found stood for Public Security Force of Macao—"would like to interrogate you."

That sounded suitably intimidating, he felt.

And sure enough, within the hour, he got a call back from a woman who identified herself as 'Ms. Troy's assistant.'

"Ms. Troy apologizes for not getting back to you, sir," said the assistant who said her name was Li-wan. "The problem is she travels extensively to other countries and just hasn't been here for a while."

Crawford perked up, thinking one of those countries might be the U.S. "Thanks for getting back to me. Why does she travel so much?" he asked. "My understanding is she's the manager there."

"She is," Li-wan said, "but she also is active in the acquisitions of other properties."

"Where?"

"All over the world," Li-wan said. "Australia, Singapore, Sri Lanka—"

"What about the U.S.?"

There was a long pause. "Yes."

"Recently?" Crawford asked.

"I...I'm not sure."

"I thought you were her assistant," Crawford said. "You don't know where she is?"

"Please understand, sir..." Li-wan's voice had bumped up an

octave higher. "Ms. Troy's schedule isn't always...predictable. A lot of things happen at the last minute."

Crawford was not buying it. "I'll ask you again, is she in the U.S. now or not?"

"I'm not sure," Li-wan said. "She was looking at a property there a little while ago—"

"Where?"

"I really can't reveal that," Li-wan said. "A lot of what Ms. Troy does is highly confidential. I'm sure you can understand, sir, we're in a very competitive bus—"

"I'll tell you what I do understand: you're giving me the runaround," Crawford said, in full kick-ass cop mode. "Unless you tell me the whereabouts of Ms. Troy right now, be expecting a visit from Constable Zhao"—another guy at his gym—"of the PSP immediately."

"She is in America," Li-wan said.

"America's a big place," Crawford said. "Where exactly?"

"Las Vegas," Li-wan said. "She's also been taking some vacation time."

"Where is she staying?" Crawford asked.

"She made her own reservations there," Li-wan said. "I really do not know. She's still got a boat there, from when she was living there three years ago."

"I got news for you, Li-wan," Crawford said. "There aren't a lot of boats in Las Vegas."

"I don't know, I've never been to the U.S.," Li-wan said.

"See, Las Vegas is in the middle of the desert."

"Mr. Crawford, I am sorry, but I can't help you further."

"Is that the same answer you're going to give Constable Zhao?"

"Yes," Li-wan said. "I really do not know anything more."

Crawford believed her. "Surely you know what her cell phone number is."

"Yes," and she gave it to Crawford.

"How often do you speak to Ms. Troy?" Crawford asked.

"Not often," Li-wan said. "She talks to one of the owners more than me."

"Give me his name and number, please," said Crawford.

Reluctantly, she did.

He felt that was all he was going to get out of her. But it was plenty.

He then called the owner of the Starworld and left a message. Later in the day, he called him again and left another message. That night he called him yet again and said he'd be flying there on Thursday and would come visit him along with three officers from the PSP. This time the bluff didn't work. He never got a call back.

After the conversation with Li-wan he went over to Ott's cubicle.

Ott was on the phone.

He waited until Ott hung up then told him about his conversation with Li-wan.

"So she's here," Ott said and a big smile lit up his face.

"Looks like it. I called her cell and left a message," Crawford said. "Something tells me I'm not going to be hearing back from her."

"Yeah, wouldn't hold your breath," Ott said.

Crawford nodded. "Remember when that guy, the manager at Harrah's, said: How he heard something about her company looking to buy a casino in Vegas?"

Ott nodded. "I remember, she had a non-compete. Couldn't work for another casino in the states for ten years."

"Exactly," Crawford said. "You remember the name of the casino?"

"No, he never said," Ott said. "Don't think he knew."

"I'm going to look into casinos there that have sold recently," Crawford said. "See if I can find out if she was involved. Easy for her to get around that non-compete."

Ott nodded. "Yeah, she could negotiate the deal, then have the Chinese guys be the actual buyers."

"Or it could be bought in the name of an LLC," Crawford said.

"Exactly," Ott said. "While you're on that, I'm gonna keep

checking every boat tied up at the Palm Beach Marina. See if one belongs to Elizabeth Jeanne Loadholt or Lisa Troy."

Crawford got up and patted Ott on the shoulder. "We're back in the game, Mort."

"I know," Ott said. "And something tells me our perp could be right under our noses."

FORTY-EIGHT

TRYING TO TRACK DOWN LISA TROY'S INVOLVEMENT IN THE purchase of a Las Vegas hotel was a dead end. Crawford couldn't find any names at all in the sale of any hotels nine months ago, only LLCs.

He eyed the stack of photos taken at the Palm Beach Marina again and picked up the one that had the yellow Vanquish in it. This time he noticed something he hadn't noticed before. The car right next to it. It was a black Jag convertible with a thin white stripe.

He took out his cell phone and dialed.

Rose Clarke answered. "Hi, Charlie."

"Hi, Rose. Question: have you parked your car at the Palm Beach Marina in the last couple of weeks?"

"Yes, a couple of times. Why?"

Crawford took a deep breath. "Do you know a woman who owns a yellow Aston Martin with a wide teal stripe?"

"Sure, that's Beth Jastrow's car. Why?"

Crawford was as amped up as he had been in a long time. "Beth Jastrow. Who is she?"

"Remember a while back I told you about The Mentors?"

"Yeah, I do."

"Well, she's one of us. She's got a boat there. I've had lunch and dinner there in the last couple of weeks."

"And is she there now?"

"No, she went somewhere on a cruise," Rose said. "Left this morning."

"I need to speak to her. Do you know how to reach her?"

"Sure," Rose said. After a moment of searching her phone, she gave him the number.

Same as the one Crawford had tried.

"She'll be back for our next meeting in three weeks, if you can wait," Rose said. "But, knowing you, you probably can't."

"Yeah, no, this is something that can't wait five minutes," Crawford said. "What's the name of the boat, Rose?"

"*Revenge*," Rose said. "It's a beautiful boat."

"Do you know where she went?'

"Sorry."

"Thanks for the info," Crawford said.

"And my reward is?"

"Lunch at the Crab Shack?"

"How 'bout dinner at La Bohéme?"

"You got a deal," Crawford said. "But it's got to wait until I wrap this up."

"So what are you waiting for?" Rose said. "Wrap it up."

"I'm trying. Oh, and by the way, that conversation about Beth Jastrow. We never had it, okay?"

"Okay. But I never asked what you want to talk to her about," Rose said.

"I know you didn't. And thank you for that," Crawford said, clicking off.

Crawford got down to Ott's office in record time. Ott was on his computer.

"We got a boat to find," Crawford said.

Ott looked up. "Didn't we do this already?" he said. "With Hector Reyes and *The Ghost*?"

FORTY-NINE

"It's not like she had to file a flight plan or something," Ott said, facing Crawford from his cubicle.

"Yeah, just haul up the anchor and go," Crawford said. "But someone's got to know where she was going."

"Yeah, maybe a friend of hers," Ott said. "Or a friend of her captain or one of the crew."

Crawford stood up. "Okay, so let's do this. I'll call Rose back, get some names and numbers of Jastrow's friends. Make a bunch of calls and see what I find out. You go back down to the marina and ask around about the captain and the crew of the *Revenge*. Maybe someone has one of their cell numbers or something."

"Yeah, okay, I'm on my way," Ott said, grabbing his jacket. "Gotta say, bro, if I was gonna go kill a bunch of people I'm not sure I'd advertise it on the back of my boat. Know what I mean?"

Crawford called every one of The Mentors, and the closest he got to locating Beth Jastrow's destination was from one of the members named Marla Fluor, who said, "I don't know, the Bahamas maybe."

The Bahamas was a big place.

Actually, he realized as he looked at his handwritten list, there was one more member he hadn't spoken to yet. Diana Quarle.

He drove down to the Palm Beach Marina and found Ott in conversation with a man who was wearing the uniform of a crewmember. On the breast pocket of his white shirt it said *Dreamchaser*.

Ott introduced the man to Crawford. His name was Dale Harris. He said he knew the first name of captain of the *Revenge* was Jerry but didn't know his last name. He said the captain of a boat called the *Mommie Dearest,* moored down at the end of the dock, would know for sure. Dale said the *Mommie Dearest*'s captain was named Archie and that Archie and the captain of the *Revenge* went fishing a lot in between cruises.

Crawford and Ott thanked him and walked down to the *Mommie Dearest.* It turned out Archie was in West Palm getting supplies for a trip but was expected back soon.

Crawford and Ott decided to hang around and wait for him. Fifteen minutes later, a man showed up pushing a large white cart down the dock. It was filled with four boxes of liquor and three cases of Heineken.

"Are you Archie?" Crawford asked the man as he pulled up to the gangplank of the *Mommie Dearest.*

"Sure am," the man said, shading his eyes.

"My name's Detective Crawford, Palm Beach Police, and this is my partner, Detective Ott," Crawford said. "Mind if we ask you a few questions?"

"No problem," Archie said. "What do you want to know?"

"We understand you're a friend of Jerry, the captain of the *Revenge?*"

"Yeah," Archie said, clearly concerned. "Something happen to him?"

"No, no, he's fine," Crawford said. "We just need to know where the *Revenge* went. What its destination is? We need to get in touch with the owner, Beth Jastrow, about something."

Archie cleared his throat. "No, sorry, I don't know, just that they left here earlier today," Archie said. "Seemed like maybe it was a spur-of-the-moment thing."

"What made you think that?" Crawford asked.

"Well, Jerry and me planned to go fishing this morning and next thing I know the boat's gone," Archie said. "Never called me or anything."

"What is his cell number?" Ott asked. "And what's Jerry's last name?"

"Remar," Archie said and gave Ott the number. "What do you need Beth Jastrow for?"

"Oh, it's not a big deal," Crawford said. "About the state boat tax."

Archie looked away, then back. "I bet she's exempt 'cause she's not a Florida resident."

"That's what we need to find out," Crawford said. "Anyway, thanks for your help."

"Yeah, appreciate it," Ott said.

"No problem," Archie said and he pushed the booze up the gangway.

As soon as he got inside the boat, Archie took out his cell phone and dialed.

"Hey, Jer, it's Archie," he said. "Just thought you might want to know, a couple Palm Beach cops are looking for Beth."

"What did they want?" Jerry asked.

"Guy said something about the boat tax," Archie said. "Just not sure I'm buying it."

"What were their names?" Jerry asked.

"Crawford and Ott. Detectives," Archie said. "You in Charleston yet?"

"Not quite," Jerry said. "Couple hours away."

"Okay, so I'd be expecting a call from this guy," Archie said. "You don't want to talk to him, don't answer."

"Thanks, man," Jerry said.

CRAWFORD WAS ON HIS WAY BACK TO THE STATION WHEN HIS cell phone rang.

"Hello."

"Hi, is this Detective Crawford?" the woman's voice asked.

"Yes, it is."

"Hi, Detective, my name is Diana Quarle," the woman said. "You left a message wanting to know about my friend, Beth Jastrow?"

"Yes, Ms. Quarle," he said. "Thanks for getting back to me. Ms. Jastrow left Palm Beach on her boat and I wondered if you knew where she was going?"

"Sure do," Diana said. "To Spoleto."

Crawford had a vague recollection that was in Italy. "Where is that?"

"It's in Charleston. South Carolina," Diana said. "It's this festival they have every year. Music, theatre, dancing, you name it."

"So she docks her boat there?" Crawford asked.

"Yes," Diana said. "I think she's meeting a friend."

"Oh, really. Do you know the name?".

"No, sorry," Diana said. "From up north, I think."

"Well, thank you, Ms. Quarle, I really appreciate it," Crawford said.

"You're welcome," Diana said. "I saw you the other day at Madeline's. Rose Clarke pointed you out."

"Yeah, Rose is a friend of mine," Crawford said.

"Lucky girl."

JERRY REMAR FOUND BETH JASTROW IN A BIKINI ON THE foredeck of the *Revenge*. She was lying on a mahogany deck chaise that had a full-length blue and white pillow cushion. On either side of her were teak tables. On top of the one to her right was a Diet Coke in a plastic glass and several magazines. On the table to her left was suntan lotion, two paperbacks, and a MacBook Air computer.

Beth Jastow liked to have a lot going on. She usually read two or three books at the same time, while also reading a magazine and the *Wall Street Journal* and the *New York Times* digital editions. She was a well-informed woman.

She didn't hear Jerry Remar approach because she was absorbed in *Architectural Digest* pictures of a house in East Hampton.

"Ms. Jastrow?" Jerry said.

She looked up and shaded her eyes. "Oh, hi, Jerry. What's up?"

"I thought you'd want to know, I got a call from a friend of mine," Jerry said. "He told me two cops were looking for you."

Beth put the magazine down on the deck and sat up. "Where?"

"At the marina."

"Did they say what they wanted?"

"Something about the boat tax."

Beth frowned but didn't say anything.

"They asked him what our destination was."

"And did he tell them?"

"No, said he didn't know."

Beth nodded and thought for a second. "Okay, thanks, I appreciate it."

Jerry started to walk away.

"Oh, Jerry," Beth said. "Cancel the berth at the Harborage Marina in Charleston. Let's tie up at that one in Mount Pleasant instead."

Jerry nodded. "Yes, ma'am."

Mount Pleasant was a town that was just over the bridge from Charleston.

Beth thrummed her fingers on the teak table then took a sip of Diet Coke. Then she put it down, picked up her cell phone and dialed.

A man answered.

"Hey, honey," she said. "I'm an hour away. Instead of the Charleston marina, I'm tying up in Mount Pleasant."

"Right around the corner from me, huh?"

"If you'd like I can drop anchor right in front of your house," Beth said.

The man laughed. "You'd run aground. It's pretty shallow."

"So what do you want to do tonight?"

"You know damn well what I want to do."

Beth laughed. "Before that."

"I've got us a reservation at Fig for seven thirty."

"Perfect," Beth said. "I love that place. You want to come to the boat and have a cocktail before?'

"Sure," said the man. "We can talk a little shop. Get that out of the way."

"I'll see you then," Beth said. "Can't wait."

FIFTY

CRAWFORD CALLED OTT AND TOLD HIM TO STOP BY HIS OFFICE
as soon as he got back to the station.

Fifteen minutes later Ott walked in. "What's up, Chuck?"

"How'd you like to go to Spoleto?"

"Where the hell is that?"

Crawford was on his computer reading about it. "Charleston, South Carolina. It's this festival up there. Classical music, opera, string bands—"

"But I'm a rock n' roll guy," Ott said.

Crawford scrolled down the schedule. "Flamenco dancers, ballet, chamber music," he read. "Oh, hey, they got Dee Dee Bridgewater."

"Who's she?"

"Shit, man, you don't know?"

Ott shook his head.

"This really amazing jazz singer."

"Well, then, what are we waiting for?"

"I checked and it's about a seven-hour drive," Crawford said, "which you can probably knock off in six. Flying doesn't make any sense 'cause like New Orleans, it's connecting flights."

"I got a full tank in the Caprice," Ott said. "Let's hit the road."

This time they decided not to bother telling Norm Rutledge until they were in Charleston.

NED CARLINO WALKED UP THE GANGWAY OF THE *REVENGE*.

A man in a white jacket, black bow tie, and a silver tray with two flutes of champagne met him at the top of the steps.

"Good evening, Mr. Carlino," the man said. "Champagne?"

"Thank you, James," Carlino said, taking one of the flutes.

"Ms. Jastrow is getting ready, but asked if you'd wait on the aft deck."

"Sure," Carlino said.

He found several lavish teak chairs with cushions laid out in a seating arrangement at the rear of the boat. Carlino did not sit, but looked out at the view. Farther down, along the beach, he could almost see his house.

Carlino was a lawyer based in Philadelphia who spent at least four months of the year going back and forth between his beach house in Mount Pleasant and his twelve hundred acre plantation an hour south. His house in Mount Pleasant was a six-bedroom brick Georgian that had expansive views of the ocean, which didn't interest Carlino in the least. What Carlino liked most about the house was the fact that his wife spent almost no time there. She had five sisters and a million friends in Philadelphia and had no interest in making new ones in South Carolina.

Carlino was no longer a practicing lawyer but a businessman who had extensive commercial real estate holdings, which included a hotel and a majority interest in a racetrack. In the last year he had sold a harness racing track outside of Philadelphia to Harrah's.

Carlino heard footsteps behind him and turned.

Beth Jastrow looked stunning in white slacks and a black top with a glittering array of sequins. She had flashing, bright eyes and, yes, a *killer* body. She raised her champagne flute, then walked up to Carlino and gave him a kiss on the lips.

"I've missed you," she said softly.

"And I you," Carlino said with a laugh. "If that's proper English."

"I get the idea," she said, putting her arm around his back. "So you want to sit?"

"Sure," said Carlino and they both sat, facing each other.

"How long are you here for?" Carlino asked.

"As long as you want me," she said. "Well, except I have to be back for a meeting in a few weeks."

"Your little philanthropic group?"

"Gotta give back once in a while, right?"

Carlino shrugged. "I wouldn't know. I'm a taker."

Jastrow laughed. "Least you're honest about it," she said. "So are you making any progress?"

Carlino killed the rest of his champagne just as the waiter walked toward them.

"Can I get you another, sir?"

"I'll have a scotch on the rocks," Carlino said.

The waiter looked at Jastrow's glass, but it was still half full.

He walked away.

"You've got him well-trained, Beth," Carlino said. "So in answer to your question: Charleston is a tough town to break into. Classic good-old-boy network. But I finally got to a few guys in high places—guys with no money but more power than they deserve."

Jastrow's eyes lit up. "My favorite kind," she said. "Men who can be persuaded by an envelope full of cash."

"Exactly."

"Well, my boss Ming Yao is ready to step up when you get the approval for the casino," Jastrow said.

Carlino leaned toward Jastrow and gave her a kiss on the lips. "I've got to hand it to you," he said. "Getting the Chinaman to go from, 'Where's Charleston, South Carolina?' to ready-to-step-up is a hell of a feat."

"Well, it was two things: showing him the demographics about all the rich Yankees with houses in Charleston," Jastrow said. "But mainly, you and your friends getting all those high-end cruise ships to stop there."

The waiter came back with Carlino's scotch on the tray.

"And I'll have another champagne, please, James," she said.

"Yes, ma'am," the waiter said and walked away.

"How are you coming with the mayor?" Jastrow asked.

Carlino shook his head and frowned. "He's the fly in the ointment," he said. "An incorruptible public servant."

"So what are you going to do about him?" Jastrow asked.

"He might have to become the victim of an accident," Carlino said.

Jastow smiled. "Oh, I hate when that happens."

"I NEVER REALIZED HOW LONG THIS DAMN STATE IS," OTT SAID. "I mean, it just goes on forever."

"Yeah, I know, almost three hundred miles from West Palm to Jacksonville alone," Crawford said.

"And then we gotta go through Georgia," Ott said. "At least we got Sirius."

Ott was bouncing back between two Sirius stations: one that played primarily Tom Petty and another Bruce Springsteen.

"Badlands" had just finished.

"Gotta love Bruce," Ott said. "But I always thought he could do better in the wife department."

"What the hell are you talking about?" Crawford said.

"I don't know, I'm not saying Patti's a dog, just think the guy coulda done a little better," Ott said. "And speaking of Bruce, what's with that whole 'working class' thing anyway? Have you seen the house in LA he just put on the market? Like sixty mil or something. Working class, my ass." Ott took a breath. "Know who else?"

"Who else what?" Crawford asked.

"Coulda done better in the wife department," Ott said.

Crawford shook his head. "Jesus, where'd this rant come from?"

"Just killin' time, Charlie. Don't have to get all tetchy."

"Whatever that means," Crawford said. "You just go off on these wacky tangents."

"Roger Federer," Ott said. "I mean, I'm sure Mrs. Federer is really nice and all but he's maybe the best tennis player ever lived and a nice looking guy to boot. Then there's Cate Blanchett's husband. She *really* coulda done better. Guy looks like Humpty Dumpty on a bad day. And, I read somewhere, the guy might be messing around with another woman."

"Okay, Mort, I have no idea what Cate Blanchett's husband looks like and don't care," Crawford said. "Can we just get back to listening to Bruce sing his songs about his sad, pathetic, blue-collar life?"

After a few minutes, Crawford got on his phone, trying to locate where the *Revenge* might be mooring. The first two marinas he tried had said no such boat was scheduled to be mooring there. Then a third one said that the *Revenge* had been scheduled to tie up there, but had cancelled a few hours before.

Crawford told Ott.

"Shit," Ott said. "You figure she knows we're after her?"

"I don't know," Crawford said. "I'm just gonna keep trying to locate the boat."

Crawford tried four more Charleston marinas but struck out with each one. Then he tried ones near but outside of Charleston. Finally he tried one in Mount Pleasant.

"Yes, I'm looking at it right now," said a man who identified himself as the harbormaster. "A couple is walking down the gangway, going toward the parking lot."

"Do me a favor," Crawford said. "See what kind of car they're getting into. And the license plate if you can."

"You got it," the harbormaster said. Then after a few moments, "It's a black Tesla X, South Carolina LE1663."

"Thanks a lot," Crawford said. "Appreciate it."

Crawford clicked off and dialed another number.

"Who're you calling?" Ott asked.

"I need to speak to someone at SLED," Crawford said.

Crawford had done some poking around and found out that SLED stood for South Carolina Law Enforcement Division based in Columbia, the state capital. They had jurisdiction for any arrest made in the state and the last thing Crawford wanted to do was to go rogue—arrest Beth Jastrow and haul her back to Palm Beach without SLED's direct involvement. That would be something that would give a defense attorney grounds to get her off.

He and Ott had already done that with David Balfour's niece and thought it was a really bad idea to do it twice in the same week.

Crawford got bumped around at SLED until finally he was talking to a man who seemed to have both the authority and the ability to grasp the fluid situation Crawford had just described to him.

"So we've located the subject's boat," Crawford said. "We know she just departed from there by car with a man. We're going to go there and try to find out where she went. What I'll do, once I've found out, is give you a call, then we can hook up."

"Sounds good," John Birkenheuer, the SLED constable said. "Just keep me posted. My partner and I will be on our way to Charleston in a few minutes."

"Will do," Crawford said, and clicked off.

He turned to Ott. "How much longer?"

Ott looked down at the odometer. "I figure another fifty miles."

"The address is 1610 Ben Sawyer Boulevard," Crawford said.

Ott nodded and put the address in his GPS.

Another thing Crawford had done on the ride up was to get a warrant issued from a West Palm Beach judge for the arrest of Beth Jastrow. He had also been instructed on the extradition process from South Carolina to Florida.

Crawford turned to Ott and patted the car's dashboard. "You think this old girl can run down a Tesla X if it has to?"

Ott glanced over at Crawford. "What do I always tell you, Charlie?"

"You tell me a lot of lame shit," Crawford said. "Oh, you mean, 'It's not about the car, it's about the driver?'"

"Bingo," Ott said, chuckling. "Even though a Tesla X can do zero to sixty in 2.9 seconds."

FIFTY-ONE

Fig on Meeting Street in Charleston doesn't look like much on the outside, but what comes out of its kitchen is spectacular. Even though Ned Carlino had called and made the reservation that same day, management scrambled so he could have the best table in the house. Ned Carlino was a prodigious tipper, a server's dream.

He and Beth Jastrow were on their first drinks.

"So the mayor," Beth was saying, almost in a whisper. "Do you have someone lined up for the accident that will soon befall him?"

Carlino laughed. "I love the way you say that. So refined and understated," he said. "It's almost like he's going to skin his knee or something."

Jastrow shrugged. "Yes, if skinning your knee is fatal."

"My brother's got a guy who was a sniper in Afghanistan."

"That ought to do it," Jastrow said, then with a smile, "but if you ever need anybody to do it for free..."

Carlino laughed. "You actually enjoy it, don't you?"

"I wouldn't go that far." Jastrow's eyes got flinty. "Those scumbags deserved everything they got."

Jastrow had shared a few of her secrets with Carlino.

The waiter approached.

Carlino held up his hand. "A few more minutes."

The waiter nodded and walked away.

"Tell me the whole story," Carlino said.

"I thought I did," Jastrow said.

"You did, but give me all the nitty-gritty details," Carlino said.

Jastrow reached for her drink and finished it in one gulp. "Okay, fasten your seat belt," she said. "So my beloved grandfather had this regular poker game every week with his asshole buddies. Lots of heavy drinking, you know, a couple of times they'd have strippers show up."

"Wait, I thought he was married?"

"He was, but that never got in the way," Jastrow said. "He'd send her over to her sister's."

Carlino nodded. "What did grandma make of that, I wonder?"

"Susie Loadholt didn't ask questions," Jastrow said. "If she did, she'd end up with bruises all over her face the next day."

She took another sip of her drink. "So this one time I made the mistake of going down to the kitchen when the game was going on," Jastrow said. "One of 'em spotted me and said, 'Hey, honey, whatcha doin'?'"

Carlino leaned toward her. "How old were you at the time?"

"Seventeen," Jastrow said, a pained expression in her eyes. "So this guy—the honorable Judge Meyer—motioned me over. Like an idiot, I walked into the den and the guy starts groping me."

"With your grandfather right there?" Even Carlino was shocked.

Jastrow was choked up.

Carlino put his hand on her arm. "You don't have to—"

"I want to," Jastrow said. "I've never told anybody else." She wiped her eyes with her napkin, "So all of a sudden all these pigs were groping me. Their hands up my skirt. All over my—"

"Beth, seriously, you don't have to—"

"I said, I want to," Jastrow said. "Next thing I know the judge is dragging me to a bedroom and my grandfather's just yukking it up with his buddies, doing nothing. Pretending like he's not seeing what's going on."

The waiter came up to them again. "No, not yet," Carlino said, waving him away.

"I remember this one guy saying something—trying to stop it—and the judge just telling him to shut the fuck up. I was hoping...but the guy just backed down."

Carlino put his hand on her arm again. "I'm sorry, honey. You shoulda killed the whole damn lot of 'em."

Jastrow tried to smile. "Well, it was only a matter of time until I got the judge. Bastard lived a lot longer than he should have, though."

"And your charming grandfather. What—"

"So I came back here a month ago. Told the guys in Macau that I was going on a little extended vacation after I did the deal in Vegas." Jastrow shrugged. "I had the boat here and I got hooked up with the girls through a mutual friend—"

"The group, you mean The Mentors?"

"Yes, we were having meetings every couple of days," Jastrow said. "And I really got into it. I liked the idea of helping women just starting out. I was thinking, 'Shit, I wish there were people like us around when I was a kid.' I was even thinking about buying a house in Palm Beach."

"But, why bother, with a boat like the *Revenge*?"

"That's true."

"So you got in touch with Grandpa?"

Jastrow nodded her head. "Yeah, even though my gut told me it was a bad idea. But some little misguided part of me wanted to hear him apologize, tell me that he loved me and how much he regretted what happened."

"So what happened?"

"I called him up, asked him to come on the boat. So he comes on board like nothing ever happened. Proceeds to go through half a bottle of Jack Daniels. Then tells me I was a bitchy little brat who never appreciated anything he ever did for me."

"You're kidding," Carlino said. "What an asshole."

"So I brought up the whole incident that night of the poker game and he pretends he doesn't even remember it. Says that if that really happened with the judge, it must have been that I was flirting with him and deserved it."

Carlino shook his head, incredulous. "Are you kidding?"

"So I politely excused myself while he's making another Jack, went back to my stateroom, and got the Glock with the silencer—same one I used on the judge three years back—and without a word put one in the fat bastard's chest."

"Atta girl," then Carlino had an afterthought. "What about the crew?"

"They're a bunch of very loyal boys who I pay *very, very* well," Jastrow said. "But just to make sure, I wrote out a check to each one of them that night for five thousand dollars, then we left the dock and went out into the ocean. They dumped the body about a mile off shore, figuring the fish would have their way with dear old grandpa," she laughed and shook her head, "but apparently they wanted no part of him."

Carlino leaned forward and kissed her. "Good fucking riddance."

He sat back and flagged the waiter down. "We're ready now." He turned back to Beth. "So while you're coming clean, what really happened to Emile?"

Emile was Emile Troy, Beth's short-lived husband.

"My dear Emile," Jastrow said, with a laugh. "So you didn't believe the first story I told you?"

Carlino shook his head. "Kind of sounded like a sanitized version. Older man meets younger woman in a bar. They get married, go to New Orleans for their honeymoon. Older man dies of unexplained illness three weeks later."

"Yeah, that's more or less what happened," Jastrow said. "Mostly less."

"Come on, tell me. I can't get enough of love stories like this."

Jastrow thought for a second then sighed. "Okay, because your childhood wasn't so lily-white," she said, "I guess I can tell you about mine."

"I'm all ears."

She put her hand on his. "So when I was seventeen, I met men hitchhiking around in the central part of Florida. And because I was strapped for cash, some of them paid me for a session in the back seat."

"Lucky them," Carlino said.

"Yeah, well, let me tell you, it was not how I planned to spend my teenage years. But a girl's gotta eat..."

"Where were you living?"

Jastrow twirled a strand of hair. "Well, let's see, there was this room behind a bar in Daytona, a fleabag motel in New Smyrna Beach in exchange for doing the owner."

"Bet he was a dreamboat."

"Oh, yeah, Brad Pitt," Jastrow said. "Then one day I got picked up by Emile Troy in a little dump of a town called Keystone Heights. Emile was basically a traveling salesman for a knife-sharpening business."

"You can make money doing that?" Carlino asked.

"Emile seemed to do all right for himself, but the main thing was he had a Caddy. A shiny, new El Dorado," Jastrow said. "So I thought, *hmm,* might as well marry the old fuck."

"How old was he?"

"Sixty-four," Jastrow said. "But he didn't look a day over eighty. So I put the idea in his head and, sure enough, we got married. I saw some show about Mardi Gras, so we decided to go to New Orleans for the honeymoon."

Carlino took a sip of his drink and put it down. "There are worse places you could have chosen."

"Yeah, except when we got there I found out he had no money to speak of. All he had was the goddamn Caddy. He suggested I go out on Bourbon Street and hook so we could pay for the hotel."

Carlino leaned back in his chair. "You're kidding," he said. "So'd you do it?"

"No way. I've got my standards," Jastrow said. "I got him to sell the Caddy instead."

"Good move," Carlino said. "Then what?"

"That night we went to bed—it *was* our honeymoon after all—and rather than do the old bastard, I smothered him with a pillow instead," Jastrow said matter-of-factly. "Took me a while to finish him off."

Carlino held up a fist. Jastrow bumped it with hers.

"Told the medical examiner he had a heart attack when we were doin' it," Jastrow said. "Guy bought it."

"That's a heartwarming story," Carlino said. "It's got it all. Love, sex, and death by pillow."

"I'm not done," Jastrow said. "After I did it, I took his wad of hundreds from the Caddy sale down to the casino and blew half of it in forty-five minutes. Absolutely no clue what I was doing."

Carlino gave her another light fist bump. "So from there you made your meteoric rise up the corporate ladder at Harrah's?"

"Yeah, screwing everybody I could," she laughed. "In both senses of the word. But after a while I figured out I was pretty damn good at the casino business. Plus, I was gonna out-work and out-hustle every-body. Then when Harrah's was thinking about putting Caesar's on the block and the Yao brothers came sniffing around, I had a meeting with them."

"Love at first sight?"

"Lust at first sight," Jastrow said. "Ming and I had a thing, then he offered me the Macau job."

"And the rest is history," Carlino said. "But going back to Emile, why'd you take his name? I mean, it only last five minutes."

"Well, Troy was a way better name than Loadholt," Jastrow said. "But mainly, I didn't want to be reminded I was related to any of those fucked up people."

"So then along came Mr. Jastrow?" Carlino said. "In Macau, I'm assuming?"

Jastrow laughed. "Oh, no, there was no Mr. Jastrow in Macau or anywhere else."

"Wait, you didn't get married again?"

Jastrow shook her head. "No, I just needed a different last name so I could negotiate the purchase of the Vegas casinos without my old boss knowing it was me. That would have violated my non-compete, could have put the kibosh on the deal. So at Starworld and in Macau people knew me as both Lisa Troy and Beth Jastrow. A little confusing, I admit, but it worked."

Carlino smiled his admiration. "So of all the names you could have picked, why Jastrow?"

"That was the name of the lawyer who got me off when I held up a liquor store way back when," Jastrow said. "After that, I started turning my life around." She burst out laughing, "Well, sort of."

FIFTY-TWO

CRAWFORD AND OTT HAD JUST CROSSED THE BRIDGE FROM Charleston to Mount Pleasant.

"I've been thinking about what happens if I show up at Jastrow's boat and ask for her," Crawford said. "The captain or whoever says she's gone out to dinner. I ask him where? He says he doesn't know. Or he tells me, then the second I leave he calls Jastrow and tells her I was there. Then we go to the restaurant or wherever they went and she's long gone."

"You raise a good point," Ott said. "So what are you thinking about doing instead?"

"Glad you asked."

CRAWFORD AND OTT PARKED IN A CORNER OF THE MARINA parking lot that was far away from the boats. Crawford walked across the lot and up onto the dock. The *Revenge* was the biggest boat there by far.

He walked up to it, then, without hesitating, walked up the gangway.

"Hello," he shouted, when he got on board. "Beth! Hey, Beth! Where are you, honey?"

A young guy in a uniform walked up to him. "Yes, sir, can I help you?"

Crawford gave him his biggest smile. "I'm looking for Beth. Ms. Jastrow."

"Sorry, sir, she's not here. Was she expecting you?"

"No," Crawford said, folding his arms over his chest, and smiling broadly. "I'm an old friend. She called me a few days ago and said she was coming to town. I was just hoping to take her out to dinner."

"Sorry, she left a little while ago for dinner," the crewman said.

"By herself? Maybe I can catch up," Crawford said.

"Sorry, with another man," the crewman said.

Crawford laughed and shifted to his other foot. "Well, that two-timing...just kidding. Know where they went? Maybe I'll have a night cap with 'em."

The crewman thought for a moment, then smiled. "A place called Fig."

"Refresh my memory," he said. "King Street, right?"

"Nah, pretty sure it's Meeting," the crewman said.

"Great, well, thanks for your help," Crawford said, putting out his hand. "If she checks in, don't tell her I stopped by. I want to surprise her."

———

CRAWFORD OPENED THE PASSENGER-SIDE DOOR. "PLACE CALLED Fig, on Meeting Street."

"Good work. How'd it go?"

Crawford smiled. "If I didn't know any better, I'd think I was Beth Jastrow's best friend."

Crawford dialed his phone.

A man answered. "Birkenheuer."

"Hey, John, it's Charlie Crawford again," he said. "I just got word that Beth Jastrow is at Fig restaurant on Meeting Street having dinner now."

"How far from there are you now, Charlie?" Birkenheuer asked.

Crawford turned to Ott. "How far—"

"Ten, twelve minutes," Ott said.

"Ten to twelve minutes," Crawford repeated. "How about you?"

"Maybe twenty," Birkenheuer said. "I'll meet you there."

"Copy that," Crawford said.

NED CARLINO HAD JUST FINISHED HIS FIFTH SCOTCH AND WAS starting to slur a little. Beth Jastrow had stopped after three—the champagne on the boat and the one vodka at Fig. Carlino had just flagged down the waiter and made an air scribble—*check, please*—and almost fallen out of his chair doing it.

"Okay, Ned," Jastrow said, "I'm officially relieving you of your driving duties. Where are your keys?"

Carlino cocked his head "Huh, whaddaya talkin' about, honeeee?"

"You're going to be co-pilot on the ride back to the boat," Jastrow said.

"Whaddaya mean? I'm fine," Carlino said.

"Yes, and you're going to be a very fine co-pilot," Jastrow said. "Giving me good directions...come on, Ned, keys, please."

Carlino shook his head, gave her a long dramatic exhale, reached in his pocket, and handed her the keys. "Okay, be careful, though, the thing's a goddamn rocket ship."

"What do you mean?" Jastrow said, taking them.

"I mean, it goes about three hundred miles an hour!"

"Not really?" Jastrow said.

"No, but just about," Carlino said, as the waiter handed him the check.

He pulled out his license and put it on the check.

"Ah, sir," the waiter said. "That's not a credit card."

Jastrow burst out laughing as Carlino, red-faced, picked it up and replaced it with an Amex card.

"I rest my case," she said.

FIFTY-THREE

CRAWFORD AND OTT TURNED FROM SOUTH BAY STREET ONTO Hasell Street, watching the GPS.

"Looks like it's about three blocks from here," Crawford said.

"And the SLED guys are right behind us?"

"Yeah," Crawford said, pointing to the restaurant a block and a half away. "There it is. Fig."

Two people came out the front door. Beth Jastrow and Ned Carlino.

"Jesus, that's her," Crawford said as Ott hit the accelerator. "We gotta do it without SLED."

Crawford hit the button that rolled down his window and reached for a bullhorn that he had ready at his feet. He picked it up and clicked it on.

"Beth Jastrow," he said into the bullhorn. "This is the police. Stop where you are and raise your hands."

Beth Jastrow did just the opposite. She started running down Meeting Street, leaving her dinner date in her dust. Just as the Caprice skidded around the corner of Hasell and Meeting, Jastrow slipped quickly into the parked Tesla and hunched over the wheel to start the car. Crawford's hand went to the Sig Sauer in his shoulder holster, but the sidewalks were packed with people. No way was he going to risk an errant shot, and no way was he going to shoot Beth Jastrow in the back either.

"Get out of the car *now*," Crawford said as they neared the rear of the Tesla.

Jastrow floored the car and it shot away from them. In an instant, she was half a block away, the sports car's engine noiselessly leaving them behind.

"Come on, Mort," Crawford exhorted, "catch up."

But the Tesla was putting more and more distance between them, now only a block from where Meeting Street dead-ended into Broad Street. Crawford and Ott were a block and a half behind as Jastrow took a skidding right onto Broad Street, heading west.

Ott had the siren and lights going now. No sign of the SLED team. Ott skidded around the turn onto Broad as Crawford dialed his phone. The Tesla blew past a few cars like they were standing still then hung a sudden, hard right onto King Street.

John Birkenheuer picked up on the first ring.

"John, we're in pursuit of suspect's black Tesla. She just went right from Broad onto King."

Ott turned onto King, narrowly missing a car coming straight at him.

"Jesus," Birkenheuer said loud enough for Ott to hear, "that's a one-way street."

"Now you fuckin' tell me," Ott muttered.

Crawford saw the Tesla two blocks up King Steet, slaloming between cars coming down the one-way street.

"Gotta pull over, Mort," Crawford said. "Too damn dangerous."

Ott pulled into a street perpendicular to King.

Crawford opened the door and ran out to King Street. He looked up it just in time to see the Tesla—facing two cars in both lanes coming toward it—fishtail across the sidewalk and slam into a four-story brick building.

Crawford started running up King Street as he saw Beth Jastrow climb out of the smoking Tesla. She shot him a glance, then disappeared down a side street.

Ott was just behind Crawford, both dodging pedestrians on the sidewalk.

A few minutes later they got to the Tesla and ran down the side street. Moments later they were back on Meeting. They looked in all directions, but no Beth Jastrow.

Crawford dialed his cell. John Birkenheuer answered. "We're at Meeting and Society," Crawford said. "We lost her."

FIFTY-FOUR

Beth Jastrow had run three long blocks and her feet were killing her. She was in the parking lot of a Harris Teeter supermarket on Bay Street, looking for a car the owners had left the keys in but having no luck. She had covered half of the parking lot already.

She saw an old lady hit her clicker and heard the whoop of the door unlocking her car. Looking around and seeing no one, Jastrow walked quickly toward the woman and shoved her as hard as she could. The women fell to the ground, keys in hand.

Jastrow reached down and yanked the keys out of her hand.

"What are you—"

Jastrow backhanded her across the mouth before the woman could finish her question. Jastrow stood, turned, flung open the car door, and got in.

Another older woman was in the passenger seat, holding her hand over her mouth, her eyes bulging.

"Get out," Jastrow hissed.

The woman reached for the door.

Jastrow reached across and grabbed her arm. "On second thought," she said. "Stay here."

The woman looked to be in her eighties with round glasses, gray wispy hair, and a slight build. She had a terrified look on her face and her lips were trembling.

"Just sit there and don't say a goddamn thing," Jastrow commanded. Then calmly, "You might want to put on your seat belt."

Jastrow started the car up and drove out of the parking lot. She reached in her pocket, pulled out her cell phone and dialed.

Her captain, Jerry Remar, answered.

"It's Beth," she said. "I want you to cast off and meet me at that marina in Edisto."

"Okay," Remar said.

"How long will it take you to get there?"

"An hour and a half, max."

"Okay, I'm probably going to get there before you," Jastrow said. "I'm gonna get on route 17. See you in a while."

"Sounds good. Where are we going after that?"

Jastrow sighed deeply. "I don't really know yet."

———

"Just got a report of a woman boosting a car at the Harris Teeter on Bay Street." John Birkenheuer had just called Crawford.

"Where's that?" Crawford asked, his cell on speaker.

"About three blocks east of where you last saw Jastrow," Birkenheuer said. "She knocked down an old woman in the parking lot and her sister was in the car."

"Jesus," Crawford said, glancing at Ott and shaking his head. "Thanks, John, I'll get back to you."

"Copy that," Birkenheuer said. "In the meantime, we've got an APB out for the car. It's a burgundy 2015 Buick Regal, South Carolina plate AR1221."

"Copy that," Crawford said, clicking off.

He and Ott were sitting in the Caprice on the side of Broad Street.

"So where would she go?" Crawford asked.

"Back to the boat?" Ott said.

Crawford thought for a second. "Nah, that might be her first instinct. But then she'd figure we found out she was at Fig from someone on the boat. So we'd know the boat was at the marina and go there."

"So she'd call the boat and tell it to meet her somewhere else?" Ott said.

"That's what I'm thinking," Crawford said. "I've got an idea."

Crawford dialed his cell phone again. Birkenheuer answered. "Yeah, John, you got a helicopter at your disposal?"

"Not in the Charleston area," he said. "Up in Columbia. But I can maybe borrow one from CPD." Charleston Police Department.

"Okay, that's good," Crawford said. "Here's what it's gonna do: Go down to the marina in Mount Pleasant, Ben Sawyer Boulevard and look for the biggest boat down there. It's got a black hull with a red T-bird as its tender."

"You mean the car on the deck, right?" Birkenheuer asked.

"Yeah, exactly."

"Copy that," Birkenheuer said.

"Thing is," Crawford said, "the boat may have already taken off. If so, the chopper's just gonna have to find it. It can only be going in one direction: toward the ocean. I'm guessing heading south. When they spot it, follow it, but stay far enough away so the guys on the boat don't know they're being followed."

"Okay," Birkenheuer said. "Makes sense."

"Oh, and John," Crawford had to pick his words carefully, "I know me and my partner are out of state guys, but I really believe the fewer the better. Like just you and us. If we've got every cop in the state going after Jastrow, I worry about her hostage. What could happen if Jastrow gets cornered. Know what I mean? She's a stone-cold killer, after all."

"I hear you," Birkenheuer said. "But I can't just tell 'em all to stand down."

"No, but you don't have to tell 'em everything we know," Crawford said. "Like where she's headed."

There was a long pause. Finally, "All right, Charlie, for now anyway."

"And can you call off that APB?" Crawford knew he was pushing it. "I've got a grave concern about that hostage."

Birkenheuer sighed. "O-kay."

"Thanks, man," Crawford said. "Will you give the chopper pilot my number and have him call when he spots the boat?" Crawford asked. "He'll be able to tell us where it's headed. Then my partner and I can go in that direction."

Crawford clicked off.

"There's also a chance we'll run across her on the road," Ott said. "If we're both headed to the same place."

"That's true," Crawford said

IT WAS A GOOD PLAN BUT IT TOOK JOHN BIRKENHEUER SOME time to reach the chief of the Charleston Police Department, who needed to authorize the use of the helicopter. The helicopter went out twenty minutes later, headed to the marina.

The *Revenge* was gone but, a couple of miles from the pier, the helicopter finally located it. The pilot called Crawford.

"Detective, this is Vern Markey, helicopter pilot for the Charleston Police Department."

"Hey, Vern, thanks for calling. Any luck?"

"Yeah, I got your boat up ahead, headed south a few miles north of Folly Beach."

"Okay, me and my partner'll get on route 17," Crawford said. "Keep us posted, please."

"Yeah, will do, but the route I'd take is Riverland to Maybank Highway, then Bohicket," Markey said. "It's a little faster."

Ott nodded.

"Okay, thanks, got it," Crawford said.

"So your theory is that the *Revenge* is gonna pull in somewhere to pick up a passenger?" Markey asked.

"Yeah, the boat's owner," Crawford said, "she's a fugitive. Wanted for murder."

"Two of 'em," Ott added.

"We'll get her," Markey said.

"We better," Crawford said.

———

OTT HAD JUST TURNED ONTO MAYBANK HIGHWAY, FIGURING Beth Jastrow had probably a twenty-minute head start on him. Crawford had John Birkenheuer on his cell phone again. "Also, John, can you call CPD or whatever jurisdiction we'll be going through and tell them to look the other way if they see a white 2016 Caprice, Florida plate XN615, going thirty miles over the speed limit. Last thing we need is to get pulled over."

"Copy that," Birkenheuer said.

"What we're hoping is that we overtake Jastrow in the Buick," Crawford said. "But I've got a feeling she'll be moving at a pretty good clip too."

"I'm just glad she's not in that Tesla," Ott said. "Nobody'd catch her. Where are you, John?"

"I'm coming down route 17," Birkenheuer said. "That's the other way to go. I just heard from the chopper pilot the *Revenge* is just past Folly Beach."

———

JASTROW DIALED HER CELL PHONE. SHE WAS ONLY GOING TEN

miles over the speed limit, because the last thing she needed was to get stopped for speeding. The jig would be up because, no doubt, every cop in South Carolina would know about the stolen car being driven by a murder suspect.

"Hi, Jerry," Jastrow said. "We're going to need to gas up at Edisto marina. Will a full tank get us to Jacksonville?"

"Yes, definitely," Jerry said.

"Good, I should be getting there in about fifteen or twenty minutes."

"Good timing," Jerry said. "We're a half hour from there."

"See you then," Jastrow said, clicking off.

Before calling Jerry Remar, she'd been on the phone making a reservation for the next day, from Jacksonville to Macau. There was a 6:00 a.m. from Jacksonville to Newark, then the bear of all flights—fifteen hours from Newark to Shanghai—then another two hours from Shanghai to Macau.

She had looked into the reciprocity between the United States and Macau long ago and felt that she'd be safe if she could just get there. Even if the U.S. came after her there, her boss had paid off enough politicians and cops so she'd get a heads-up if anything was in the works to arrest and deport her.

Her cell phone rang. She looked at the display. It was Ned Carlino.

"Sorry, Ned," she said. "Had to run."

"Literally," he said. "And I was so looking forward to spending the night with you."

"Another time," she said, thinking *If you want to come to Macau, that is.*

"By the way," he said, still a little bit of a slur in his voice. "Where's my car?"

"Ah, bad news, Ned," she said. "It's over on King Street. I'm afraid I had a little accident."

"What happened?"

"Hit a house."

There was a long pause. Then like he had suddenly sobered up. "So how am I supposed to get home?"

That's your problem, Jastrow thought, *I've got bigger ones.*

"Uber," she said, and clicked off.

She checked the GPS on the Buick and it looked like the marina was no more than fifteen minutes away.

She realized now that she'd only miss one thing about the United States: The Mentors. She loved the group, and they were doing some really good things. She felt that being part of the group helped make up for all of the bad things she had done in her life. Well, at least made a small dent anyway. She wondered what the other group members would think when the word got out about the real Beth Jastrow.

FIFTY-FIVE

"BOAT'S TAKING A RIGHT AFTER EDISTO CREEK," VERN MARKEY said to Crawford. "There is a marina a mile ahead on Big Bay Creek."

"Know what it's called?" Crawford asked.

"I think the Edisto Marina," Markey said.

"That's probably where they're going," Crawford said. "Thanks, Vern."

Crawford clicked off and Googled the marina. "6702 Dockside," he said to Ott.

"Ten minutes from here," Ott said.

Crawford dialed John Birkenheuer. "Just got off with Markey. Looks like the *Revenge* is heading to Edisto Marina on Dockside. How far away from there are you?"

Birkenheuer didn't respond right away. "Umm, maybe twenty-five minutes," he said finally.

"Do I have your authorization, on behalf of SLED, to arrest Beth Jastrow if we get there before you and she's there?" Crawford asked, wanting to make sure everything was by the book. "Don't want her getting away if you're not on scene."

"Yeah, definitely," Birkenheuer said. "Object is to take her down, not stand on ceremony."

"Thanks, I agree," Crawford said. "See you there."

"Later."

It was 9:35 when Crawford and Ott got to the marina. They drove around with their headlights off but didn't see a burgundy Buick Regal. Then they drove along the dock and didn't see the *Revenge* either. Crawford had a sinking feeling that maybe Beth Jastrow was meeting the boat somewhere else.

Ott parked the Caprice in a far corner of the parking lot.

"Why don't you stay here," Crawford said, pointing, "I'll go to the other end."

"Okay," Ott said. "What do you think the odds are she's gonna be packing?"

"Slim," Crawford said. "Can't see her bringing a piece on a dinner date."

Crawford walked down to the end of the driveway and hid behind a building that had restroom signs on it. Within two minutes he heard a car. He peeked out behind a corner of the building. A black Ford 150 pickup. The driver got out and walked down to the dock.

Crawford's cell phone rang. It was Vern Markey.

"Yeah, Vern?"

"The *Revenge* just turned into Big Bay Creek," Markey said. "Where you at?"

"Just got to the marina."

"Okay, I'll hang around to see what happens," Markey said. "Be careful, man."

"Thanks."

He heard another car drive onto the dirt parking lot.

He peeked around the corner of the building. It was a burgundy Buick Regal. He ducked back behind the building.

The Buick pulled into a spot twenty feet away. The car door opened and he heard footsteps on the driveway. A woman walked past him toward the dock.

He came up behind her and she didn't hear him. He put his Sig Sauer up against her back.

"Detective Crawford," he said. "You're under arrest for murder. Along with grand theft auto, assault, and attempting to elude police officers."

"Please, please, please," the old lady said. "I am not that woman."

Crawford took a step to her side. "Sorry, ma'am. Where—"

He swung around and saw the Buick accelerating in reverse, kicking up a shower of gravel.

Just as quickly, Mort Ott suddenly pulled behind the Buick and cut it off. Crawford ran to the front of the car, Sig Sauer in both hands.

"Get out," Crawford shouted to the driver. He saw Ott get out of the Caprice with his Glock raised.

The Buick's door opened as Crawford and Ott walked around to the driver's side.

Jastrow didn't even hesitate. "I have seven hundred thousand dollars on my boat if you let me go."

"Attempting to bribe law enforcement officers just got added to your charges," Crawford said, getting face to face with her.

Ott walked up to Jastrow, pulling out his handcuffs. "That was very tempting. Now put your hands behind your back."

Crawford reached in his pocket, pulled out his cell phone, and dialed.

"Hey, John, how far from Edisto Marina are you now?"

"Fifteen minutes."

"Good," Crawford said. "'Cause we got our fugitive."

"Nice goin', man," Birkenheuer said.

"See you in a few," Crawford said, clicking off and dialing again.

"Hey, Vern, we got her. Thanks for all your help. You can head back up to Charleston now."

"Pleasure doin' business with you fellas," Markey said.

Crawford clicked off.

John Birkenheuer showed up fifteen minutes later and charged Beth Jastrow on behalf of SLED. Birkenheuer said he had spoken to his superior who said to take her into custody and transport her up to Columbia. That wasn't what Crawford had in mind.

"What's your boss's name, John?" Crawford said. "I want to have a conversation with him."

Birkenheuer, a stocky man with a shaved head, gave him the name and number. Crawford dialed it. The man's name was Jim Emery.

"Hi, Jim, this is Charlie Crawford, Palm Beach PD. I'm here with John Birkenheuer and his partner. We just took in my fugitive from Florida, Beth Jastrow."

"Hey, Charlie, yeah, John told me," Emery said. "Nice work."

"So here's my thinking," Crawford said, "we're gonna extradite her anyway, so why don't I just take her back to Florida now. Save you all the trouble."

"I don't know," Emery said. "It is our jurisdiction."

Crawford guessed that Emery was looking to get a feather in his cap for SLED's role in the take down of a multiple murderer. The publicity wouldn't hurt.

"How 'bout if it goes down as your bust?" Crawford said, scrambling. "I'm tight with a reporter who'd write something like, 'SLED detectives, John Birkenheuer and—" he turned to Birkenheuer's partner, "I'm sorry, what's your name?"

"Ted Copeland."

"'Yeah, 'SLED detectives John Birkenheuer and Ted Copeland arrested Beth Jastrow tonight, a Florida fugitive suspected of double-homicide, in a joint effort with two Palm Beach, Florida detectives —'" Crawford paused, then continued. "And, ah, 'the suspect was remanded to the Florida detectives to be transported back to Florida.' How's that sound, Jim? You guys get the credit."

Jim Emery didn't answer right away. Finally, "Just one little addition."

"What's that?"

"'SLED detectives, John Birkenheuer and Ted Copeland, under the supervision of constable James D. Emery, arrested Beth Jasper tonight—'"

"Jastrow."

"Yeah," said Emery, "and then all the rest just like you said."

BETH JASTROW SAID NOTHING DURING THE RIDE BACK DOWN TO Palm Beach. They got there at almost four in the morning and put Jastrow in the cell in the basement of the station at 345 County Road. Right next to Camilo Vega, his two accomplices, and Jenny Montgomery.

Then Crawford and Ott went out the back of the building toward their cars.

"Nice driving, by the way, Mort," Crawford said as they faced each other in the parking lot.

Ott lowered his voice. "Nice navigating, Charlie,"

"Thanks."

Ott chuckled. "Particularly around all those South Carolina cops."

FIFTY-SIX

CRAWFORD'S RUDELY JANGLING CELL PHONE WOKE HIM UP AT eight thirty.

"Hello."

"Nice going," said Norm Rutledge. "When were you going to tell me about Beth Jastrow?"

"Hey, Norm," Crawford said. "I remember calling you once at eleven at night and you bit my head off."

"Yeah, but this time you got a cop killer," Rutledge said. "If we can prove it, that is."

Crawford was staring up at his popcorn ceiling. "We can prove it."

"How do you know?"

"'Cause Ott and me and a South Carolina cop went on her yacht and got a guy to confess that they dumped Loadholt's body out in the ocean."

"No shit," Rutledge said. "That's good news. How'd you do it?"

Crawford propped his head up on his two pillows. "Isolated the captain and crew and talked to 'em one at a time. Told 'em they'd get accessory to murder if they didn't talk. Captain said he didn't know what we were talking about. Same with the second guy. So we put heavy pressure on the third one. Said we'd let him off if he told us what happened. Eventually he talked."

"You got it on tape?"

"Yeah, along with Jastrow offering me seven hundred thou to let her go."

Rutledge whistled. "Shit, I would have taken it."

He probably would have.

"Hey, Norm, you mind if I go back to sleep now? I had a really long night."

"Yeah, guess you earned it. See you when you roll in."

Crawford clicked off and put his cell on his bedside table.

Five minutes later as he was drifting off it rang again.

Fuck!

"Hello," Crawford said irritably.

"Hey, Chas," his brother Cam said. "Did I catch you at a bad time?"

"No, you're not in a bar are you?"

"No, my drinking days are over. Where are you?"

"In bed."

"In bed? It's nine o'clock."

"8:47, to be exact," Crawford said.

"You're not sick, are you?"

"Sick of everyone calling me," Crawford said. "No, I just had a long night."

"With Dominica, I hope?"

"No, Jesus, what's with all the questions? Why'd you call?"

"So they're letting me out in five days. They think I've turned over a new leaf."

"Have you?"

"Yeah, I have," Cam said. "Plus I met this woman here. Think I want to marry her."

"For chrissake, Cam, last time I checked you were still married."

"Yeah, but the divorce papers have been drawn up," Cam said.

"And don't worry, I won't be rushing into anything. I'm just telling you, I really like her."

"Well, good, I'm happy for you and look forward to meeting her," Crawford said.

"We'll come down maybe and visit you."

"I'd like that. You keep doin' that stuff they teach you there. That DBT or whatever. Walking the straight and narrow."

"I plan to," Cam said. "Talk later."

"Later."

Crawford decided he might as well get up or turn his phone off. As he got to his feet, it rang again. He looked to see who it was.

"Good morning, Dominica."

"It is a good morning, right?" she said. "You got your killer?"

"Yeah, we got her. Had to go up to South Carolina to get her."

"So I heard," Dominica said. "Well, nice going."

"Thanks."

"So when are we going waterskiing again?"

"Oh, God, I forgot. It's Saturday."

"Don't say that," Dominica said. "I've been really looking forward to it."

"So have I," Crawford said. "I just kind of lost track of time. I'll pick you up at three thirty." He had a sudden afterthought. "Sure I can't talk you into wearing that green bikini?"

FIFTY-SEVEN

"I really miss our meetings on the *Revenge*," Rose Clarke said.

The Mentors—minus one—were meeting in Rose's living room. It was ten in the morning and they were drinking coffee, with the exception of Diana Quarle, who had a teacup and saucer in her lap.

"I know, with that nice James always ready to fetch you another drink," Diana said.

"So what's the latest?" Elle T. Graham asked. "I've been out of town."

"Well, if you go by what you read in the *Morning News*, Beth was pretty justified in doing what she did," Rose said. "I mean, getting raped at seventeen with her grandfather, the police chief, right there. Not doing a thing to stop it."

"Question is, is the reporter getting his info from Beth's defense attorney or from people who were actually there when it happened?" Marla Fluor asked.

"Good point," Rose said.

Marla was shaking her head. "Can you imagine a life like that?"

Fluor said. "Reading between the lines, she had to be a prostitute just to stay alive."

"You don't even need to read between the lines," Elle said. "The reporter pretty much said it."

"The tip-off was that time she beat the hell out of that guy in the hotel in Atlanta," Rose said. "I mean, that was just pure rage pouring out. Like that guy represented a lot of men in her early life."

"Yeah, like her grandfather and that judge, for starters," Marla said.

They all nodded.

"You know, I have a theory," Rose said.

"Okay, let's hear it," said Diana.

"I'm guessing that the writer Beth discovered—up in wherever-the-hell-it-was, Michigan—was really Beth spilling her sad tale," Rose said. "Seemed pretty autobiographical, right?"

"Holy shit," Marla said. "I think you're right. Which is why she was never gonna meet with us."

"Exactly," Rose said.

"Brilliant theory, Rose. So you think the book was her way of getting the whole thing off her chest?" Diana asked. "Like a big catharsis maybe."

"Maybe," Rose said, taking a sip of her coffee.

Elle was nodding. "You're absolutely right, now that I think about it," she said. "Some of those things in the book really happened to her."

"Okay," said Elle. "So here's the big question: do we take our *not inconsiderable* power and influence and support her. Try to make it so she doesn't spend the rest of her life in prison or—"

"In prison?" Rose said. "I heard the prosecution is going for the death penalty. She did kill a police chief and a judge, don't forget."

"Plus they're also looking into the death of her husband in New Orleans," Diana said.

"Oh, yeah, that's right," Rose said.

"She had a husband?" Elle asked.

"Yeah, for about a week," Diana said. "When she was young."

A long silence followed. A lot of sips of coffee and tea. Several long looks out the window at the ocean.

"Yes, of course, we do," Rose said finally. "We have to. The poor woman's all alone."

As one, the four friends nodded.

FIFTY-EIGHT

FACT OF THE MATTER WAS, DOMINICA LOOKED STUNNING IN A black one-piece bathing suit. And the woman could water ski like she had learned to do it before she walked. Crawford and Dominica were with David Balfour on his boat, which was a Scarab: fast and loud. It had two seats looking forward and two looking back. Balfour had the wheel next to his niece Lila. Crawford sat in one of the seats, looking back at Dominica who was effortlessly slaloming back and forth over the wake. They were on the Intracoastal Waterway, slightly north of Palm Beach.

Dominica went wide, kicking up a twenty-foot wake. Crawford got the sense she was showing off for him a little. He liked it. She was so damned athletic and muscular. Dominica went to the same gym that Rose used—some little boutique place in Palm Beach—and they had the same trainer. If he had to guess, he'd bet they had an unspoken competition for the best body in Palm Beach.

Crawford had silently rebuked himself before for being shallow. For the emphasis he put on the physical aspect of a woman. No matter how pure her soul, big her cerebellum, or exemplary her character. Yes, he was a shallow man, and damned if he could change it.

Dominica raised her toned right arm then let go of the rope.

"She's down," Crawford yelled.

Balfour cut the engine and turned the wheel to his left, circling back to pick up Dominica.

"She's really good," Lila said, turning to Crawford.

"Yeah, I know," Crawford said. "Problem is she's really good at everything."

"Like what else?" Lila asked.

"You name it: surfing, tennis, cooking...Scrabble—"

"Scrabble?"

"Yeah, she kills me at it," Crawford said as the boat approached Dominica.

"That's pathetic, Charlie," Balfour chimed in. "And you went to an Ivy League college."

"Yeah, not a lot of Scrabble courses there."

Dominica was ten feet away, smiling up at Crawford and shading her eyes.

"Good job," Crawford said. "I don't know how you can stay up so long. My arms get tired."

Dominica shrugged. "'Cause it's so smooth. Like glass"

Crawford reached down, grabbed her arms, and pulled her up into the boat. Then he reached over, got a towel, and handed it to her.

She toweled off and looked at him. "Okay, big boy, you're next."

Lila had already skied.

"You ready for another go?" Crawford asked Lila.

"I will, but not right now," she said. "It's your turn, Charlie."

Crawford felt suddenly uncertain. "There aren't any snakes in there, are there?" He had flashed back to a murder scene where twenty-four cottonmouths had been dumped into a man's backyard the year before. A woman had been killed by them, and when he went to investigate it was the creepiest, most terrifying crime scene he had ever seen.

"A big, brave homicide detective scared of a little snake,"

Dominica said with a smirk. "I didn't see a one...just a few twelve-foot alligators."

"Seriously?" Crawford said, making no move to take his shirt off and jump in the water.

"No, *not* seriously," Dominica said and laughed.

"How 'bout you, David?" Crawford said to Balfour, who had the boat idling. "Why don't you go? I can drive."

Lila laughed. "You big chicken, Charlie. Come on the water's really nice and warm."

"Yeah, 'cause of all the snakes and gators peeing in it," Crawford said.

Lila and Balfour laughed, Dominica shook her head and smiled.

Reluctantly, hesitantly, fearfully he stood up and started to take his shirt off. "What about sharks?"

"Yeah, Charlie," Dominica said. "And the Loch Ness monster too."

"Wiseass," Crawford said, taking his shirt off.

Dominica tossed him the life jacket. He put it on.

"Get in there, you big wimp," Dominica said.

Crawford meekly sidled toward the gunwale. Hesitantly, he stepped up to it.

He looked back at Balfour for support. Balfour motioned with his hand for him to jump in.

He did. It really was warm, but the water was so dark. He tried to not imagine what lurked beneath as he grabbed the ski rope.

Dominica tossed a water ski at him. It skimmed across the surface and he caught it.

"I'm thinking maybe get up on two," he said. "Then drop one."

"Up to you," Dominica shouted back.

That really would be wimpy.

"Nah, I guess I can do one," he said. He got his left foot into the ski. He raised his arm and Balfour hit the boat's throttle.

He wobbled a little at first, but was able to get up.

He raised his fist, exuberantly to Dominica. She shot him a big smile and a thumbs-up.

The surface of the Intracoastal was incredibly smooth. He stayed in the wake at first, directly behind the boat, just going straight. Then he remembered back to how rough it was on Lake Waramaug in Connecticut, where he'd first learned to ski. And Lake Sunapee in New Hampshire, where he'd first gotten up on one ski.

Snakes, gators, and sharks out of his mind, he shot across the wake, his legs straight, fast and feeling suddenly confident. It had been at least five years since he last skied, but it was like it was yesterday. He cut across the wake again then cut hard to his left, shooting up a big spray. There was a short pause as the boat caught up. Then it tugged hard at his arms and shoulders and he cut across the wake again. He jumped when he hit the wake and caught a little air.

He remembered his brother Evan calling him a hot dog once. Maybe so, but wasn't that the whole idea? To push it a little? Hell, worst case was you'd fall.

He whipped across the glassy water—faster than the times before —then cut it hard.

Too hard. His legs went out from under him and he smacked down with his shoulder and head then flipped over. It felt like the wind was knocked out of him.

He looked toward the boat, which was circling back to him. Slowly, he began to breathe easier.

"You okay?" Dominica called out, a concerned look on her face.

He nodded. "Yeah, I'm fine," he said as she drew closer.

"That was quite a header," she said, leaning toward him to help him out.

"Yeah," he said, taking her hand. "I was just trying to be better than you at something," she pulled him up, "should've known better."

DAVID BALFOUR HAD TWO BOATS. THE SKI BOAT AND A YACHT. A

small yacht but a yacht nevertheless. They were tied up at the Palm Beach Marina, two much larger yachts on either side. Balfour was grilling steaks on the aft deck, while Lila, Dominica, and Crawford were nursing cocktails, seated in a semi-circle of plushly cushioned teak furniture. Balfour had mixed up a batch of rum drinks called Southsides, which, he explained, were a drink native to the north shore of Long Island. He told the others that a friend had sent him six bottles of mix made by a bartender at a club up there who guarded the secret of its ingredients like Colonel Sanders guarded his Kentucky Fried Chicken recipe.

"These things are really good," Crawford told Balfour.

"Strong too," Dominica said, raising her glass.

"Hey, nothing's too good for my two favorite cops," Balfour said, pointing. "By the way, did you notice who my neighbor is, Charlie?"

Crawford craned his neck in the direction Balfour was pointing and first saw the black hull. Then, on the upper deck, the resplendent red Thunderbird.

"No, didn't even notice," Crawford said, as Balfour came and sat down.

"So what's the real story there?" Balfour asked. "I've heard so many different things about her."

"I've got to be careful what I say," Crawford said. "They'll be a trial coming up."

"Well, what about the Aileen Wuornos thing?" Balfour asked, leaning closer to Crawford.

"Who's Aileen Wuornos?" Lila asked.

"Before your time," Balfour said to his niece. "She was this serial killer who killed like ten men. She was basically a prostitute who would get picked up by men hitchhiking. Then they'd do...whatever they did, and she'd kill 'em."

"But what did that have to do with Beth Jastrow?" Dominica asked, looking to Crawford.

Crawford just motioned to Balfour. "Let's hear what David has heard."

"Well, the way I heard it Beth Jastrow may have been on a similar course, though she only killed one man. Until the judge and her grandfather, that is," Balfour said. "And when she was young, she supposedly went and visited Wuornos before Wuornos hooked up with Old Sparky."

"Okay," Lila said, "I hate to be so dumb but...Old Sparky?"

Crawford and Balfour laughed.

"It's the nickname for the electric chair," Balfour said.

Lila nodded. "Oh, right, now I know what you're talking about."

"But," Crawford said, "Wuornos was actually executed by lethal injection. They stopped using 'Old Sparky' back in 2000."

Dominica turned to Crawford. "Is that true? Beth Jastrow went and visited Aileen Wuornos?"

Crawford shrugged. "I don't really know."

Balfour turned to Dominica. "Charlie playing dumb."

Dominica laughed. "Yeah, I know."

"No," Crawford said. "All it is, is Charlie not repeating hearsay."

"All right," Lila said, standing up, "I'm going into the galley to make my famous salad."

Dominica stood up. "I'll join you."

Lila nodded. "We'll leave them to talk about women serial killers."

The two walked away.

Balfour stood up. "Come on, Charlie, I gotta flip those steaks."

They walked over to the grill. "Jesus," Crawford said. "I've never seen steaks that thick."

Balfour flipped one, then the other, then turned to Crawford. "I just want to say two things, Charlie."

"Okay."

"First, I want to thank you again for bringing Lila home," Balfour said. "For dropping everything and doing what you did. And also, for not bringing in the cavalry."

"You're welcome." Crawford said. "And number two?"

Balfour took a step toward Crawford. "Number two, don't fuck it up."

"What?"

"With Dominica," Balfour said. "In case you haven't noticed, she's—"

"Trust me, David, I have noticed," Crawford said. "The problem is my job. I get so damn busy when I'm on a—"

"Don't be an idiot, Charlie," Balfour said. "You're just gonna have to figure out how to make it work. Besides, Palm Beach ain't Chicago. Last time I checked, murders are still pretty rare here."

FIFTY-NINE

CRAWFORD WOKE UP IN THE MIDDLE OF THE NIGHT IN A COLD sweat. Maybe it was the header he took waterskiing or three of Balfour's Southside drinks. Then he started remembering the dream. It was one of those dreams where you come close to waking up screaming, though Crawford had never had one that went that far. But still, it was scary as hell—in 3-D and Technicolor. Snakes and gators and, yes, even the goddamn Loch Ness monster in a cameo, chasing him all around the most peaceful, tranquil place in the world: Lake Waramaug in New Preston, Connecticut, where he'd learned how to water ski. It was a CGI-fright world.

"You okay, Charlie?" the voice beside him said.

Then it all came back to him.

It was Dominica. And *ohmigod*, they'd just had the most *incredible* love-making session of all time. Must have gone on for at least two hours. Right before he collapsed in utter and complete exhaustion and the ghouls of the netherworld crept into his bone-chilling, forbidding nocturnal world.

He laughed. "Yeah, just had a crazy dream."

"I could tell," said Dominica. "Like you were in the middle of World War Three."

Crawford leaned across and kissed her.

He never really got back to sleep.

At 6:00 a.m. he slid out of bed, got into his well-worn Dartmouth sweat pants, Nike flip-flops, and Fruit of the Loom t-shirt. First stop, of course, was Dunkin' Donuts, where Janelle, server extraordinaire with the melt-your-heart smile, fixed him up. A veggie egg white flatbread extravaganza—for Dominica. Then the wake-up wrap and the big n' toasted for him. Oh, and, a double order of hash browns for the voracious Dominica.

Next stop was Swifty's newsstand over on Congress and Okeechobee. Okay, on a cop's salary the Sunday *New York Times* seemed to cost about as much as a cheap Japanese car these days, but it was a must-have on a rainy Sunday.

He drove back to his apartment overlooking the parking lot of Publix when the sappy, old Louis Armstrong song, "What a Wonderful World," came on the radio. Sappy, maybe, but even for a Rolling Stones guy, the song hit the spot. Dunkin' Donuts five-star cuisine, a rainy day perfect for staying inside, *"All the News That's Fit to Print,"* the best-looking, nicest, smartest, funniest woman in Palm Beach—and, for that matter, Florida and, quite possibly, the world. What more could a guy ask for?

THE END

AFTERWORD

I hope you liked *Palm Beach Bones*. If you did, please **leave a quick review on Amazon**. Thank you!

Charlie Crawford and Mort Ott return for another murder investigation in *Palm Beach Pretenders*—**now available on Amazon**.

And to receive an email when the next Charlie Crawford Palm Beach Mystery comes out, be sure to sign up for my free author newsletter at **tomturnerbooks.com/news**.

Best,
Tom

PALM BEACH PRETENDERS
(EXCERPT)

ONE

IF YOU GO TO THE MAR-A-LAGO WEBSITE, YOU WILL SEE PHOTOS of catered weddings, which take place at the club. One shows an exterior pathway leading to an ornate, white arch, where men and women are united in holy matrimony. A profusion of palm trees sway in the breeze over rows of white wooden chairs on either side of the path. The wedding in the photos appears to be fairly small, seating a hundred or so guests.

Today's wedding party was much larger, and the white wooden chairs looked tiny because the average guest weighed between two hundred fifty and three hundred pounds. It was the wedding of the son of legendary college football coach Paul Pawlichuk, who'd recently signed a five-year contract for nine million dollars per year. Rich, the bridegroom, was a linebacker for the Miami Dolphins and made even more than his father, though it was Paul who was the member of the Mar-a-Lago Club. Rich was marrying Addison, the younger sister of Carla Carton, the lead actress in the hugely successful Netflix series *Bad Karma*. Not much was known about the bride except that she'd recently been a Miss Universe runner-up and was a woman who demanded things be done her way.

Rich's Miami Dolphin teammates and friends were sitting in the fragile-looking white chairs, along with a number of former college football players who had remained friendly with their coach, Paul. Fortunately, and somewhat surprisingly, as the ceremony came to a close and all rose to watch and photograph the ring exchange and protracted kiss between Addison and Rich, it appeared that all the white chairs had survived intact. The only casualty was the well-tended and recently mown lawn, into which countless chair legs had sunk three or four inches below the dark-green zoysia grass.

The ceremony concluded, the bride and groom were walking down the aisle, followed by the wedding party. As they headed to the area where the reception would be held, three waves of white-jacketed waiters made their way into the crowd with trays of fluted glasses filled with champagne.

"Thanks," Paul Pawlichuk said as he reached for a glass, then proceeded to drain it in one long gulp.

His wife Mindy, aware of her husband's prodigious appetites in so many areas, thought nothing of it when Paul grabbed a second flute off another waiter's tray on the fly.

"Beautiful ceremony, didn't you think?" Mindy asked her husband as their daughter Janice approached them with her husband George Figueroa and young son in tow.

"Very nice," Paul said, then under his breath, muttered, "But the padre kind of dragged it out a little."

The "padre" was a renowned monsignor from Miami who spoke too slow and flowery for Paul's taste.

"Hey, hon," Paul said, kissing his daughter Janice and ignoring his son-in-law the way he always did.

Janice shook her head. "You do see George standing next to me, Dad...and your grandson?"

Paul nodded. "Hey, Jorge, how's it goin', bro?"

Paul called everyone 'bro' except his brother.

Janice looked furious. "It's not Jorge, for God's sake."

Paul refrained from saying what he was thinking, *Well, it used to be*, and instead gave his four-year-old grandson a pat on his under-sized head.

Janice turned to her mother and whispered under her breath. "You believe that tramp?" she said, flicking her head in the direction of the TV star and bride's sister. "Decked out like some Las Vegas hooker."

"Hey, hey," her mother said. "A little reverence on your brother's wedding day."

"Well, it's true," Janice said, as she caught her father sneaking a glance at Carla.

***

ACROSS THE ROOM, CARLA HAD WALKED UP TO ONE OF THE two outside bars and was talking to an older man who had followed her there. He was Robert Polk, the billionaire owner of Polk Global.

Carla leaned close to Polk and asked under her breath, "When was the last time you spoke to Alex?"

Polk glanced around to make sure no one was within hearing distance. "I went up to Deerfield and saw him play in a soccer match," he said, "Took him out for dinner afterward."

Carla frowned. "That was way back in the fall, for God's sake," she said. "It's spring now."

"Well, you had him for Thanksgiving and Christmas," Polk said.

"Yes, but there was a lot of time in between."

"What can I tell you, I've been busy as hell lately," Polk said. "When does he hear from Yale?"

"In a couple of weeks," Carla looked concerned. "It's a sure thing, right?"

Polk nodded and took a sip of his champagne.

Carla's sister Addison, clad in her twenty-thousand-dollar Zac Posen wedding dress, walked up to them.

"There she is," Carla said, giving her sister a big hug and kiss.

"Such a beautiful ceremony. And, oh my God, your flowers are *so* gorgeous—"then turning to Polk—"you remember Robert?"

"Of course, hello, Robert," Addison Pawlichuk said, then turned to her sister. "Well, it's official, I just married into the Polish royal family of football."

"Mazel tov," Carla said, raising her drink.

Addison laughed. "That's Jewish, not Polish."

"Close enough," Carla said. "You got a real mixed bag of people here. Which makes for the best weddings, they tell me."

"We'll see about that," Addison said.

Carla, looking over her sister's shoulder, zeroed in on her husband, Duane Truax. "Which one of your bridesmaids is Duane impressing with his race-track heroics now?"

Addison turned around and looked. "Oh, that's Chelsea."

"Is she the Prada model?" Carla asked.

"Yes, exactly, living with a chef at Nobu," Addison said.

"Where's he?"

"Working."

Carla nodded knowingly. "While the cat's away, I guess."

Addison laughed.

Robert Polk took a step closer to hear better.

Carla, still looking at her husband and the young model, shook her head disdainfully. "I've seen that look in his eye. I bet he just told her he was Driver of the Year."

Addison turned to her sister. "He was?"

"Yeah, back in 2005."

Addison glanced over at the six-piece band, which had segued into something slow after having just finished a bouncy number.

"Would you like to dance?" Polk asked Carla, sounding very formal.

Carla rolled her eyes and raised her eyebrows at her sister. "You mean, would I like you to tromp all over my toes?"

Addison tried to suppress a laugh. Polk looked stung.

Carla couldn't care less. "No, thanks," she said, looking away from Polk. "I'm going to go talk to my old friend, the movie director. It's been a while."

Addison glanced to where her sister was looking. A short man in his fifties with slicked-back blond hair and a ring in his ear was talking to a young woman.

"Movie director?" Addison said with a knowing smile. "I'd say you just gave him a promotion."

Carla laughed. "Okay, how about...director of short features where none of the actors wear clothes."

Addison patted her sister's shoulder and smiled. "Yeah, exactly, the kind that never have much of a plot."

"But plenty of skin," Carla whispered, then gave Robert Polk a kiss that barely grazed his cheek. "Bye, Robert, nice to see you."

"I'll give you a call," Polk said.

"Go ahead, but I'm going to be busy as hell," Carla zinged him.

Carla walked over to the man with the slicked-back blond hair. He was talking to a woman—late teens or early twenties—who had boobs so tightly packed into her dress that they looked like they were struggling to come out for air.

"Hello, Xavier," Carla said.

The short man swung around and came eye level with Carla's expensive Bvlgari diamond necklace.

"Well, hello, Carla," Xavier Duke said.

Carla glanced at the young woman. "Hi, I'm Carla."

The woman's baby blues lit up at having been addressed by the well-known actress.

"And this is my friend, Taylor Whitcomb," Duke said.

"Hi, so nice to meet you," Taylor said. "I love your show."

"Well, thank you," Carla said. "Wait, are you related to Rennie and Wendy?"

Taylor laughed. "Daughter."

"Well, I'll be damned," Carla said. "I haven't seen them in such a long time. Do they still live in New York and have a house down here?"

"Yes," Taylor said. "Sure do."

"Well, please give them my best," Carla said.

"I definitely will," Taylor said.

Carla turned back to Duke and said flirtatiously, "So how 'bout a dance, big boy?"

Big boy he wasn't, but game he was. "I'd love to," Duke said, then to Taylor, "See you in a little bit."

Xavier Duke had no original parts left on his face. Two years ago, he'd had a major facelift to expunge the bags under his eyes, and the plastic surgeon had thrown in a complimentary Kirk Douglas cleft chin. All of his crow's feet, frown lines and smoker's lines had been lasered into oblivion. His teeth had been bleached to an extreme, almost unnatural white.

Duke and Carla made their way to the dance floor, then she dropped her voice...and her smile. "A hundred thousand dollars," she said, suddenly all business.

"Add a zero," Duke said.

"Fuck that."

"It's like a tip to you."

"Two hundred is the best I'm doing," she said.

"You've got until Monday," Duke said.

Carla pulled back from him. "And you've got until I make a phone call."

She didn't have some big *goombah* on speed-dial but figured there was no harm in implying she did. Carla walked away quickly, headed for the bar.

She watched Paul Pawlichuk walk across the room with a drink in his hand and decided to follow him. He seemed to be heading in the direction of Mar-a-Lago's living room. She looked around to see if anyone was watching and, seeing no one, walked faster until she was right behind him. As he got to the door, she reached between his legs and goosed him.

He swung around and, seeing her, broke into a wide smile.

"Hello, Paul," she said. "You weren't looking for me, by any chance?"

He touched her on the shoulder.

"I'm just going to take care of a little business with my son-in-law, then I plan to give you my complete, undivided attention."

ACKNOWLEDGMENTS

I've run out of people to thank.

So Serena and Georgie, world's greatest daughters, thanks for putting up with all my nonsense.

ABOUT THE AUTHOR

A native New Englander, Tom dropped out of college and ran a bar in Vermont...into the ground. Limping back to get his sheepskin, he then landed in New York where he spent time as an award-winning copywriter at several Manhattan advertising agencies. After years of post-Mad Men life, he made a radical change and got a job in commercial real estate. A few years later he ended up in Palm Beach, buying, renovating and selling houses while getting material for his novels. On the side, he wrote *Palm Beach Nasty*, its sequel, *Palm Beach Poison*, and a screenplay, *Underwater*.

While at a wedding, he fell for the charm of Charleston, South Carolina. He spent six years there and completed a yet-to-be-published series set in Charleston. A year ago, Tom headed down the road to Savannah, where he just finished a novel about lust and murder among his neighbors.

Learn more about Tom's books at:
www.tomturnerbooks.com

facebook.com/tomturner.books